AUNT PHILLIS'S CABIN;

OR,

SOUTHERN LIFE AS IT IS.

BY MRS. MARY H. EASTMAN.

Philadelphia:
Lippincott, Grambo & Co.
1852.

AUNT PHILLIS'S CABIN;

OR,

SOUTHERN LIFE AS IT IS.

BY

Mrs. MARY H. EASTMAN.

TENTH THOUSAND.

PHILADELPHIA:
LIPPINCOTT, GRAMBO & CO.
1852.

Eastman, Mary H. (Mary Henderson), 1818-1887

Born in Virginia and raised near Washington, D.C., Mary Henderson Eastman married artist and army officer Seth Eastman at West Point in 1835. In 1841, Mary Eastman accompanied her husband to Fort Snelling on the upper Mississippi River. Residing there seven years, Mrs. Eastman learned the Sioux language and tribal customs and legends, which she wove into literary romances. Eastman's first book, Dahcotah, which her husband illustrated, appeared in 1849, and its success encouraged her literary career. She published further volumes of Indian tales (1853-1855), a fictional response to Uncle Tom's cabin (1852), and sentimental fiction on other subjects (1856-1879).

PREFACE.

A WRITER on Slavery has no difficulty in tracing back its origin. There is also the advantage of finding it, with its con tinued history, and the laws given by God to govern his own in stitution, in the Holy Bible. Neither profane history, tradition, nor philosophical research are required to prove its origin or existence; though they, as all things must, come forward to sub stantiate the truth of the Scriptures. God, who created the human race, willed they should be holy like himself. Sin was com mitted, and the curse of sin, death, was induced: other punish ments were denounced for the perpetration of particular crimes —the shedding of man's blood for murder, and the curse of slavery. The mysterious reasons that here influenced the mind of the Creator it is not ours to declare. Yet may we learn enough from his revealed word on this and every other subject to confirm his power, truth, and justice. There is no Christian duty more insisted upon in Scripture than reverence and obe dience to parents. " Honor thy father and thy mother, that thy days may be long 'in the land which the Lord thy God giveth thee." The relation of child to parent resembles closely that of man to his Creator. He who loves and honors his God will assuredly love and honor his parents. Though it is evidently the duty of every parent so to live as to secure the respect and affection of his child, yet there is nothing in the Scriptures to

PREFACE.

authorize a cliild treating with disrespect a parent, though he be unworthy in the greatest degree.

The human mind, naturally rebellious, requires every com mand and incentive to submission. The first of the ten com mandments, insisting on the duty owing to the Creator, and the fifth, on that belonging to our parents, are the sources of all order and good arrangement in the minor relations of life; and on obedience to them depends the comfort of society.

Jleverence to age, and especially where it is found in the p^r-son of those who by the will of God were the authors of their being, is insisted upon in the Jewish covenant—not indeed less required now; but as the Jews were called from among the heathen nations of the earth to be the peculiar people of God, they were to show such evidences of this law in their hearts, by their conduct, that other nations might look on and say, " Ye are the children of the Lord your God."

It was after an act of a child dishonoring an aged father, that the prophecy entailing slavery as a curse on a portion of the human race was uttered. Nor could it have been from any feeling of resentment or revenge that the curse was made known by the lips of a servant of God; for this servant of God was a parent, and with what sorrow would any parent, yea, the worst of parents, utter a malediction which insured such punishment and misery on a portion of his posterity! Even the blessing which was promised to his other children could not have consoled him for the sad necessity. He might not resist the Spirit of God: though with perfect submission he obeyed its dictates, yet with what regret! The heart of any Christian parent will answer this appeal!

We may well imagine some of the reasons for the will of God in thus punishing Ham and his descendants. Prior to the unfilial act which is recorded, it is not to be supposed he had been a righteous man. Had he been one after God's own heart, he would not have been guilty of such a sin. What must that child be, who would openly dishonor and expose an erring parent, borne down with the weight of years, and honored by God as Noah had been! The very act of disrespect to Noah, the chosen of God, implies wilful contempt of God himself. Ham was not a young man either: he had not the excuse of the impetuosity of youth, nor its thoughtlessness—he was himself an old man; and there is every reason to believe he had led a life at variance with God's laws. When he committed so gross and violent a sin, it may be, that the curse of God, which had lain tranquil long, was roused and uttered against him: a curse not conditional, not implied—now, as then, a mandate of the Eternal.

Among the curses threatened by the Levites upon Mount Ebal, was the one found in the 16th verse of the 27th chapter of Deuteronomy : " Cursed be he that setteth light by his father or his mother." By the law of Moses, this sin was punished with death: " Of the son which will not obey the voice of his father or the voice of his mother/' " all the men of his city shall stone him with stones that he die." (Deut. xxi. 21.) God in his wisdom instituted this severe law in early times; and it must convince us that there were reasons in the Divine mind for insisting on the ordinance exacting the most perfect submission and reverence to an earthly parent.

" When, after the deluge," says Josephus, " the earth was settled in its former condition, Noah set about its cultivation; and when he had planted it with vines, and when the fruit was ripe, and he had gathered the grapes in the season, and the wine was ready for use, he offered a sacrifice and feasted, and, being inebriated, fell asleep, and lay in an unseemly manner. When Ham saw this, he came laughing, and showed him to his brothers." Does not this exhibit the impression of the Jews as regards the character of Ham ? Could a man capable of such an act deserve the blessing of a just and holy God ?

" The fact of Noah's transgression is recorded by the inspired historian with that perfect impartiality which is peculiar to the Scriptures, as an instance and evidence of human frailty and imperfection. Ham appears to have been a bad man, and probably he rejoiced to find his father in so unbecoming a situation, that, by exposing him, he might retaliate for the reproofs which he had received from his parental authority. And perhaps Canaan first discovered his situation, and told it to Ham. The conduct of Ham in exposing his father to his brethren, and their behaviour in turning away from the sight of his disgrace, form a striking contrast."— *Scoffs Com.*

We are told in Gen. ix. 22, " And Ham, the father of Canaan, saw the nakedness of his father, and told his two brethren without;" and in the 24th, 25th, 26th, and 27th verses we read, "And Noah awoke from his wine, and knew what his younger son had done unto him; and he said, Cursed be Canaan, a servant of servants shall he be unto his brethren. And he said, Blessed be the Lord God of Shem, and Canaan shall be his servant. God shall enlarge Japheth, and he shall dwell in the tents of Shem, and Canaan shall be his servant." Is it not preposterous that any man, any Christian, should read these verses and say slavery was not instituted by God as a curse on Ham and Canaan and their posterity ?

And who can read the history of the world and say this curse has not existed ever since it was uttered?

"The whole continent of Africa," says Bishop Newton, "was peopled principally by the descendants of Ham; and for how many ages have the better parts of that country lain under the dominion of the Romans, then of the Saracens, and now of the Turks! In what wickedness, ignorance, barbarity, slavery, misery, live most of the inhabitants! And of the poor negroes, how many hundreds every year are sold and bought like beasts in the market, and conveyed from one quarter of the world to do the work of beasts in another!"

But does this curse authorize the slave-trade? God forbid. He commanded the Jews to enslave the heathen around them, saying, "they should be their bondmen forever;" but he has given no such command to other nations. The threatenings and reproofs uttered against Israel, throughout the old Testament, on the subject of slavery, refer to their oppressing and keeping in slavery their own countrymen. Never is there the slightest imputation of sin, as far as I can see, conveyed against them for holding in bondage the children of heathen nations.

Yet do the Scriptures evidently permit slavery, even to the present time. The curse on the serpent, ("And the Lord God said unto the serpent, Because thou hast done this, thou art cursed above all cattle and above every beast of the field,") uttered more than sixteen hundred years before the curse of Noah upon Ham and his race, has lost nothing of its force and true meaning. "Cursed is the ground for thy sake: in sorrow shalt thou eat of it, all the days of thy life," said the Supreme Being. Has this curse failed or been removed?

Remember the threatened curses of God upon the whole Tewish tribe if they forsook his worship. Have not they been fulfilled?

However inexplicable may be the fact that God would appoint the curse of continual servitude on a portion of his creatures, will any one dare, with the Bible open in his hands, to say the fact does not exist? It is not ours to decide why the Supreme Being acts! "We may observe his dealings with man, but we may not ask, until he reveals it, Why hast thou thus done?

"Cursed is every one who loves not the Lord Jesus Christ." Are not all these curses recorded, and will they not all be fulfilled? God has permitted slavery to exist in every age and in almost every nation of the earth. It was only commanded to the Jews, and it was with them restricted to the heathen, ("referring entirely to the race of Ham, who had been judicially condemned to a condition of servitude more than eighteen hundred years before the giving of the law, by the mouth of Noah, the medium of the Holy Ghost.") No others, at least, were to be enslaved "forever." Every book of the Old Testament records a history in which slaves and God's laws concerning them are spoken of, while, as far as profane history goes back, we cannot fail to see proofs of the existence of slavery. "No legislator of history," says Voltaire, "attempted to abrogate slavery. Society was so accustomed to this degradation of the species, that Epictetus, who was assuredly worth more than his master, never expresses any surprise at his being a slave." Egypt, Sparta, Athens, Carthage, and Rome had their thousands of slaves. In the Bible, the best and chosen servants of God owned slaves, while in profane history the purest and greatest men did the same. In the very nation over whose devoted head hung the curse of God, slavery, vindictive, lawless, and cruel slavery, has prevailed. It is said no nation of the earth has equalled the Jewish in the enslaving of negroes, except the negroes themselves; and examination will prove that the descendants of Ham and Canaan have, as God foresaw, justified by their conduct the doom which he pronounced against them.

But it has been contended that the people of God sinned in holding their fellow-creatures in bondage ! Open your Bible, Christian, and read the commands of God as regards slavery—the laws that he made to govern the conduct of the master and the slave!

But again— we live under the glorious and new dispensation of Christ; and He came to establish God's will, and to confirm such laws as were to continue in existence, to destroy such rules as were not to govern our lives !

"When there was but one family upon the earth, a portion of the family was devoted to be slaves to others. God made a covenant with Abraham : he included in it his slaves. " He that is born in thy house, and he that is bought with thy money," are the words of Scripture. A servant of Abraham says, " And the Lord has blessed my master greatly, and he is become great, and he hath given him flocks and herds, and silver and gold, and men-servants and maid-servants, and camels and asses."

The Lord has called himself the God of Abraham and 5 Isaac and Jacob. These holy men were slaveholders !

The existence of slavery then, and the sanction of God on his own institution, is palpable from the time of the pronouncing of the curse, until the glorious advent of the Son of God. When he came, slavery existed in every part of the world.

Jesus Christ, the Son of God, came from heaven and dwelt upon the earth : his mission to proclaim the will of God to a world sunk in the lowest depths of iniquity. Even the dear and chosen people of God had departed from him—had forsaken his worship, and turned aside from his commands.

He was born of a virgin. He was called Emmanuel. He was God with us.

Wise men traveled from afar to behold the Child-God—they

2*

knelt before him—they opened their treasures—they presented to them gifts. Angels of God descended in dreams, to ensure the protection of his life against the king who sought it. He emerged from infancy, and grew in favour with God and man. He was tempted but not overcome—angels came again from heaven to minister to him. He fulfilled every jot and tittle of the law, and entered upon the duties for which he left the glories of heaven.

That mission was fulfilled. " The people which sat in dark ness saw great light, and to them which sat in the region and shadow of death light is sprung up."

Look at his miracles—the cleansing of the leper, the healing of the sick, the casting out unclean spirits, the raising of the dead, the rebuking of the winds and seas, the control of those possessed with devils—and say, was he not the Son of God—yea, was he not God ?

Full of power and goodness he came into the world, and light and glory followed every footstep. The sound of his voice, the glance of his eye, the very touch of the garment in which his assumed mortality was arrayed, was a medicine mighty to save. He came on an errand of mercy to the world, and he was all powerful to accomplish the Divine intent; but, did he eman cipate the slave ? The happiness of the human race was the object of his coming; and is it possible that the large portion of them then slaves could have escaped his all-seeing eye ! Did he condemn the institution which he had made ? Did he establish universal freedom ? Oh ! no; he came to redeem the world from the power of sin; his was no earthly mission; he did not inter fere with the organization of society. He healed the sick servant of the centurion, but he did not command his freedom; nor is there a word that fell from his sacred lips that could be construed into

a condemnation of that institution which had existed from the early ages of the world, existed then, and is continued now. The application made by the Abolitionist of the golden rule is absurd : it might then apply to the child, who would have his father no longer control him; to the appentice, who would no longer that the man to whom he is bound should have a right to direct him. Thus the foundations of society would be shaken, nay, destroyed. Christ would have us deal with others, not as they desire, but as the law of God demands: in the condition of life in which we have been placed, we must do what we conscientiously believe to be our duty to our fellow-men.

Christ alludes to slavery, but does not forbid it. "And the servant abideth not in the house forever, but the son abideth ever. If the Son therefore shall make you free, you are free indeed."

In these two verses of the Gospel of St. John, there is a manifest allusion to the fact and condition of slaves. Of this fact the Saviour took occasion, to illustrate, by way of similitude, the condition of a wicked man, who is the slave of sin, and to show that as a son who was the heir in a house could set a bondman free, if that son were of the proper age, so he, the Son of God, could set the enslaved soul free from sin, when he would be free in deed." Show me in the history of the Old Testament, or in the life of Christ, authority to proclaim as a sin the holding of the race of Ham and Canaan in bondage.

In the times of the apostles, what do we see ? Slaves are still in bondage, the children of Ham are menials as they were before. Christ had come, had died, had ascended to heaven, and slavery still existed. Had the apostles authority to do it away ? Had Christ left it to them to carry out, in this instance, his revealed will?

"Art thou," said Paul, "called being a slave? care not for it; but if thou mayest be made free, use it rather. Let every man abide in the same calling wherein he is called." " Let as many servants as are under the yoke count their own masters worthy of all honor, that the name of God and his doctrines be not blasphemed. And they that have believing masters, let them not despise them, because they are brethren, but rather do them service, because they are faithful and beloved, partakers of the benefit."

It is well known and often quoted that the holy apostle did all he could to restore a slave to his master—one whom he had been the means of making free in a spiritual sense. Yet he knew that God had made Onesimus a slave, and, wnen he had fled from his master, Paul persuaded him to return and to do his duty toward him. Open your Bible, Christian, and carefully read the letter of Paul to Philemon, and contrast its spirit with the incendiary publications of the Abolitionists of the present day. St. Paul was not a fanatic, and therefore could not be an Abolitionist. The Christian age advanced and slavery continued, and we approach the time when our fathers fled from persecution to the soil we now call our own, when they fought for the liberty to which they felt they had a right. Our fathers fought for it, and our mothers did more when they urged forth their husbands and sons, not knowing whether the life-blood that was glowing with religion and patriotism would not soon be dyeing the land that had been their refuge, and where they fondly hoped they should find a happy home. Oh, glorious parentage ! Children of America, trace no farther back—say not the crest of nobility once adorned thy father's breast, the gemmed coronet thy mother's brow—stop here! it is enough that they earned for thee a home—a free, a happy home. And what did they say to the slavery that existed then and had been entailed upon them by the English govern-ment? Their opinions are preserved among us—they were dictated by their position and necessities—and they were wisely formed. In the North, slavery was useless; nay, more, it was a drawback to the prosperity of that section of the Union—it was dispensed with. In other sections, gradually, our people have seen their condition would be more prosperous without slaves—they have emancipated them. In the South, they are necessary : though an evil, it is one that cannot be dispensed with; and here they have been retained, and will be retained, unless God should manifest his will (which never yet has been done) to the contrary. Knowing that the people of the South still have the views of their revolutionary forefathers, we see plainly that many of the North have rejected the opinions of theirs. Slaves were at the North and South considered and recognized as property, (as they are in Scripture.) The whole nation sanctioned slavery by adopting the Constitution which provides for them, and for their restoration (when fugitive) to their owners. Our country was then like one family—their souls had been tried and made pure by a united struggle—they loved as brothers who had suffered together. Would it were so at the present day!

The subject of slavery was agitated among them; many difficulties occurred, but they were all settled—and, they thought, effectually. They agreed then, on the propriety of giving up run away slaves, unanimously. Mr. Sherman, of Connecticut, " saw no more impropriety in the public seizing and surrendering a slave or servant than a horse I" (Madison's Papers.) This was then considered a compromise between the North and South. Henry Clay and Daniel Webster—the mantle of their illustrious fathers descended to them from their own glorious times. The slave-trade was discontinued after a while. As long as England needed the

sons and daughters of Africa to do her bidding, she trafficked in the flesh and blood of her fellow-creatures; but our immortal fathers put an end to the disgraceful trade. They saw its heinous sin, for they had no command to enslave the heathen; but they had no command to emancipate the slave; therefore they wisely forbore farther to interfere. They drew the nice line of distinction between an unavoidable evil and a sin.

Slavery was acknowledged, and slaves considered as property all over our country, at the North as well as the South—in Pennsylvania, New York, and New Jersey. Now, has there been any law reversing this, except in the States that have become free ? Out of the limits of these States, slaves are property, according to the Constitution. In the year 1798, Judge Jay, being called on for a list of his taxable property, made the following observation:—" I purchase slaves and manumit them at proper ages, when their faithful services shall have afforded a reasonable retribution." "As free servants became more common, he was gradually relieved from the necessity of purchasing slaves." (See Jay's Life, by his son.)

Here is the secret of Northern emancipation: they were relieved from the necessity of slavery. Rufus King, for many years one of the most distinguished statesmen of the country, writes thus to John B. Coles and others:—" I am perfectly anxious not to be misunderstood in this case, never having thought myself at liberty to encourage or assent to any measure that would affect the security of property in slaves, or tend to disturb the political adjustment which the Constitution has made respecting them."

John Taylor, of New York, said, " If the weight and influence of the South be increased by the representation of that which they consider a part of their property, we do not wish to diminish them. The right by which this property is held is derived

from the Federal Constitution; we have neither inclination nor power to interfere with the laws of existing States in this particular ; on the contrary, they have not only a right to reclaim their fugitives whenever found, but, in the event of domestic violence, (which God in his mercy forever avert!) the whole strength of the nation is bound to be exerted, if needful, in reducing it to subjection, while we recognize these obligations and will never fail to perform them."

How many more could be brought! opinions of great and good men of the North, acknowledging and maintaining the rights of the people of the South. Everett, Adams, Cambrelengj and a host of others, whose names I need not give. "Time was," said Mr. Fletcher in

Boston, (in 1835, at a great meeting in that city,) "when such sentiments and such language would not have been breathed in this community. And here, on this hallowed spot, of all places on earth, should they be met and rebuked. Time was, when the British Parliament having declared 'that they had a right to bind us in all cases whatsoever/ and were attempting to bind our infant limbs in fetters, when a voice of resistance and notes of defiance had gone forth from this hall, then, when Massachussets, standing for her liberty and life, was alone breasting the whole power of Britain, the generous and gallant Southerners came to our aid, and ours refused not to hold communion with slaveholders. When the blood of our citizens, shed by a British soldiery, had stained our streets and flowed upon the heights that surround us, and sunk into the earth upon the plains of Lexington and Concord, then when he, whose name can never be pronounced by American lips without the strongest emotion of gratitude and love to every American heart,— when he, that slaveholder, (pointing to a full-length portrait of Washington,) who, from this canvass, smiles

upon his children with paternal benignity, came with other slave holders to drive the British myrmidons from this city, and in this hall our fathers did not refuse to hold communion with them.

" With slaveholders they formed the confederation, neither asking nor receiving any right to interfere in their domestic relations : with them, they made the Declaration of Independence."

To England, not to the United States, belongs whatever odium may be attached to the introduction of slavery into our country. Our fathers abolished the slave-trade, but permitted the continuation of domestic slavery.

Slavery, authorized by God, permitted by Jesus Christ, sanctioned by the apostles, maintained by good men of all agv3S, is still existing in a portion of our beloved country. How long it will continue, or whether it will ever cease, the Almighty Ruler of the universe can alone determine.

I do not intend to give a history of Abolition. Born in fanaticism, nurtured in violence and disorder, it exists too. Turning aside the institutions and commands of God, treading under foot the love of country, despising the laws of nature and the nation, it is dead to every feeling of patriotism and brotherly kindness; full of strife and pride, strewing the path of the slave with thorns and of the master with difficulties, accomplishing nothing good, forever creating disturbance.

The negroes are still slaves—"while the American slave holders, collectively and individually, ask no favours of any man or race that treads the earth. In none of the attributes of men, mental or physical, do they acknowledge or fear superiority else-w.here. They stand in the broadest light of the knowledge, civilization, and improvement of the age, as much favored of Heaven as any other of the sons of Adam. ;;

AUNT PHILLIS'S CABIN.

CHAPTER I.

THERE would be little to strike the eye of a traveler accustomed to picturesque scenes, on approaching the

small town of L . Like most of the settlements in

Virginia, the irregularity of the streets and the want of similarity in the houses would give an unfavorable first impression. The old Episcopal church, standing at the entrance of the town, could not fail to be attractive from its appearance of age; but from this alone. No monuments adorn the churchyard; head-stones of all sizes meet the eye, some worn and leaning against a shrub or tree for support, others new and white, and glistening in the sunset. Several family vaults, unpretending in their appearance, are perceived on a closer scrutiny, to which the plants usually found in burial-grounds are clinging, shadowed too by large trees. The walls where they are visible are worn and discolored, but they are almost covered with ivy, clad in summer's deepest green. Many a stranger stopped his horse in passing by to wonder at its look of other days; and some, it may be, to wish they were sleeping in the shades of its mouldering walls.

The slight eminence on which the church was built, commanded a view of the residences of several gentlemen of fortune who lived in the neighborhood. To the nearest one, a gentleman on horseback was directing his way. The horse required no direction, in truth, for so accustomed was he to the ride to Exeter, and to the good fare he enjoyed on arriving there, that neither whip nor spur was necessary; he traced the familiar road with evident pleasure.

The house at Exeter was irregularly built; but the white stone wings and the look-out over the main building gave an appearance of taste to the mansion. The fine old trees intercepted the view, though adding greatly to its beauty. The porter's lodge, and the wide lawn entered by its open gates, the gardens at either side of the building, and the neatness and good condition of the out-houses, all showed a prosperous state of affairs with the owner. Soon the large porch with its green blinds, and the sweet-brier entwining them, came in view, and the family party that occupied it were discernible. Before Mr. Barbour had reached the point for alighting from his horse, a servant stood in readiness to take charge of him, and Alice Weston emerged from her hiding-place among the roses, with her usual sweet words of welcome. Mr. Weston, the owner of the mansion and its adjoining plantation, arose with a dignified but cordial greeting; and Mrs. Weston, his sister-in-law, and Miss Janet, united with him in his kind reception of a valued guest and friend.

Mr. Weston was a widower, with an only son; the young gentleman was at this time at Yale College. He had been absent for three years; and so anxious was he to graduate with honor, that he had chosen not to return to Virginia until his course of study should be completed. The family had visited him during the first year of his exile, as he called it, but it had now been two years since he had seen any member of it. There was an engagement between him and his cousin, though Alice was but fifteen when it was formed. They had been associated from the earliest period of their lives, and Arthur declared that should he return home on a visit, he would not be able to break away from its happiness to the routine of a college life: he yielded therefore to the earnest entreaties of his father, to remain at New Haven until he graduated.

Mr. Weston will stand for a specimen of the southern gentleman of the old school. The bland and cheerful expression of his countenance, the arrangement of his soft fine hair, the fineness of the texture and the perfect cleanliness of every part of his dress, the plaiting of his old-fashioned shirt ruffles, the whiteness of his hand, and the sound of his clear, well-modulated voice—in fact, every item of his appearance—won the good opinion of a stranger; while the feelings of his heart and his steady course of Christian life, made him honored and reverenced as he deserved. He possessed that requisite to the character of a true gentleman, a kind and charitable heart.

None of the present members of his family had any lawful claim upon him, yet he cherished them with the utmost affection. He requested his brother's widow, on the death of his own wife, to assume the charge of his house; and she was in every respect its mistress. Alice was necessary to his happiness, almost to his existence; she was the very rose in his garden of life. He had never had a sister, and he regarded Alice as a legacy from his only brother, to whom he had been most tenderly attached: had she been uninteresting, she would still have been very dear to him; but her beauty and her many graces of appearance and character drew closely together the bonds of love between them ; Alice returning, with the utmost warmth, her uncle's affection.

Mrs. Weston was unlike her daughter in appearance, Alice resembling her father's family. Her dark, fine eyes were still full of the fire that had beamed from them in youth ; there were strongly-marked lines about her mouth, and her face when in repose bore traces of the warfare of past years. The heart has a writing of its own, and we can see it on the countenance; time has no power to obliterate it, but generally deepens the expression. There was at times too a sternness in her voice and manner, yet it left no unpleasant impression; her general refinement, and her fine sense and education made her society always desirable.

Cousin Janet, as she was called by them all, was a dependant and distant relation; a friend faithful and unfailing ; a bright example of all that is holy and good in the Christian character. She assisted Mrs. Weston greatly in the many cares that devolved on the mistress of a plantation, especially in instructing the young female servants in knitting and sewing, and in such household duties as would make them useful in that state of life in which it had pleased God to place them. Her heart was full of love to all God's creatures; the servants came to her with their little ailings and grievances, and she had always a soothing remedy—some little specific for a bodily sickness, with a word of advice and kindness, and, if the case required it, of gentle reproof for complaints of another nature. Cousin Janet was an old maid, yet many an orphan and friendless child had shed tears upon her bosom; some, whose hands she had folded together in prayer as they knelt beside her, learning from her lips a child's simple petition, had long ago laid down to sleep for ever; some are living still, surrounded by the halo of their good influence. There was one, of whom we shall speak by-and-by, who was to her a source of great anxiety, and the constant subject of her thoughts and fervent prayers.

Many years had gone by since she had accepted Mr. Weston's earnest entreaty to make Exeter her home; and although the bread she eat was that of charity, yet she brought a blessing upon the house that sheltered her, by her presence : she was one of the chosen ones of the Lord. Even in this day, it is possible to entertain an angel unawares. She is before you, reader, in all the dignity of old age, of a long life drawing to a close; still to the last, she works while it is yet day!

With her dove-colored dress, and her muslin three-cornered handkerchief, pinned precisely at the waist and over her bosom, with her eyes sunken and dim, but expressive, with the wrinkles so many and so deep, and the thin, white folds of her satin-looking hair parted under her cap; with her silver knitting-sheath attached to her side, and her needles in ever busy hands, Cousin Janet would perhaps first arrest the attention of a stranger, in spite of the glowing cheek and golden curls that were contrasting with her. It was the beauty of old age and youth, side by side. Alice's face in its full perfection did not mar the loveliness of hers; the violet eyes of the one, with their long sweep of eyelash, could not eclipse the mild but deep expression of the other. The rich burden of glossy hair was lovely, but so were the white locks; and the slight but rounded form was only compared in its youthful grace to the almost shadowy dignity of old age.

It was just sundown, but the servants were all at home after their day's work, and they too were enjoying the pleasant evening time. Some were seated at the door of their cabins, others lounging on the grass, all at ease, and without care. Many of their comfortable cabins had been recently whitewashed, and were adorned with little gardens in front; over the one nearest the house a multiflora rose was creeping in full bloom. Singularly musical voices were heard at intervals, singing snatches of songs, of a style in which the servants of the South especially delight; and not unfrequently, as the full chorus was shouted by a number, their still more peculiar laugh was heard above it all, Mr. Barbour had recently returned from a pleasure tour in our Northern States, had been absent for two months, and felt that he had not in as long a time wit nessed such a scene of real enjoyment. He thought it

would have softened the heart of the sternest hater of Southern institutions to have been a spectator here; it might possibly have inclined him to think the sun of his Creator's beneficence shines over every part of our favored land.

"Take a seat, my dear sir," Mr. Weston said, "in our sweetbrier house, as Alice calls it; the evening would lose half its beauty to us, if we were within."

"Alice is always right," said Mr. Barbour, "in every thing she says and does, and so I will occupy this arm chair that I know she placed here for me. Dear me! what a glorious evening! Those distant peaks of the Blue Ridge look bluer than I ever saw them before."

"Ah! you are glad to tread Virginia soil once more, that is evident enough," said Mr. Weston. "There is no danger of your getting tired of your native state again."

" Who says I was ever tired of her ? I challenge you to prove your insinuation. I wanted to see this great New England, the < great Norrurd,' as Bacchus calls it, and I have seen it; I have enjoyed seeing it, too; and now I am glad to be at home again."

"Here comes Uncle Bacchus now, Mr. Barbour," said Alice ; " do look at him walk. Is he not a curiosity ? He has as much pretension in his manner as if he were really doing us a favor in paying us a visit."

"The old scamp," said Mr. Barbour, "he has a frolic in view; he wants to go off to-morrow either to a camp-meeting, or a barbecue. He looks as if he were hooked together, and could be taken apart limb by limb."

Bacchus had commenced bowing some time before he reached the piazza, but on ascending the steps he made a particularly low bow to his master, and then in the same manner, though with much less reverence, paid his respects to the others.

"Well, Bacchus?" said Mr. Weston.

" How is yer health dis evenin, master ? You aint been so well latterly. We'll soon have green corn though, and that helps dispepsy wonderful."

"It may be good for dyspepsia, Bacchus," said Mr. Weston, "but it sometimes gives old people choleramorbus, when they eat it raw; so I advise you to remember last year's experience, and roast it before you eat it."

" I shall, indeed," replied Bacchus; " 'twas an awful time I had last summer. My blessed grief! but I thought my time was done come. But de Lord was mighty good to me, he brought me up again—Miss Janet's physic done me more good though than any thing, only it put me to sleep, and I never slept so much in my born days."

"You were always something of a sleeper, I am told, Bacchus," said Cousin Janet; "though I have no doubt the laudanum had that effect; you must be more prudent; old people cannot take such liberties with them selves."

" Lor, Miss Janet, I aint so mighty ole now; besure I aint no chicken nother; but thar's Aunt Peggy; she's what I call a raal ole nigger; she's an African. Miss Alice, aint she never told you bout de time she seed an elerphant drink a river dry?"

"Yes," said Alice, "but she dreamed that."

" No, Miss, she actually seed it wid her own eyes. They's mighty weak and dim now, but she could see out of 'em once, I tell ye. It's hot nuff here sometimes, but Aunt Peggy says it's winter to what 'tis in Guinea, whar she was raised till she was a big gall. One day when de sun was mighty strong, she seed an elerphant a comin along. She runned fast enough, she had no 'casion to grease her heels wid quicksilver; she went mighty fast, no doubt; she didn't want dat great beast's hoof in her wool. Y r ou and me seed an elerphant de time we was in Wash ington, long wid master, Miss Alice, and I thought 'bout Aunt Peggy that time. 'Twas a 'nageree we went to. You know I held you in my arms over de people's heads to see de monkeys ride.

" Well, Aunt Peggy say she runned till she couldn't run no longer, so she dumb a great tree, and sat in de branches and watched him. He made straight for de river, and he kicked up de sand wid his hoofs, as he went along, till he come to de bank; den he begins to drink, and he drinks, I tell you. Aunt Peggy say every swaller he took was least a gallon, and he drunk all dat blessed mornin. After a while she seed de water gitting very low, and last he gits enuff. He must a got his thirst squinched by dat time. So Aunt Peggy, she waded cross de river, when de elephant had went, and two days arter dat, de river was clean gone, bare as my hand. Master," continued Bacchus, "I has a great favor to ax of you."

"Barbecue or campmeeting, Bacchus?" said Mr. Bar-bour.

"If you please, master," said he, addressing Mr. Wes-ton, but at the same time giving an imploring look to Mr. Barbour, "to 'low me to go way to-morrow and wait at de barbecue. Mr. Semmes, he wants me mightily; he says he'll give me a dollar a day if I goes. I'll sure and be home agin in the evenin."

"lam afraid to give you permission," said Mr. Wes-ton ; " this habit of drinking, that is growing upon you, is a disgrace to your old age. You remember you were picked up and brought home in a cart from campmeeting this summer, and I am surprised that you should so soon ask a favor of me."

"I feels mighty shamed o' that, sir," said Bacchus, " but I hope you will 'scuse it. Niggers aint like white people, no how; they can't 'sist temptation. I've repented wid tears for dat business, and 'twont happen agin, if it please the Lord not to lead me into temptation."

"You led yourself into temptation," said Mr. Weston; " you took pains to cross two or three fences, and to go round by Norris's tavern, when, if you had chosen, you could have come home by the other road."

« True as gospel, ma'am," said Bacchus, " I don't deny de furst word of it; the Lord forgive me for backsliding; but master's mighty good to us, and if he'll overlook that little misfortune of mine, it shan't happen agin."

" You call it a misfortune, do you, Bacchus ?" said Mr. Barbour; " why, it seems to me such a great Christian as you are, would have given the right name to it, and called it a sin. I am told you are turned preacher ?"

" No, sir," said Bacchus, « I aint no preacher, I warn't called to be; I leads in prayer sometimes, and in general I rises de tunes."

" Well, I suppose I can't refuse you," said Mr. Weston ; " but come home sober, or ask no more permissions."

" God bless you, master; don't be afeard: you'll see you can trust me. I aint gwine to disgrace our family no more. I has to have a little change sometimes, for Miss Janet knows my wife keeps me mighty straight at home. She 'lows me no privileges, and if I didn't go off some times for a little fun, I shouldn't have no health, nor sper-rets nother."

" You wouldn't have any sperrits, that's certain," said Alice, laughing; «I should like to see a bottle of whisky in Aunt Phillis's cabin."

Bacchus laughed outright, infinitely overcome at the suggestion. "My blessed grief! Miss

Alice," said he, " she'd make me eat de bottle, chaw up all de glass, swaller it arter dat. I aint ever tried dat yet—best not to, I reckon. No, master, I intends to keep sober from this time forrurd, till young master comes back; den I shall git high, spite of Phillis, and 'scuse me, sir, spite of de devil hisself. When is he comin, any how, sir?"

"Next year, I hope, Bacchus," said Mr. Weston.

"Long time, sir," said Bacchus; "like as not he'll never see old Aunt Peggy agin. She's failin, sir, you can see by de way she sets in de sun all day, wid a long switch in her hand, trying to hit de little niggers as dey go by. Sure sign she's gwine home. If she wasn't alto gether wore out, she'd be at somefin better. She's sarved her time cookin and bakin, and she's gwine to a country whar there's no 'casion to cook any more. She's a good old soul, but wonderful cross sometimes."

" She has been an honest, hard-working, and faithful servant, and a sober one too," said Mr. Weston.

"I understand, sir," said Bacchus, humbly; "but don't give yourself no oneasiness about me! I shall be home to morrow night, ready to jine in at prayers."

"Very well—that will do, Bacchus," said Mr. Weston, who felt anxious to enjoy the society of his friend.

" Good evenin to you all," said Bacchus, retreating with many bows.

We will see how Bacchus kept his word, and for the present leave Mr. Weston to discuss the subjects of the day with his guest; while the ladies paid a visit to Aunt Peggy, and listened to her complaints of " the flies and the little niggers," and the thousand and one ailings that be long to the age of ninety years.

CHAPTER II.

" You rode too far this afternoon, Alice, you seem to be very tired," said Mr. Weston.

" No, dear uncle, I am not fatigued; the wind was cold, and it makes me feel stupid."

"Why did not Walter come in?" asked Mr. Weston. "I saw him returning with you by the old road."

"He said he had an engagement this evening," replied Alice, as she raised her head from her uncle's shoulder.

"Poor Walter !" said Cousin Janet; "with the education and habits of a gentleman, he is to be pitied that it is only as a favor he is received, among those with whom he may justly consider himself on an equality."

"But is not Walter our equal?" asked Alice. Cousin Janet held her knitting close to her eyes to look for a dropped stitch, while Mr. Weston replied for her :

"My love, you know, probably, that Walter is not an equal by right of birth to those whose parents held a fair and honorable position in society. His father, a man of rare talents, of fascinating appearance, and winning address, was the ruin of all connected with him. (Even his mother, broken-hearted by his career of extravagance and dissipa tion, found rest in the termination of a life that had known no rest.) His first wife, (not Walter's mother,) a most interesting woman, was divorced from him by an unjust decision of the law, for after her death circumstances transpired that clearly proved her innocence. Walter's mother was not married, as far as is known ; though some believe she was, and that she concealed it in consequence of the wishes and threats of Mr. Lee, who was ashamed to own the daughter of a tradesman for his wife."

"But all this is not Walter's fault, uncle," said Alice.

"Assuredly not; but there is something due to our long established opinions. Walter should go to a new country, where these things are not known, and w r here his education and talents would advance him. Here they are too fresh in the memory of many. Yet do I feel most kindly to wards him, though he rather repels the interest we take in him by his haughty coldness of manner. The attachment between him and my son from their infancy draws me towards him. Arthur writes, though, that his letters are very reserved and not frequent. What can be the meaning of it?"

" There was always a want of candor and generosity in Walter's disposition," remarked Alice's mother.

"You never liked him, Anna," said Mr. Weston; "why was it?"

"Arthur and Walter contrast so strongly," answered Mrs. Weston. "Arthur was always perfectly honest and straight-forward, even as a little child; though quiet in his way of showing it, he is so affectionate in his disposi tion. Walter is passionate and fickle, condescending to those he loves, but treating with a proud indifference every one else. I wonder he does not go abroad, he has the command of his fortune now, and here he can never be happily situated; no woman of delicacy would ever think of marrying him with\that stain on his birth."

"How beautiful his mother was, Cousin Janet!" said Mr. Weston. " I have never seen more grace and refine ment. I often look at Walter, and recall her, with her beautiful brown hair and blue eyes. How short her course was, too ! I think she died at eighteen."

" Do tell me about her, uncle," said Alice.

" Cousin Janet can, better than I, my darling. Have you never told Alice her history, cousin ?"

"No, it is almost too sad a tale for Alice's ear, and there is something holy, in my mind, in the recollection of

the sorrows of that young person. I believe she was a wife, though an unacknowledged one. If the grave would give up its secrets—but it will, it will—the time will come for justice to all, even to poor Ellen Haywood.

" That young creature was worse than an orphan, for her father, thriving in business at one time, became dissipated and reckless. Ellen's time was her own; and after her mother's death her will was uncontrolled. Her education was not good enough to give her a taste for self-improve ment. She had a fine mind, though, and the strictest sense of propriety and dignity. Her remarkable beauty drew towards her the attention of the young men of her own class, as well as those of good family; but she was always prudent. Poor girl! knowing she was motherless and friendless, I tried to win her regard; I asked her to come to the house, with some other young girls of the neighborhood, to study the Bible under my poor teachings ; but she declined, and I afterwards went to see her, hoping to persuade her to come. I found her pale and delicate, and much dispirited. Thanking me most earnestly, she begged me to excuse her, saying she rarely went out, on account of her father's habits, fearing something might occur during her absence from home. I was surprised to find her so depressed, yet I do not remember ever to have seen any thing like guilt, in all the interviews with her, from that hour until her death.

"Ellen's father died; but not before many had spoken lightly of his daughter. Mr. Lee was constantly at the house; and what but Ellen's beauty could take him there ! No one was without a prejudice against Mr. Lee, and I have often wondered that Ellen could have overlooked what every one knew, the treatment his wife had received. You will think," continued Cousin Janet, "that it is be cause I am an old maid, and am full of notions, that 1 cannot imagine how a woman can love a man who has been divorced from his wife. I, who have never loved as tho

novelists say, have the most exalted ideas of marriage. It is in Scripture, the type of

Christ's love to the church. Life is so full of cares; there is something holy in the thought of one heart being privileged to rest its burden on another. But how can that man be loved who has put away his wife from him, because he is tired of her? for this is the meaning of the usual excuses—incompatibility of temper, and the like. Yet Ellen did love him, with a love passing description ; she forgot his faults and her own position; she loved as I would never again wish to see a friend of mine love any creature of the earth.

" Time passed, and Ellen was despised. Mr. Lee left abruptly for Europe, and I heard that this poor young woman was about to become a mother. I knew she was alone in the world, and I knew my duty too. I went to her, and I thank Him who inclined me to seek this wandering lamb of his fold, and to be (it may be) the means of leading her back to His loving care and protection. I often saw her during the last few weeks of her life, and she was usually alone ; Aunt Lucy, her mother's servant, and her own nurse when an infant, being the only other occupant of her small cottage.

« Speaking of her, brings back, vividly as if it happened yesterday, the scene with which her young life closed. Lucy sent for me, as I had charged her, but the messenger delayed, and in consequence, Ellen had been some hours sick when I arrived. Oh! how lovely her face appears to my memory, as I recall her. She was in no pain at the moment I entered; her head was supported by pillows, and her brown hair fell over them and over her neck. Her eyes were bright as an angel's, her cheeks flushed to a crimson color, and her white, beautiful hand grasped a cane which Dr. Lawton had just placed there, hoping to relieve some of her symptoms by bleeding. Lucy stood by, full of anxiety and affection, for this faithful servant loved her as she loved her own life. My heart reproached

me for my unintentional neglect, but I was in a moment by her side, supporting her head upon my breast.

"It is like a dream, that long night of agony. The patience of Ellen, the kindness of her physician, and the devotion of her old nurse—I thought that only a wife could have endured as she did.

" Before this, Ellen had told me her wishes as regards her child, persuaded that, if it should live, she should not survive its birth to take care of it. She entreated me to befriend it in the helpless time of infancy, and then to appeal to its father in its behalf. I promised her to do so, always chiding her for not hoping and trusting. ‹ Ellen,' I would say, « life is a blessing as long as God gives it, and it is our duty to consider it so.'

" 'Yes, Miss Janet, but if God give me a better life, shall I not esteem it a greater blessing ? I have not deserved shame and reproach, and I cannot live under it. Right glad and happy am I, that a few sods of earth will soon cover all.'

" Such remarks as these," continued Cousin Janet, " convinced me that there was grief, but not guilt, on Ellen's breast, and for her own sake, I hoped that she would so explain to me her past history, that I should have it in my power to clear her reputation. But she never did. Truly, 'she died and made no sign,' and it is reserved to a future day to do her justice.

"I said she died. That last night wore on, and no word of impatience or complaint escaped her lips. The agony of death found her quiet and composed. Night advanced, and the gray morning twilight fell on those features, no longer flushed and excited. Severe faintings had come on, and the purple line under the blue eyes heralded the approach of death. Her luxuriant hair lay in damp masses about her; her white arms were cold, and the moisture of death was gathering there too. 'Oh ! Miss Ellen,' cried old Lucy, 'you will be better soon—bear up a little longer.'

" 'Ellen dear,' I said, 'try and keep up.' But who can give life and strength save One?—and

He was calling to her everlasting rest the poor young sufferer.

" 'Miss Ellen,' again cried Lucy, 'you have a son; speak to me, my darling;' but, like Rachel of old, she could not be thus revived, 'her soul was in departing.'

"Lucy bore away the child from the chamber of death, and I closed her white eyelids, and laid her hands upon her breast. Beautiful was she in death: she had done with pain and tears forever.

"I never can forget," continued Cousin Janet, after a pause of a few moments, "Lucy's grief. She wept unceasingly by Ellen's side, and it was impossible to arouse her to a care for her own health, or to an interest in what was passing around. On the day that Ellen was to be buried, I went to the room where she lay prepared for her last long sleep. Death had laid a light touch on her fair face. The sweet white brow round which her hair waved as it had in life—the slightly parted lips—the expression of repose, not only in the countenance, but in the attitude in which her old nurse had laid her, seemed to indicate an awakening to the duties of life. But there was the coffin and the shroud, and there sat Lucy, her eyes heavy with weeping, and her frame feeble from long fasting, and indulgence of bitter, hopeless grief.

" It was in the winter, and a severe snow-storm, an unusual occurrence with us, had swept the country for several clays ; but on this morning the wind and clouds had gone together, and the sun was lighting up the hills and river, and the crystals of snow were glistening on the evergreens that stood in front of the cottage door. One ray intruded through the shutter into the darkened room, and rested on a ring, which I had never observed before, on Ellen's left hand. It was on the third finger, and its appearance there was so unexpected to me, that for a moment my strength forsook me, and I leaned against the table on which the coffin rested, for support.

« 'Lucy,' I said, 'when was that placed there?'

" <I put it there, ma'am.'

« ' But what induced you ?'

" ' She told me to do so, ma'am. A few days before she was taken sick, she called me and took from her bureau-drawer, that ring. The ring was in a small box. She was very pale when she spoke—she looked more like death than she does now, ma'am. I know'd she wasn't able to stand, and I said, ' Sit down, honey, and then tell me what you want me to do.'

"'Mammy,' said she, 'you've had a world of trouble with me, and you've had trouble of your own all your life; but I am not going to give you much more I shall soon be where trouble cannot come.'

"'Don't talk that way, child,' said I, 'you will get through with this, and then you will have something to love and to care for, that will make you happy again.'

" 'Never in this world,' said she ; 'but mammy, I have one favor more to ask of you—and you must promise me to do it.'

" 'What is it, Miss Ellen?' said I; 'you know I would die for you if 'twould do you any good.'

" 'It is this,' she said, speaking very slowly, and in a low tone, ' when I am dead, mammy, when you are all by yourself, for I am sure you will stay by me to the last, I wTant you to put this ring on the third finger of my left hand—will you remember ?—on the third finger of my left hand.' She said it over twice, ma'am, and she was whiter than that rose that lays on her poor breast.'

"' Miss Ellen,' says I, ' as sure as there's a God in heaven you are Mr. Lee's wife, and why don't you say so, and stand up for yourself? Don't you see how people sneer at you when they see you?'

" 'Yes, but don't say any more. It will soon be over.

I made a promise, and I will keep it; God will do me justice when he sees fit.'

" 'But, Miss Ellen,' says I, 'for the sake of the child'— " ' Hush ! mammy, that is the worst of all; but I will trust in Him. It's a dreadful sin to love as I have, but God has punished me. Do you remember, dear mammy, when I was a child, how tired I would get, chasing butter flies while the day lasted, and when night came, how I used to spring, and try to catch the lightning-bugs that were flying around me—and you used to beg me to come in and rest or go to bed, but I would not until I could no longer stand ; then I laid myself on your breast and forgot all my weariness ? So it is with me now; I have had my own way, and I have suffered, and have no more strength to spend; I will lie down in the grave, and sleep where no one will reproach me. Promise me you will do what I ask you, and I will die contented.'

" 'I promised her, ma'am, and I have done it.' " 'It is very strange, Lucy,' said I, 'there seems to have been a mysterious reason why she would not clear herself; but it is of no use to try and unravel the mystery. She has no friends left to care about it; we can only do as she said, leave all to God.'

" 'Ah ma'am,' said Lucy, 'what shall I do now she is gone? I have got no friend left; if I could only die too— Lord have mercy upon me.'

" ' You have still a friend, Lucy,' I said. ' One that well deserves the name of friend. You must seek Him out, and make a friend of Him. Jesus Christ is the friend of the poor and desolate. Have you no children, Lucy ?' " ' God only knows, ma'am.'

" ' What do you mean ?' I said. ' Are they all dead ?'

" ' They are gone, ma'am—all sold. I ain't seen one of them for twenty years. Days have come and gone, and nights have come and gone, but day and night is all the same to me. You did not hear, may be, for grand folks don't often hear of the troubles of the poor slave—that one day I had seven children with me, and the next they were all sold ; taken off, and I did not even see them, to bid them good-by. My master sent me, with my mistress to the country, where her father lived, (for she was sickly, and he said it would do her good,) and when we came back there was no child to meet me. I have cried, ma'am, enough for Miss Ellen, but I never shed a tear for my own.'

" < But what induced him, Lucy, to do such a wicked thing ?'

" < Money, ma'am, and drinking, and the devil. He did not leave me one. My five boys, and my two girls, all went at once. My oldest daughter, ma'am, I was proud of her, for she was a handsome girl, and light-colored too—she went, and the little one, ma'am. My heart died in me. I hated him. I used to dream I had killed him, and I would laugh out in my sleep, but I couldn't murder him on her account. My mistress, she cried day and night, and called him cruel, and she would say, < Lucy, I'd have died before I would have done it.' I couldn't murder him, ma'am, 'twas my mistress held me back.'

" ' No, Lucy,' said I, «'twas not your mistress, it was the Lord; and thank Him that you are not a murderer. Did you ever think of the consequences of such an act?'

" < Lor, ma'am, do you think I cared for that ? I wasn't afraid of hanging.'

"' I did not mean that, Lucy. I meant, did you not fear His power, who could not only kill your body, but destroy your soul in hell ?'

"'I didn't think of any thing, for a long time. My mistress got worse after that, and I nursed her until she died ; poor Miss Ellen was a baby, and I had her too. When master died I thought it was no use for me to wish him ill, for the hand of the Lord was heavy on him, for true. 'Lucy,' he said, 'you are a kind nurse to me, though I sold your children, but I've had no rest since.' I couldn't make him feel worse, ma'am, for he was going to his account with all his sins upon him.'

"' This is the first time Lucy,' I said, 'that I have ever known children to be sold away from their mother, and I look upon the crime with as great a horror as you do.'

"'Its the only time I ever knowed it, ma'am, and every body pitied me, and many a kind thing was said to me, and many a hard word was said of him ; true enough, but better be forgotten, as he is in his grave.'

" Some persons now entered, and Lucy became absorbed in her present grief; her old frame shook as with a tempest, when the fair face was hid from her sight. There were few mourners; Cousin Weston and I followed her to the grave. I believe Ellen was as pure as the white lilies Lucy planted at her head."

"Did Lucy ever hear of her children?" asked Alice.

" No, my darling, she died soon after Ellen. She was quite an old woman, and had never been strong."

"Uncle," said Alice, "I did not think any one could be so inhuman as to separate mother and children."

"It is the worst feature in slavery," replied Mr. Weston, "and the State should provide laws to prevent it; but such a circumstance is very uncommon. Haywood, Ellen's father, was a notoriously bad man, and after this wicked act was held in utter abhorrence in the neighborhood. It is the interest of a master to make his slaves happy, even were he not actuated by better motives. Slavery is an institution of our country; and while we are privileged to maintain our rights, we should make them comfortable here, and fit them for happiness here after."

" Did you bring Lucy home with you, Cousin Janet ?" asked Alice.

" Yes, my love, and little Walter too. He was a dear baby—now he is a man of fortune, (for Mr. Lee left him his entire property,) and is under no one's control. He will always be very dear to me. But here comes Mark with the Prayer Book."

" Lay it here, Mark," said Mr. Weston, " and ring the bell for the servants. I like all who can to come and unite with me in thanking God for His many mercies. Strange, I have opened the Holy Book where David says, (and we will join with him,) 'Praise the Lord, oh ! my soul, and all that is within me, praise his holy name.' '

CHAPTER III.

AFTER the other members of the family had retired, Mr. Weston, as was usual with him, sat for a while in the parlor to read. The closing hour of the day is, of all, the time that we love to dwell on the subject nearest our heart. As, at the approach of death, the powers of the mind rally, and the mortal, faint and feeble, with but a few sparks of decaying life within him, arouses to a sense of his condition, and puts forth all his energies, to meet the hour of parting with earth and turning his face to heaven ; so, at the close of the evening, the mind, wearied with its day's travelling, is about to sink into that repose as necessary for it as for the body—that repose so often compared to the one in which the tired struggler with life, has " forever wrapped the drapery of his couch about him, and laid down to pleasant dreams." Ere yielding, it turns with energy to the calls of memory, though it is so soon to forget all for a while. It hears voices long since hushed, and eyes gaze into it that have looked their last upon earthly visions. Time is forgotten, Affection for a while holds her reign, Sorrow appears with her train of reproachings and remorse, until exhaustion comes to its aid, and it obtains the relief so bountifully provided by Him who knoweth well our frames. With Mr. Weston this last hour was well employed, for he not only read, but studied the Holy Scriptures. Possessed of an unusually placid temperament, there had occurred in his life but few events calculated to change the natural bent of his disposition. The death of his wife was indeed a bitter grief; but he had not married young, and she had lived so short a time, that after a while he returned to his usual train of reflection. But for the constant presence of his son, whose early education he superintended, he would have doubted if there ever had been a reality to the remembrance of the happy year he had passed in her society.

With his hand resting on the sacred page, and his heart engrossed with the lessons it taught, he was aroused from his occupation by a loud noise proceeding from the kitchen. This was a most unusual circumstance, for besides that the kitchen was at some distance from the house, the servants were generally quiet and orderly. It was far from being the case at present. Mr. Weston waited a short time to give affairs time to right themselves, but at length determined to inquire into the cause of the confusion.

As he passed through the long hall, the faces of his ancestors looked down upon him by the dim light. There was a fair young lady, with an arm white as snow, unconcealed by a sleeve, unless the fall of a rich border of lace from her shoulder could be called by that name. Her golden hair was brushed back from her forehead, and fell in masses over her shoulders. Her face was slightly turned, and there was a smile playing about her mouth.

Next her was a grave-looking cavalier, her husband. There were old men, with powdered hair and the rich dress of bygone times.

There were the hoop and the brocades, and the stomacher, and the fair bosom, against which a rose leaned, well satisfied with its lounging place. Over the hall doors, the antlers of the stag protruded, reminding one that the chase had been a favorite pastime with the self-exiled sons of Merry England.

Such things have passed away from thee, my native State! Forever have they gone, and the times when over waxed floors thy sons and daughters gracefully performed the minuet. The stately bow, the graceful curtsey are seen no more; there is hospitality yet lingering in thy halls, but fashion is making its way there too. The day when there was a tie between master and slave,—is that departing, and why?

Mr. Weston passed from the house under a covered way to the kitchen, and with a firm but slow step, entered. And here, if you be an Old or a New Englander, let me introduce you—as little at home would be Queen Victoria holding court in the Sandwich Islands, as you here. You may look in vain for that bane of good dinners, a cooking stove; search forever for a grain of saleratus or soda, and it will be in vain. That large, round block, with the wooden hammer, is the biscuit-beater; and the cork that is lifting itself from the jug standing on it, belongs to the yeast department.

Mr. Weston did not, nor will we, delay to glance at the well-swept earthen floor, and the bright tins in rows on the dresser, but immediately addressed himself to Aunt Peggy, who, seated in a rush-bottomed chair in the corner, and rocking herself backwards and forwards, was talking rapidly.

And oh! what a figure had Aunt Peggy; or rather, what a face. Which was the blacker, her eyes or her visage; or whiter, her eyeballs or her hair? The latter, uncon-fined by her bandanna handkerchief as she generally wore it, standing off from her head in masses, like snow. And who that had seen her, could forget that one tooth projecting over her thick underlip, and in constant motion as she talked.

"It's no use, Mister Bacchus," said she, addressing the old man, who looked rather the worse for wear, "it's no use to be flinging yer imperence in my face. I'se worked my time; I'se cooked many a grand dinner, and eat 'em too. You'se a lazy wagabond yerself."

"Peggy," interposed Mr. Weston.

"A good-for-nothing, lazy wagabond, yerself," continued Peggy, not noticing Mr. Weston, "you'se not worth de hommony you eats."

"Does you hear that, master?" said Bacchus, appealing to Mr. Weston; "she's such an old fool."

"Hold your tongue, sir," said Mr. Weston; while Mark, ready to strangle his fellow-servant for his impertinence, was endeavoring to drag him out of the room.

"Ha, ha," said Peggy, "so much for Mr. Bacchus going to barbecues. A nice waiter he makes."

"Do you not see me before you, Peggy?" said Mr. Weston, "and do you continue this disputing in my presence? If you were not so, old, and had not been so faithful for many years, I would not excuse such conduct. You are very ungrateful, when you are so well cared for; and from this time forward, if you cannot be quiet and set a good example in the kitchen, do not come into it."

"Don't be afeard, master, I can stay in my own cabin. If I has been well treated, it's no more den I desarves. I'se done nuff for you and yours, in my day; slaved my self for you and your father before you. De Lord above knows I dont want ter stay whar dat ole drunken nigger is, no how. Hand me my cane, dar, Nancy, I ain't gwine to 'trude my 'siety on nobody." And Peggy hobbled off, not without a most contemptuous look at Bacchus, who was making unsuccessful efforts to rise in compliment to his master.

"As for you, Bacchus," said Mr. Weston, "never let this happen again. I will not allow you to wait at barbecues, in future."

" Don't say so, master, if you please; dat ox, if you could a smelled him roastin, and de whiskey-punch," and Bacchus snapped his finger, as the only way of concluding the sentence to his own satisfaction.

"Take him off, Mark," said Mr. "Weston, " the drunken old rascal."

" Master," said Bacchus, pushing Mark off, " I don't like de way you speak to me ; faint 'spectful."

"Carry him off," said Mr. Weston, again. "John, help Mark."

"Be off wid yourselves, both of ye," said Bacchus; "if ye don't, I'll give you de devil, afore I quits."

"I'll shut your mouth for you," said Mark, "talking so before master; knock him over, John, and push him out."

Bacchus was not so easily overcome. The god whose namesake he was, stood by him for a time. Suddenly the old fellow's mood changed; with a patronizing smile he turned to Mr. Weston, and said, "Master, you must 'scuse me: I aint well dis evening. I has the dyspepsy; my suggestion aint as good as common. I think dat ox was done too much."

Mr. Weston could not restrain a smile at his grotesque appearance, and ridiculous language. Mark and John took advantage of the melting mood which had come over him, and led him off without difficulty. On leaving the kitchen, he went into a pious fit, and sung out

"When I can read my title clar."

Mr. Weston heard him say, "Don't, Mark; don't squeeze an ole nigger so; do you 'spose you'll ever get to Heaven, if you got no more feelins than that?"

"I hope," said Mr. Weston, addressing the other servants, "that you will all take warning by this scene. An honest and respectable servant like Bacchus, to degrade himself in this way—it gives me great pain to see it.

5

William," said he, addressing a son of Bacchus, who stood by the window, "did you deliver my note to Mr, Walter?"

« Yes, sir; he says he'll come to dinner ; I was on my way in to tell you, but they was making such a fuss here."

"Very well," said Mr. Weston. "The rest of you go to bed, quietly; I am sure there will be no more disturbance to-night."

But, what will the Abolitionist say to this scene ? Where were the whip and the cord, and other instruments of torture ? Such consideration, he contends, was never shown in the southern country. With Martin Tupper, I say,

"Hear reason, oh! brother; Hear reason and right."

It has been, that master and slave were friends; and if this cannot continue, at whose door will the sin lie?

The Abolitionist says to the slave, Go! but what does he do that really advances his interest ? He says to the master, Give up thine own! but does he offer to share in the loss ? No; he would give to the Lord of that which costs him nothing.

Should the southern country become free, should the eyes of the world see no stain upon her escutcheon, it will not be through the efforts of these fanatics. If white labor could be substituted for black, better were it that she should not have this weight upon her. The emancipation of her slaves will never be accomplished by interference or force. Good men assist in colonizing them, and the Creator may thus intend to christianize benighted Africa. Should this be the Divine will, oh! that from every port, steamers were going forth, bearing our colored people to their natural home!

CHAPTER IV.

MY readers must go with me to a military station at the North, and date back two years from the time of my story. The season must change, and instead of summer sunsets and roses, we will bring before them three feet of snow, and winter's bleakest winds.

Neither of these inconvenienced the company assembled in the comfortable little parlor of Captain Moore's quarters, with a coal-grate almost as large as the room, and curtains closely drawn over the old style windows: Mrs. Moore was reduced to the utmost extremity of her wits to make the room look modern; but it is astonishing, the genius of army ladies for putting the best foot foremost. This room was neither square nor oblong; and though a mere box in size, it had no less than four doors (two belonged to the closets) and three windows. The closets were utterly useless, being occupied by an indomitable race of rats and mice; they had an impregnable fortress somewhere in the old walls, and kept possession, in spite of the house-keeping artillery Mrs. Moore levelled against them. The poor woman gave up in despair; she locked the doors, and determined to starve the garrison into submission.

She was far more successful in • other respects, having completely banished the spirits of formality and inhospi-tality that presided in these domains. The house was outside the fort, and had been purchased from a citizen who lived there, totally apart from his race; Mrs. Moore had the comfort of hearing, on taking possession, that all sorts of ghosts were at home there; but she was a cheerful kind of woman, and did not believe in them any more than sho

did in clairvoyance, so she set to work with a brave heart, and every thing yielded to her sway, excepting the aforesaid rats and mice.

Her parlor was the very realization of home comfort. The lounge by the three windows was covered with small figured French chintz, and it was a delightful seat, or bed, as the occasion required. She had the legs of several of the chairs sawed off, and made cushions for them, covered with pieces of the chintz left from the lounge. The arm chairs that looked at each other from either side of the fire place, not being of velvet, were made to sit in.

In one corner of the room, (there were five,) a fine-toned guitar rested against the wall; in another, was a large fly-brush of peacock's feathers, with a most unconscionable number of eyes. In the third, was Captain Moore's sword and sash. In the fourth, was Mrs. Moore's work-basket, where any amount of thimbles, needles, and all sorts of sewing implements could be found. And in the fifth corner was the baby-jumper, its fat and habitual occupant being at this time oblivious to the day's exertions; in point of fact, he was up stairs in a red pine crib, sound asleep with his thumb in his mouth.

One of Chickering's best pianos stood open in this wonderful little parlor, and Mrs. Moore rung out sweet sounds from it evening after evening. Mrs. M. was an industrious, intelligent Southern woman; before she met Captain Moore, she had a sort of antipathy to dogs and Yankees; both, however, suddenly disappeared, for after a short acquaintance, she fell desperately in love with the captain, and allowed his great Newfoundland dog, (who had saved the captain, and a great number of boys from drowning,) to lick her hand, and rest his cold, black nose on her lap ; on this evening Neptune lay at her feetj and was another ornament of the parlor. Indeed, he should have been mentioned in connection with the baby-jumper, for wherever the baby was in the day time, there was Neptune, but he seemed to

think that a Newfoundland dog had other duties incumbent upon him in the evening than watching babies, so he listened attentively to the music, dozing now and then. Sometimes, during a very loud strain, he would suddenly rouse and look intently at the coal-fire ; but finding himself mistaken, that he had only dreamed it was a river, and that a boy who was fishing on its banks had tumbled in, and required his services to pull him out, would fall down on the rug again and take another nap.

I have said nothing of this rug, which Neptune thought was purchased for him, nor of the bright red carpet, nor of the nice china candlesticks on the mantel-piece, (which could not be reached without a step-ladder,) nor of the silver urn, which was Mrs. Moore's great-grandmother's, nor of the lard-lamp which lit up every thing astonishingly, because I am anxious to come to the point of this chapter, and cannot do justice to all these things. But it would be the height of injustice, in me, to pass by Lieutenant Jones's moustaches, for the simple reason, that since the close of the Mexican war, he had done little else but cultivate them. They were very brown, glossy, and luxuriant, entirely covering his upper lip, so that it was only in a hearty laugh that one would have any reason to suppose he had cut his front teeth; but he had, and they were worth cutting, too, which is not always the case with teeth. The object of wearing these moustaches was, evidently, to give himself a warlike and ferocious appearance; in this, he was partially successful, having the drawbacks of a remarkably gentle and humane countenance, and a pair of mild blue eyes. He was a very good-natured young man, and had shot a wild turkey in Mexico, the tail of which he had brought home to Mrs. Moore, to be made into a fan. (This fan, too, was in the parlor, of which may be said what was once thought of the schoolmaster's head, that the only wonder was, it could contain so much.)

Next to Mr. Jones we will notice a brevet-second lieutenant, just attached to the regiment, and then introduce a handsome bachelor captain. (These are scarce in the army, and should be valued accordingly.) This gentleman was a fine musician, and the brevet played delightfully on the flute; in fact, they had had quite a concert this evening. Then there was Colonel Watson, the commanding officer, who had happened in, Mrs. Moore being an especial favorite of his; and there was a long, lean, gaunt-looking gentleman, by the name of Kent. He was from Vermont, and was an ultra Abolitionist. They had all just returned from the dining-room, where they had been eating cold turkey and mince pies; and though there was a fair chance of the nightmare some hours hence, yet for the present they were in an exceedingly high state of health and spirits.

Now, Mrs. Moore had brought from Carolina a woman quite advanced in life. She had been a very faithful servant, and Mrs. Moore's mother, wishing her daughter to have the benefit of her services, and feeling perfect confidence in Polly's promise that under no circumstances would she leave her daughter without just cause, had concluded that the best way of managing affairs would be to set her free at once. She did so; but Polly being one of those persons who take the world quietly, was not the least elated at being her own mistress; she rather felt it to be a kind of experiment to which there was some risk attached. Mrs. Moore paid her six dollars a month for her services, and from the time they had left home together until the present moment, Polly had been a most efficient servant, and a sort of friend whose opinions were valuable in a case of emergency.

For instance, Captain Moore was a temperance man, and in consequence, opposed to brandy, wine, and the like being kept in his house. This was quite a trouble to his wife, for she knew that good mince pies and pudding sauces could not be made without a little of the wherewithal; so she laid her difficulties before Aunt Polly, and begged her to advise what was best to do.

" You see, Aunt Polly, Captain Moore says that a good example ought to be set to the soldiers; and that since the Mexican war the young officers are more inclined to indulge than they used to be; that he feels such a responsibility in the case that he can't bear the sight of a bottle in the house."

"Well, honey," said Aunt Polly, "he says he likes my mince pies, and my puddins, mightily; and does he 'spect me to make 'em good, and make 'em out of nothin, too ?"

" That's what I say, Aunt Polly, " for you know none of us like to drink. The captain belongs to the Tempe rance Society; and I don't like it, because it gets into my head, and makes me stupid; and you never drink any thing, so if we could only manage to get him to let us keep it to cook with."

"As to that, child," said Aunt Polly, "I mus have it to cook with, that's a pint settled; there aint no use 'spu-tin about it. If he thinks I'm gwine to change my way of cookin in my old age, he's mightily mistaken. He need'nt think I'm gwine to make puddins out o' one egg, and lighten my muffins with snow, like these ere Yankees, 'kase I aint gwine to do it for nobody. I sot out to do my duty by you, and I'll do it; but for all that, I aint bound to set to larnin new things this time o' day. I'll cook Carolina fashion, or I wont cook at all."

"Well, but what shall I do?" said Mrs. Moore; "you wouldn't have me do a thing my husband disapproves of, would you?"

« No, that I wouldn't, Miss Emmy," said Aunt Polly. My old man's dust and ashes long ago, but I always done what I could to please him. Men's mighty onreasonable, the best of 'em, but when a woman is married she ought to do all she can for the sake of peace. I dont see what a man has got to do interferin with the cookin, no how;

a woman oughter 'tend to these matters. 'Pears to me, Mr. Moore, (captain, as you calls him,) is mighty fidjetty about bottles, all at once. But if he cant bear the sight of a brandy bottle in the house, bring 'em down here to me; I'll keep 'em out of his sight, I'll be bound. I'll put 'em in the corner of my old chist yonder, and I'd like to see him thar, rummagin arter brandy bottles or any thing else."

Mrs. Moore was very much relieved by this suggestion, and when her husband came in, she enlarged on the ne cessity of Polly's having her own way about the cooking, and wound up by saying that Polly must take charge of all the bottles, and by this arrangement he would not be an noyed by the sight of them.

" But, my dear," said he, " do you think it right to give such things in charge of a servant?"

"Why, Aunt Polly never drinks."

"Yes, but Emmy, you don't consider the temptation."

"La, William, do hush; why if you talk about tempta tion, she's had that all her life, and she could have drank herself to death long ago. Just say yes, and be done with it, for it* has worried me to death all day, and I want it settled, and off my mind."

"Well, do as you like," said Captain Moore, "but re member, it will be your fault if any thing happens."

" Nothing is going to happen," said Mrs. Moore, jumping up, and seizing the wine and brandy bottles by the necks, and descending to the lower regions with them.

" Here they are, Aunt Polly. William consents to your having them; and mind you keep them out of sight."

" Set 'em down in the cheer thar, I'll take care of 'em, I jist wanted son\e brandy to put in these potato puddins. I wonder what they'd taste like without it."

But Mrs. Moore could not wait to talk about it, she was up stairs in another moment, holding her baby on Nep tune's back, and more at ease in her mind than she had

been since the subject was started, twenty-four hours before.

There was but one other servant in the house, a middle-aged woman, who had run away from her mistress in Boston; or rather, she had been seduced off by the Aboli tionists. While many would have done well under the circumstances, Susan had never been happy, or comfort able, since this occurred. Besides the self-reproach that annoyed her, (for she had been brought on from Georgia to nurse a sick child, and its mother, a very feeble person, had placed her dependence upon her,) Susan was illy cal culated to shift for herself. She was a timid, delicate woman, with rather a romantic cast of mind ; her mistress had always been an invalid, and was fond of hearing her favorite books read aloud. For the style of books that Susan had been accustomed to listen to, as she sat at her sewing, Lalla Rookh would be a good specimen; and, as she had never been put to hard work, but had merely been an attendant about her mistress' room, most of her time was occupied in a literary way. Thus, having an excel lent memory, her head was a sort of store-room for love sick snatches of song. The Museum men would represent her as having snatched a feather of the bird of song; but as this is a matter-of-fact kind of story, we will observe, that Susan not being naturally very strong-minded, and her education not more advanced than to enable her to spell out an antiquated valentine, or to write a letter with a great many small i's in it, she is rather to be considered the victim of circumstances and a soft heart. She was, nevertheless, a conscientious woman; and when she left Georgia, to come North, had any one told her that she would run away,' she w r ould have answered in the spirit, if not the expression, of the oft quoted, "Is thy servant a dog?"

She enjoyed the journey to the North, the more that the little baby improved very much in strength; she had had,

at her own wish, the entire charge of him from his birth.

The family had not been two days at the Revere House before Susan found herself an object of interest to men who were gentlemen, if broadcloth and patent-leather boots could constitute that valuable article. These indi viduals seemed to know as much of her as she did of her self, though they plied her with questions to a degree that quite disarranged her usual calm and poetic flow of ideas. As to "Whether she had been born a slave, or had been kidnapped ? Whether she had ever been sold ? How many times a week she had been whipped, and what with? Had she ever been shut up in a dark cellar and nearly starved? Was she allowed more than one meal a day? Did she ever have any thing but sweet potato peelings ? Had she ever been ducked ? And, finally, she was desired to open her mouth, that they might see whether her teeth had been extracted to sell to the dentist ?"

Poor Susan! after one or two interviews her feelings were terribly agitated; all these horrible suggestions might become realities, and though she loved her home, her mis tress, and the baby too, yet she was finally convinced that though born a slave, it was not the intention of Providence, but a mistake, and that she had been miraculously led to this Western Holy Land, of which Boston is the Jerusalem, as the means by which things could be set to rights again.

One beautiful, bright evening, when her mistress had rode out to see the State House by moonlight, Susan kissed the baby, not without many tears, and then threw herself, trembling and dismayed, into the arms and tender mercies of the Abolitionists. They led her into a distant part of the city, and placed her for the night under the charge of some people w r ho made their living by receiving the newly ransomed. The next morning she was to go off, but she found she had reckoned without her host, for when she thanked the good people for her night's lodging and the

hashed cod-fish on which she had tried to breakfast, she had a bill to pay, and where was the money? Poor Susan! she had only a quarter of a dollar, and that she had asked her mistress for a week before, to buy a pair of side-combs.

"Why, what a fool you be," said one of the men; "Didn't I tell you to bring your mistress' purse along?"

"And did you think I was going to steal besides run ning off from her and the poor baby?" answered Susan.

"It's not stealing," said the Abolitionist. "Haven't you been a slaving of yourself all your life for her, and I guess you've a right to be paid for it. I guess you think the rags on your back good wages enough?"

Susan looked at her neat dress, and thought they were very nice rags, compared to the clothes her landlady had on; but the Abolitionist was in a hurry.

"Come," said he, "I'm not going to spend all my time on you; if you want to be free, come along; pay what you owe and start."

"But I have only this quarter," said Susan, despairingly.

"I don't calculate to give runaway niggers their supper, and night's lodging and breakfast for twenty-five cents," said the woman. "I aint so green as that, I can tell you. If you've got no money, open your bundle, and we can make a trade, like as not."

Susan opened her bundle, (which was a good strong carpet bag her mistress had given her,) and after some hesitation, the woman selected as her due a nice imitation of Cashmere shawl, the last present her mistress had given her. It had cost four dollars. Susan could hardly give it up; she wanted to keep it as a remembrance, but she already felt herself in the hands of the Philistines, and she fastened up her carpet-bag and set forward. She was carried off in the cars to an interior town, and directed to the house of an Abolitionist, to whom she was to hire herself.

Her fare was paid by this person, and then deducted from her wages—her wages were four dollars a month.

She cooked and washed for ten in family; cleaned the whole house, and did all the chores, except sawing the wood, which the gentleman of the house did himself. She was only required to split the hard, large knots—the oldest son splitting the easy sticks for her. On Saturday, the only extra duty required of her was to mend every item of clothing worn in the family; the lady of the house making them herself. Susan felt very much as if it was out of the frying pan into the fire; or rather, as if she had been transferred from one master to another. She found it took all her wages to buy her shoes and stockings and flannel, for her health suffered very much from the harsh climate and her new mode of life, so she ventured to ask for an increase of a dollar a month.

"Is that your gratitude," was the indignant reply, "for all that we've done for you? The idea of a nigger wanting over four dollars a month, when you've been working all your life, too, for nothing at all. Why everybody in town is wondering that I keep you, when white help is so much better."

"But, ma'am," replied Susan, "they tell me here that a woman gets six dollars a month, when she does the whole work of a family."

"A white woman does," said this Abolitionist lady, "but not a nigger, I guess. Besides, if they do, you ought to be willing to work cheaper for Abolitionists, for they are your friends."

If "save me from my friends," had been in Lalla Rookh, Susan would certainly have applied it, but as the quotation belonged to the heroic rather than the sentimental department, she could not avail herself of it, and therefore went on chopping her codfish and onions together, at the rate of four dollars a month, and very weak eyes, till some good wind blew Captain Moore to the command of his company, in the Fort near the town.

After Mrs. Moore's housekeeping operations had fairly commenced, she found it would be necessary to have a person to clean the house of four rooms, and to help Neptune mind the baby. Aunt Polly accordingly set forward on an exploration. She presented quite an unusual appearance as regards her style of dress. She wore a plaid domestic gingham gown; she had several stuff ones, but she declared she never put one of them on for any thing less than « meetin." She had a black satin Methodist bonnet, very much the shape of a coal hod, and the color of her own complexion, only there was a slight shade of blue in it. Thick gloves, and shoes, and stockings; a white cotton apron, and a tremendous blanket shawl completed her costume. She had a most determined expression of countenance; the fact is, she had gone out to get a house-servant, and she didn't intend to return without one.

I forgot to mention that she walked with a cane, having had a severe attack of rheumatics since her arrival in "the great Norrurd," and at every step she hit the pavements in such a manner as to startle the rising generation of Abolitionists, and it had the good effect of preventing any of them from calling out to her, "Where did you get your face painted, you black nigger, you?" which would otherwise have occurred.

Susan was just returning from a grocery store with three codfish in one hand, and a piece of salt pork and a jug of molasses in the other, when she was startled by Aunt Polly's unexpected appearance, bearing down upon her like a man of war.

Aunt Polly stopped for a moment and looked at her intensely, while Susan's feelings, which, like her poetry, had for some time been quite subdued by constant collision with a cooking stove, got the better of her, and she burst into tears. Aunt Polly made up her mind on the spot; it was, as she afterwards expressed it, « <Ameracle,' meeting that poor girl, with all that codfish and other stuff in her hand."

Susan did not require too much encouragement to tell her lamentable tale, and Aunt Polly in return advised her to leave her place when her month was up, informing the family of her intention, that they might supply themselves. This Susan promised to do, with a full heart, and Aunt Polly having accomplished her mission, set out on her return, first saying to Susan, however, "We'll wait for you, you needn't be afeard, and I'll do your work 'till you come, .'taint much, for we puts out our washin. And you need'nt be sceard when you see the sogers, they aint gwine to hurt you, though they do look so savage."

Susan gave notice of her intention, and after a season of martyrdom set forward to find Captain Moore's quarters. She had no difficulty, for Polly was looking out for her, with her pipe in her mouth. " Come in, child," said she, " and warm yourself; how is your cough ? I stewed some molasses for you, 'gin you come. We'll go up and see Miss Emmy, presently; she 'spects you."

Susan was duly introduced to Mrs. Moore who was at the time sitting in the captain's lap with the baby in hers, and Neptune's forepaws in the baby's. The captain's temperance principles did not forbid him smoking a good cigar, and at the moment of Susan's entrance, he was in the act of emitting stealthily a cloud of smoke into his wife's face. After letting the baby fall out of her lap, and taking two or three short breaths with strong symptoms of choking, Mrs. Moore with a husky voice and very red eyes, welcomed Susan, and introduced her to the baby and Neptune, then told Aunt Polly to show her where to put her clothes, and to make her comfortable in every respect.

Aunt Polly did so by baking her a hoe-cake, and broiling a herring, and drawing a cup of strong tea. Susan went to bed scared with her new happiness, and dreamed she was in Georgia, in her old room, with the sick baby in her arras.

Susan's friends, the Abolitionists, were highly indignant at the turn affairs had taken. They had accordingly a new and fruitful subject of discussion at the sewing societies and quilting bees of the town. In solemn conclave it was decided to vote army people down as utterly disagreeable. One old maid suggested the propriety of their immediately getting up a petition for disbanding the army; but the motion was laid on the table in consideration of John Quincy

Adams being dead and buried, and therefore not in a condition to present the petition. Susan became quite cheerful, and gained twenty pounds in an incredibly short space of time, though strange rumors continued to float about the army. It was stated at a meeting of the F. S. F. S. T. W. T. R. (Female Society for Setting the World to Hights) that « army folks were a low, dissipated set, for they put wine in their puddin sauce."

I do not mean to say liberty is not, next to life, the greatest of God's earthly gifts, and that men and women ought not to be happier free than slaves. God forbid that I should so have read my Bible. But such cases as Susan's do occur, and far oftener than the raw-head and bloody-bones' stories with which Mrs. Harriet Beecher Stowe has seeen fit to embellish that interesting romance, Uncle Tom's Cabin.

CHAPTER V.

CAPT. MOORE suddenly seized the poker, and commenced stirring the fire vigorously. Neptune rushed to his covert under the piano, and Mrs. Moore called out, " Dont, dear, for heaven's sake."

"Why, it's getting cold," said Captain Moore, apologeti cally. " Don't you hear the wind ?"

"Yes, but I don't feel it, neither do you. The fire can not be improved. See how you have made the dust fly! You never can let well alone."

" That is the trouble with the Abolitionists," said Colonel "Watson. "They can't let well alone, and so Mr. Kent and his party want to reorganize the Southern country."

"There is no well there to let alone," said Mr. Kent, with the air of a Solomon.

"Don't talk so, Mr. Kent," said Mrs. Moore, entreat-ingly, "for I can't quarrel with you in my own house, and I feel very much inclined to do so for that one sentence."

"Now," said the bachelor captain, "I do long to hear you and Mr. Kent discuss Abolition. The colonel and I may be considered disinterested listeners, as we hail from the Middle States, and are not politicians. Captain Moore cannot interfere, as he is host as well as husband; and Mr. Jones and Scott have eaten too much to feel much in terest in any thing just now. Pray, tell Mr. Kent, my dear madam, of Susan's getting you to intercede with her mis tress to take her back, and see what he says."

"I know it already," said Mr. Kent, "and I must say that I am surprised to find Mrs. Moore inducing a fellow-creature to return to a condition so dreadful as that of a

Southern slave. After having been plucked from the fire, it should be painful to the human mind to see her thrown in again."

"Your simile is not a good one, Mr. Kent," said Mrs. Moore, with a heightened color. "I can make a better. Susan, in a moment of delirium, jumped into the fire, and she called on me to pull her out. Unfortunately, I cannot heal all the burns, for I yesterday received an an swer to my letter to her mistress, who positively refuses to take her back. She is willing, but Mr. Casey will not consent to it. He says that his wife was made very sick by the shock of losing Susan, and the over-exertion neces sary in the care of her child. The baby died in Boston; and they cannot overlook Susan's deserting it at a hotel, without any one to take charge of it; they placing such perfect confidence in Susan, too. He thinks her presence would constantly recall to Mrs. Casey her child's death; besides, after having lived among Abolitionists, he fancies it would not be prudent to bring her on the plantation. Having attained her freedom, he says she must make the best of it. Mrs. Casey enclosed me ten dollars to give to Susan, for I wrote her she was in bad health, and had very little clothing when she came to me. Poor girl! I could hardly persuade her to take the money, and soon after, she brought it to me and asked me to keep it for her, and not to change the note that came from home. I felt very sorry for her."

"She deserves it," said Mr. Kent.

"I think she does," said Mrs. Moore, smiling, "though for another reason."

Mr. Kent blushed as only men with light hair, and light skin, and light eyes, can blush.

"I mean," said Mr. Kent, furiously, "she deserves her refusal for her ingratitude. After God provided her friends who made her a free woman, she is so senseless as to want to go back to be lashed and trodden under foot again, as the slaves of the South are. I say, she deserves it for being such a fool."

"And I say," said Mrs. Moore, "she deserves it for deserting her kind mistress at a time when she most needed her services. God did not raise her up friends because she had done wrong."

"You are right, Emmy, in your views of Susan's conduct; but you should be careful how you trace motives to such a source. She certainly did wrong, and she has suffered; that is all we can say. We must do the best we can to restore her to health. She is very happy with us now, and will, no doubt, after a while, enjoy her liberty: it would be a most unnatural thing if she did not."

"But how is it, Mr. Kent," said the colonel, "that after you induce these poor devils to give up their homes, that you do not start them in life; set them going in some way in the new world to which you transfer them. You do not give them a copper, I am told."

"We don't calculate to do that," said Mr. Kent.

"I believe you," said Mrs. Moore, maliciously.

Mr. Kent looked indignant at the interruption, while his discomfiture was very amusing to the young officers, they being devoted admirers of Mrs. Moore's talents and mince pies. They laughed heartily; and Mr. Kent looked at them as if nothing would have induced him to overlook their impertinence but the fact, that they were very low on the list of lieutenants, and he was an abolition agent. "We calculate, sir, to give them their freedom, and then let them look out for themselves."

"That is, you have no objection to their living in the same world with yourself, provided it costs you nothing," said the colonel.

"We make them free," said Mr. Kent. "They have their right to life, liberty, and the pursuit of happiness. They are no longer enslaved, body and soul. If I see a man with his hands and feet chained, and I break those chains, it is all that God expects me to do; let him earn his own living."

"But suppose he does not know how to do so," said Mrs. Moore, "what then? The occupations of a negro at the South are so different from those of the people at the North."

"Thank God they are, ma'am," said Mr. Kent, grandly. "We have no overseers to draw the blood of their fellow creatures, and masters to look on and laugh. We do not snatch infants from their mothers' breasts, and sell them for w'hisky/'

"Neither do we," said Mrs. Moore, her bosom heaving with emotion; «no one but an Abolitionist could have had such a wicked thought. No wonder that men who glory in breaking the laws of their country should make such misstatements."

"Madam," said Mr. Kent, "they are facts; we can prove them; and we say that the slaves of the South shall be free, cost what it will. The men of the North have set out to emancipate them, and they will do it if they have to wade through fire, water, and blood."

«You had better not talk in that style when you go South," said Captain Moore, "unless you have an unconquerable prejudice in favor of tar and feathers."

"Who cares for tar and feathers?" said Mr. Kent; " there has been already a martyr in the ranks of Abolition, and there may be more. Lovejoy died a glorious martyr's death, and there are others ready to do the same."

" Give me my cane, there, captain, if you please," said Colonel Watson, who had been looking at Mr. Kent's blazing countenance and projecting eyes, in utter amazement. " Why, Buena Vista was nothing to this. Good night, madam, and do tell Susan not to jump into the fire again; I wonder she was not burned up while she was there. Come, captain, let us make our escape while we can."

The captain followed, bidding the whole party good night, with a smile. He had been perfectly charmed with the Abolition discussion. Mr. Jones had got very sleepy, and he and Mr. Scott made their adieu. Mr. Kent, with some embarrassment, bade Mrs. Moore good night. Mrs. Moore begged him to go South and be converted, for she believed his whole heart required changing. Captain Moore followed them to the door, and shivered as he inhaled the north-easter. « Come, Emmy," said he, as he entered, rubbing his hands, "you've fought for your country this night; let's go to bed."

Mrs. Moore lit a candle, and put out the lard-lamp, wondering if she had been impolite to Mr. Kent. She led the way to the staircase, in a reflective state of mind; Neptune followed, and stood at the foot of the steps for some moments, in deep thought; concluding that if there should be danger of any one's falling into a river up there, they would call him and let him know, he went back, laid down on the soft rug, and fell asleep for the night.

****

It does not take long to state a fact. Mr. Kent went to Washington on Abolition business,—through the introduction of a senator from his own State he obtained access to good society. He boarded in the same house with a Virginian who had a pretty face, very little sense, but a large fortune. Mr. Kent, with very little difficulty, persuaded her he was a saint, ready to be translated at the shortest notice. He dropped his Abolition notions, and they were married. At the time that my story opens, he is a planter, living near Mr. "Weston, and we will hear of him again.

CHAPTER VI.

ARTHUR WESTON is in his college-room in that far-famed city, New Haven. He is in the act of replacing his cigar in his mouth, after having knocked the ashes off it, when we introduce to him the reader. Though not well employed, his first appearance must be prepossessing; he inherited his mother's clear brunette complexion, and her fine expressive eyes. His very black hair he had thrown entirely off his forehead, and he is now reading an Abolition paper which had fallen into his hands. There are two other young men in the room, one of them Arthur's friend, Abel Johnson; and the other, a young man by the name of Hubbard.

"Who brought this paper into my room ?" said Arthur, after laying it down on the table beside him.

"I was reading it," said Mr. Hubbard, "and threw it aside."

""Well, if it makes no difference to you, Mr. Hubbard, I'd prefer not seeing any more of these publications about me. This number is a literary curiosity, and deserves to be preserved; but as I do not file papers at present, I will just return it, after expressing my thanks to you for affording me the means of obtaining valuable information about the Southern country."

"What is it about, Arthur," said Abel Johnson, "it is too hot to read this morning, so pray enlighten me ?"

"Why, here," said Arthur, opening the paper again, "here is an advertisement, said to be copied from a Southern paper, in which, after describing a runaway slave, it says: «I will give four hundred dollars for him alive, and the same sum for satisfactory proof that he has been killed.' Then the editor goes on to say, 'that when a planter loses a slave, he becomes so impatient at not capturing him, and is so angry at the loss, that he then does what is equivalent to inducing some person to murder him by way of revenge.' Now, is not this infamous?"

"But it is true, I believe," said Mr. Hubbard.

"It is not true, sir," said Arthur, "it is false, totally and entirely false. Why, sir, do you mean to say, that the life of a slave is in the power of a master, and that he is not under the protection of our laws?"

"I am told that is the case," said Mr. Hubbard.

"Then you are told what is not true; and it seems to me, you are remarkably ignorant of the laws of your country."

"It is not my country," said Mr. Hubbard, "I assure you. I lay no claims to that part of the United States where slavery is allowed."

"Then if it is not your country, for what reason do you concern yourself so much about its affairs?"

"Because," replied Mr. Hubbard, "every individual has the right to judge for himself, of his own, and of other countries."

"No, not without proper information," said Arthur. "And as you have now graduated and intend to be a lawyer, I trust you will have consideration enough for the profession, not to advance opinions until you are sufficiently informed to enable you to do so justly. Every country must have its poor people; you have yours at the North, for I see them—we have ours; yours are white, ours are black. I say yours are white; I should except your free blacks, who are the most miserable class of human beings I ever saw. They are indolent, reckless, and impertinent. The poorer classes of society, are proverbially improvident—and yours, in sickness, and in old age, are often victims of want and suffering. Ours in such circumstances, are kindly cared for, and are never considered a burden;

our laws are, generally speaking, humane and faithfully administered. We have enactments which not only protect their lives, but which compel their owners to be moderate in working them, and to ensure them proper care as regards their food."

"But," said Mr. Hubbard, "you have other laws, police-laws, which deprive them of the most innocent recreations, such as are not only necessary for their happiness, but also for their health."

"And if such laws do exist," said Arthur, "where is the cause? You may trace it to the interference of meddling, and unprincipled men. They excite the minds of the slaves, and render these laws necessary for the very protection of our lives. But without this interference, there would be no such necessity. In this Walsh's Appeal, which is now open before me, you will find, where Abel left off reading, these remarks, which show that not only the health and comfort of the slaves, but also their feelings, are greatly considered. «The master who would deprive his negro of his property—the product ~»f his poultry-house or his little garden; who would force him to work on holidays, or at night; who would deny him common recreations, or leave him without shelter and provision, in his old age, would incur the aversion of the community, and raise obstacles to the advancement of his own interest and external aims."

"Then," said Mr. Hubbard, "you mean to say, he is kind from self-interest alone."

"No, I do not," replied Arthur; "that undoubtedly, actuates men at the South, as it does men at the North; but I mean, to say, so universal is it with us to see our slaves well treated, that when an instance of the contrary nature occurs, the author of it is subject to the dislike and odium of his acquaintances."

"But," said Mr. Hubbard, "that does not always protect the slaves—which shows that your laws are sometimes

ineffectual. They are not always secure from ill-treatment."

"But, do your laws always secure you from ill-treatment?" said Arthur.

" Of course," said Mr. Hubbard, " the poorest person in New England is as safe from injustice and oppression, as the highest in the land."

"Nonsense," said Arthur, " don't you think I can judge for myself, as regards that ? Abel, do tell Mr. Hubbard of our little adventure in the bakehouse."

"With pleasure," said Abel, "especially as you two have not let me say a word yet. Well, Mr. Hubbard, Arthur and I having nothing else to do, got hungry, and as it was a fine evening, thought we would walk out in search of something to satisfy our appetites, and there being a pretty girl in Brown's bakehouse, who waits on customers, we took that direction. Arthur, you know, is engaged to be married, and has no excuse for such things, but I having no such ties, am free to search for pretty faces, and to make the most of it when I find them. We walked on, arm-in-arm, and when we got to the shop, there stood Mrs. Brown behind the counter, big as all out doors, with a very red face, and in a violent perspiration; there was something wrong with the old lady 'twas easy to see."

" 'Well, Mrs. Brown,' said Arthur, for I was looking in the glass cases and under the counter for the pretty face, ' have you any rusk ?'

"'Yes, sir, we always have rusk,' said Mr. Brown, tartly.

"'Will you give us some, and some cakes, or whatever you have? and then we will go and get some soda water, Abel.'

" Mrs. Brown fussed about like a <bear with a sore head,' and at last she broke out against that gal.

" 'Where on earth has she put that cake ?' said she. 'I

sent her in here with it an hour ago; just like her, lazy, good-for-nothing Irish thing. They're nothing but white niggers, after all, these Irish. Here, Ann,' she bawled out, 'come here!'

" ' Coming,' said Ann, from within the glass door.

" ' Come this minute,' said the old woman, and Ann's pretty Irish face showed itself immediately.

" 'Where's that 'lection cake I told you to bring here?'

"'You didn't tell me to bring no cake here, Mrs. Brown,' said Ann.

" ' I did, you little liar, you,' said Mrs. Brown. ' You Irish are born liars. Go, bring it here.'

" Ann disappeared, and soon returned, looking triumphant. ' Mr. Brown says he brought it in when you told him, and covered it in that box—so I aint such a liar, after all.'

" ' You are,' said Mrs. Brown, i and a thief too.'

"Ann's Irish blood was up.

" 'I'm neither,' said she; 'but I'm an orphan, and poor; that's why I'm scolded and cuffed about.'

" Mrs. Brown's blood was up too, and she struck the poor girl in the face, and her big, hard hand was in an instant covered with blood, which spouted out from Ann's nose.

"'Now take that for your impudence, and you'll get worse next time you go disputing with me.'

" ' I declare, Mrs. Brown,' said Arthur, ' this is, I thought, a free country. I did not know you could take the law into your own hands in that style.'

" 'That gal's the bother of my life,' said Mrs. Brown. 'Mr. Brown, he was in New York when a ship come, and that gal's father and mother must die of the ship-fever, and the gal was left, and Mr. Brown calculated she could be made to save us hiring, by teaching her a little. She's smart enough, but she's the hard-headedest, obstinatest thing I ever see. I can't make nothin' of her. You might as well try to draw blood out of a turnip as to get any good out of her.'

7

"< You got some good blood out of her,' said I, < at any rate,' for Mrs. Brown was wiping her hands, and the blood looked red and healthy enough; «but she is not a turnip, that's one thing to be considered.'

"'Well, Mrs. Brown, good evening,' said Arthur. 'I shall tell them at the South how you Northern people treat your white niggers.'

"'I wish to the Lord,' said Mrs. Brown, <we had some real niggers. Here I am sweatin, and workin, and bakin, all these hot days, and Brown he's doin nothin from morn ing 'till night but reading Abolition papers, and tendin Abolition meetings. I'm not much better than a nigger myself, half the time.'

"Now,'* said Arthur, "Mr. Hubbard, I have been for tunate in my experience. I have never seen a slave woman struck in my life, though I've no doubt such things are done; and I assure you when I saw Mrs. Brown run the risk of spoiling that pretty face for life, I wondered your laws did not protect < these bound gals,' or < white niggers,' as she calls them."

"You see, Hubbard," said Abel, "your philanthropy and Arthur's is very contracted. He only feels sympathy for a pretty white face, you for a black one, while my en larged benevolence induces me to stand up for all female <phizmahoganies,' especially for the Hottentot and the Ma dagascar ones, and the fair sex of all the undiscovered islands on the globe in general."

"You don't think, then," said Mr. Hubbard, argumenta-tively, "that God's curse is on slavery, do you?"

"In what sense?" asked Arthur. "I think that slavery is, and always was a curse, and that the Creator intended what he said, when he first spoke of it, through Noah."

" But, I mean," said Mr. Hubbard, " that it will bring a curse on those who own slaves."

"No, sir," said Arthur, " God's blessing is, and always has been on my father, who is a slaveholder; on his

father, who was one; and on a good many more I could mention. In fact, I could bring forward quite a respecta ble list who have died in their beds, in spite of their egre gious sin in this respect. There are Washington, Jeffer son, Madison, Marshall, Calhoun, Henry Clay, and not a few others. In this case, the North, as has been said, says to her sister South, < Stand aside, for I am holier than thou!' that is, you didn't need them, and got rid of them."

" We were all born free and equal," said Mr. Hubbard, impressively.

"Equal!" said Abel, "there is that idiot, with his tongue hanging out of his mouth, across the street: was he born equal with you?"

"It strikes me," said Arthur, "that our slaves are not born free."

"They ought to be so, then," said Mr. Hubbard.

"Ah! there you arraign the Creator," said Arthur; "I must stop now."

" What do you think is the meaning of the text < Cursed be Canaan, a servant of servants shall he be unto his brethren,' Hubbard?" said Abel.

"I don't think*it justifies slavery," said Hubbard.

" Well, what does it mean ?" said Abel. " It must mean something. Now I am at present between two doctrines; so I am neither on your nor on Arthur's side. If I can't live one way I must another ; and these are hard times. If I can't distinguish myself in law, divinity, or physic, or as an artist, which I would prefer, I may turn planter, or may turn Abolition agent. I must do something for my living. Having no slaves I can't turn planter ; there fore there is more probability of my talents finding their way to the Abolition ranks ; so give me all the information you can on the subject."

" Go to the Bible," said Mr. Hubbard, " and learn your duty to your fellow-creatures."

" Well, here is a Bible my mother sent here for Arthur and myself, with the commentaries. This is Scott's Com mentary. Where is Canaan?" said he, turning over the leaves; " he is very hard to be got at."

"You are too far over," said Arthur, laughing, "you are not in the habit of referring to Scott."

"Here it is," said Abel, < Cursed be Canaan, a servant of servants shall he be unto his brethren.' And in another verse we see < God shall enlarge Japheth, and he shall dwell in the tents of Shem, and Canaan shall be his ser vant.' So we are Japheth and Shem, and the colored population are Canaan. Is that it, Arthur?" said Abel.

" See what Scott says, Abel," said Arthur; " I'm not a commentator."

"Well, here it is,—'There is no authority for altering the text, and reading, as some do, Cursed be Ham, the* father of Canaan, yet the frequent mention of Ham, as the father of Canaan, suggests the thought that the latter was also criminal. Ham is thought to be second, and not the youngest son of Noah; and if so, the words, < Knew what his younger son had done,' refers to Canaan, his grandson. Ham must have felt it a very mortifying rebuke, when his own father was inspired on this occasion to predict the durable oppression and slavery of his posterity. Canaan was also rebuked, by learning that the curse would espe cially rest on that branch of the family which should descend from him ; for his posterity were no doubt princi pally, though not exclusively, intended.'"

" Now," continued Abel, " I shall have to turn planter, and get my niggers as I can; for I'll be hanged if it wasn't a curse, and a predicted one, too."

" That does not make it right," said Mr. Hubbard.

"Don't it," said Abel; "well, if it should be fated for me to turn parson, I shan't study divinity with you, for my mother has told me often, that God's prophecies were right, and were fulfilled, too; as I think this one has been."

" I suppose, then, you think slavery will always conti nue, Mr. Weston?" said Hubbard.

" Well, I am only a man, and cannot prophesy, but I think, probably not. Slavery is decreasing throughout the world. The slave trade is about being abolished on the coast of Africa. You Abolitionists are getting a good many off from our southern country, and our planters are setting a number of theirs free, and sending them to Africa. I know a gentleman in Georgia who liberated a number, and gave them the means to start in Liberia as free agents and men. He told me he saw them on board, and watched the ship as she disappeared from his sight. At last he could not detect the smallest trace of her, and then such a feeling of intense satisfaction occupied his breast as had been a stranger there until that time. < Is it possible that they are gone, and I am no longer to be plagued with them ? They are free, and I am free, too.' He could hardly give vent to his feelings of relief on the occasion."

"And are they such trouble to you, Arthur?" asked Abel.

« No, indeed," said Arthur, « not the. least. My father treats them well, and they appear to be as well off as the working classes generally are. I see rules to regulate the conduct of the master and slave in Scripture, but I see no where the injunction to release them; nor do I find laid down the sin of holding them. The fact is, you northern people are full of your isms; you must start a new one every year. I hope they will not travel south, for I am tired of them. I should like to take Deacon and Mrs. White back home with me. Our servants would be afraid of a man who has worked sixteen hours a day half his lifetime."

"Deacon White is worth twenty thousand dollars," said Abel, " every cent of which he made mending and making common shoes."

"What does he do with it?" said Arthur.

" Hoards it up," said Abel, "and yet an honester man never lived. Did I not tell you of the time I hired his horse and chaise? I believe not; well, it is worth waiting for. The deacon's old white horse is as gray and as docile as himself; the fact is, the stable is so near the house, that the horse is constantly under the influence of < Old Hundred;" he has heard the good old tune so often, that he has a solemn way of viewing things. Two or three weeks ago I wanted to take my sister to see a relative of ours, who lives seven or eight miles from here, and my mother would not consent to my driving her, unless I hired the deacon's horse and chaise—the horse, she said, could not run if he wanted to. So I got him, and Harriet asked Kate Laune to go too, as the chaise was large enough for all three; and we had a good time. We were gone all day, and after I took the girls home, I drove round to the deacon's house and jumped out of the chaise to pay what I owed.

« You know what a little fellow the deacon is, and he looked particularly small that evening, for he was seated in his arm-chair reading a large newspaper which hid him all but his legs. These are so shrunken that I wonder how his wife gets his stockings small enough for him.

" < Good evening, Mrs. White,' said I, for the old lady was sitting on the steps knitting.

"«Mercy's sake, deacon,' said she, <put down your newspaper; don't you see Mr. Johnson?'

" < The deacon did not even give me a nod until he had scrutinized the condition of the horse and chaise, and then he said, <How are you?'

"<Not a screw loose in me, or the horse and chaise either, for I had two girls with me, and I'm courting one of them for a quarter, so I drove very carefully. I am in a hurry now, tell me what I am to pay you?'

^'Twelve and a half cents,' said the deacon, slowly raising his spectacles from his nose.

" 'No!' said I. < Twelve and a half cents! «Why, I have had the horse all day.'

" ' That is my price,' said the deacon.

" 'For a horse and chaise, all day?' said I. Why, deacon, do charge me something that I aint ashamed to pay you.'

'"That is iny regular price, and I can't charge you any more.'

" I remonstrated with him, and tried to persuade him to take twenty-five cents—but, no. I appealed to Mrs. White; she said the ' deacon hadn't ought to take more than the horse and chaise was worth.' However, I induced him to take eighteen and three-quarter cents, but he was uneasy about it, and said he was afraid he was imposing on me.

" The next morning I was awakened at day-dawn—there was a man, they said, who wanted to see me on pressing business, and could not wait. I dressed in a hurry, wondering what was the cause of the demand for college-students. I went down, and there stood the deacon, looking as if his last hour were come. ' Mr. Abel,' he said, 'I have passed a dreadful restless night, and I couldn't stand it after the day broke—here's your six and a quarter cents —I hadn't ought have charged you more than my usual price.' I was angry at the old fellow for waking me up, but I could not help laughing, too."

" 'Twas very ugly of you, Mr. Abel, to persuade me to take so much,' said he; ' you're Avelcome to the horse and chaise whenever you want it, but twelve and a half cents is my usual price."

"Now," said Mr. Hubbard, "he is like the Portuguese devils; when they are good, they are too good—I should distrust that man."

"He is close to a farthing," said Abel, "but he is as honest as the day. Why he has the reputation of a saint.

Harriet says she wishes he wore a long-tailed coat instead of a short jacket, so that she could hang on and get to heaven that way."

« My sister saw Mrs. White not long ago, and compli mented her on her new bonnet being so very becoming to her. <Now I want to know !' said Mrs. White; 'why I thought it made me look like a fright.'

« 'But what made you get a black one,' said Harriet, «why did you not get a dark green or a brown one ?'

" 'Why, you see,' said Mrs. White, < the deacon's health is a failin'; he's dreadful low in the top knots lately, and I thought as his time might come very soon, I might as well get a black one while I was a getting. We're all born to die, Mise Harriet; and the deacon is dwindlin' away.'"

The young men laughed, and Arthur said " What will he do with his money? Mrs. White will not wear the black bonnet long if she have twenty thousand dollars; she can buy a new bonnet and a new husband with that."

" No danger," said Abel, "Deacon White has made his will, and has left his wife the interest of five thousand dollars; at her death the principal goes, as all the rest, to aid some benevolent purpose.

" But there are the letters; what a bundle for you, Arthur ! That is the penalty of being engaged. Well I must wait for the widow White, I guess she'll let me have the use of the horse and chaise, at any rate."

Mr. Hubbard arose to go, and Arthur handed him his newspaper. « That is a valuable document, sir, but there is one still more so in your library here; it is a paper pub lished the same month and year of the Declaration of Independence, in which are advertised in the New England States negroes for sale ! Your fathers did not think we were all born free and equal it appears."

"We have better views now-a-days, said Mr. Hubbard; the Rev. Mr. H. has just returned from a tour in the

Southern States, and he is to lecture to-night, won't you go and hear him?"

« Thank you, no," said Arthur. "I have seen some of this reverend gentleman's statements, and his friends ought to advise him to drop the reverend for life. He is a fit subject for an asylum, for I can't think a man in his senses would lie so."

" He is considered a man of veracity," said Mr. Hub-bard, " by those who have an opportunity of knowing his character."

"Well, I differ from them," said Arthur, "and shall deprive myself of the pleasure of hearing him. Good evening, sir."

« Wouldn't he be a good subject for tar and feathers, Arthur ? They'd stick, like grim death to a dead nigger," said Abel.

"He is really such a fool," said Arthur, "that I have no patience with him ; but you take your usual nap, and I will read my letters."

CHAPTER VII.

WE will go back to the last evening at Exeter, when we left Mr. Weston to witness the result of Bacchus's attendance at the barbecue. There were other hearts busy in the quiet night time. Alice, resisting the offers of her maid to assist her in undressing, threw herself on a lounge by the open window. The night air played with the curtains, and lifted the curls from her brow. Her bloom, which of late had been changeful and delicate, had now left her cheek, and languid and depressed she abandoned herself to thought. So absorbed was she, that she was not aware any one had entered the room, until her mother stood near, gently reproving her for thus exposing herself to the night air. « Do get up and go to bed," she said. " Where is Martha ?"

"I did not want her," said Alice; "and am now going to bed myself. What has brought you here?"

" Because I felt anxious about you," said Mrs. Weston, "and came, as I have often before, to be assured that you were well and enjoying repose. I find you still up; and now, my daughter, there is a question I have feared to ask you, but can no longer delay it. By all the love that is between us, by the tie that should bind an only child to a widowed mother, will you tell me what are the thoughts that are oppressing you ? I have been anxious for your health, but is there not more cause to fear for your happiness ?"

"I am well enough, dear mother," said Alice, with some irritation of manner, "Do not concern yourself about me. If you will go to bed, I will too."

"You cannot thus put me off," said Mrs. Weston. " Alice, I charge you, as in the presence of God, to tell me truly: do you love Walter Lee?"

" It would be strange if I did not," said Alice, in a low voice. " Have we not always been as brother and sister?"

" Not in that sense, Alice ; do not thus evade me. Do you love him with an affection which should belong to your cousin, to whom you are solemnly engaged, who has been the companion of your childhood, and who is the son of the best friend that God ever raised up to a widow and a fatherless child?"

Alice turned her head away, and after a moment answered, "Yes, I do, mother, and I'cannot help it." But on turning to look at her mother, she was shocked at the expression of agony displayed on her countenance. Her hand was pressed tightly over her heart, her lips quivered, and her whole person trembled. It was dreadful to see her thus agitated; and Alice, throwing her arms around her mother exclaimed, "What is it, dearest mother? Do not look so deathlike. I cannot bear to see you so."

Oh! they speak falsely who say the certainty of evil can be better borne than suspense. Watcher by the couch of suffering, sayest thou so ? Now thou knowest there is no hope, thy darling must be given up. There is no mistaking that failing pulse, and that up-turned eye. A few hours ago, there was suspense, but there was hope; death was feared, but not expected; his arm was outstretched, but the blow was not descending; now, there is no hope.

Mrs. Weston had long feared that all was not well with Alice—that while her promise was given to one, her heart had wandered to another; yet she dreaded to meet the appalling certainty; now with her there is no hope. The keen anguish with which she contended was evident to her daughter, who was affrighted at her mother's appearance. So much so, that for the first time for months she entirely forgot the secret she had been hiding in her heart. The young in their first sorrow dream there are none like their own. It is not until time and many cares have bowed us to the earth, that we look around, beholding those who have suffered more deeply than ourselves.

Accustomed to self-control, Mrs. Weston was not long in recovering herself; taking her daughter's hand within her own, and looking up in her fair face, "Alice," she said, " you listened with an unusual interest to the details of suffering of one whom you never saw. I mean Walter Lee's mother; she died. I can tell you of one who has suffered, and lived.

"It is late, and I fear to detain you from your rest, but something impels me that I cannot resist. Listen, then, while I talk to you of myself. You are as yet almost un acquainted with your mother's history."

"Another time, mother; you are not well now," said Alice.

" Yes, my love, now. You were born in the same house that I was; yet your infancy only was passed where I lived until my marriage. I was motherless at an early age; in deed, one of the first remembrances that I recall is the bright and glowing summer evening when my mother was carried from our plantation on James River to the opposite shore, where was our family burial-ground. Can I ever forget my father's uncontrolled grief, and the sorrow of the ser vants, as they followed, dressed in the deepest mourning. I was terrified at the solemn and dark-looking bier, the black plumes that waved over it, and all the dread accom paniments of death. I remember but little for years after this, save the continued gloom of my father, and his con stant affection and indulgence toward me, and occasionally varying our quiet life by a visit to Richmond or Washing ton.

« My father was a sincere and practical Christian. He was averse to parting with me; declaring, the only solace he had was in directing my education, and being assured of my happiness.

"My governess was an accomplished and amiable lady, but she was too kind and yielding. I have always retained the most grateful remembrance of her care. Thus, though surrounded by good influences, I needed restraint, where there was so much indulgence. I have sometimes ventured to excuse myself on the ground that I was not taught that most necessary of all lessons: the power of governing my self. The giving up of my own will to the matured judg ment of others.

« The part of my life that I wish to bring before you now, is the year previous to my marriage. Never had I received an ungentle word from my father; never in all my waywardness and selfwill did he harshly reprove me. He steadily endeavored to impress on my mind a sense of the constant presence of God. He would often say, < Every moment, every hour of our lives, places its impress on our condition in eternity. Live, then, as did your mother, in a state of waiting and preparation for that ac count which we must all surely give for the talents entrusted to our care.' Did I heed his advice ? You will hardly believe me, Alice, when I tell you how I repaid his tender ness. I was the cause of his death."

«It could never be, mother," said Alice, weeping, when she saw the tears forcing their way down her mother's cheek. "You are excited and distressed now. Do not tell me any more to-night, and forget what I told you."

Mrs. Weston hardly seemed to hear her. After a pause of a few moments, she proceeded:

" It was so, indeed. I, his only child, was the cause of his death; I, his cherished and beloved daughter, committed an act that broke his he^art, and laid the foundation of sorrows for me, that I fear will only end with my life.

"Alice, I read not long since of a son, the veriest wretch on earth; he was unwilling to grant his poor aged father a subsistence from his abundance; he embittered the fail ing years of his life by unkindness and reproaches. One day, after an altercation between them, the son seized his father by his thin, white hair, and dragged him to the corner of the street. Here, the father in trembling tones implored his pity. < Stop, oh! stop, my son,' he said, 'for I dragged my father here. God has punished me in your sin.'

"Alice, can you not see the hand of a just God in this retribution, and do you wonder, when you made this acknowledgment to me to-night, the agony of death overcame me? I thought, as I felt His hand laid heavily upon me, my punishment was greater than I could beaf; my sin would be punished in your sorrow; and naught but sorrow would be your portion as the wife of Walter Lee.

" Do not interrupt me, it is time we were asleep, but I shall soon have finished what I have to say. My father and Mr. Weston were friends in early life, and I was thrown into frequent companionship with my husband, from the time when we were very young. His appearance, his talents, his unvaried gayety of disposition won my regard. For a time, the excess of dissipation in which he indulged was unknown to us, but on our return to Virginia after an absence of some months in England, it could no longer be concealed. His own father joined with mine in prohibiting all intercourse between us. For a time his family considered him as lost to them and to himself; he was utterly regardless of aught save what contributed to his own pleasures. I only mention this to excuse my father in your eyes, should you conclude he was too harsh in the course he insisted I should pursue. He forbade him the house, and refused to allow any correspondence between us; at the same time he promised that if he would perfectly reform from the life he was leading, at the end of two years he would permit the marriage. I promised in return to bind myself to these conditions. Will you believe it, that seated on my mother's grave, with my head upon my kind father's breast, I vowed, that as I hoped for Heaven I would never break my promise, never see him again, without my father's permission, until the expiration of this period; and yet I did break it. I have nearly done. I left home secretly. I was married; and I never saw my father's face again. The shock of my disobedience was too hard for him to bear. He died, and in vain have I sought a place of repentance, though I sought it with tears.

" I have suffered much; but though I cannot conceal from you that your father threw away the best portion of his life, his death was not without hope. I cling to the trust that his sins were washed away, and his soul made clean in the blood of the Saviour. Then, by the memory of all that I suffered, and of that father whose features you bear, whose dying words gave testimony to my faithfulness and affection to him, I conjure you to conquer this unfortunate passion, which, if yielded to, will end in your unceasing misery.

« There was little of my large fortune left at your father's death; we have been almost dependant on your uncle. Yet it has not been dependance; he is too generous to let us feel that. On your father's death-bed, he was all in all to him—never leaving him; inducing him to turn his thoughts to the future opening before him. He taught me where to look for comfort, and bore with me when in my impatient grief I refused to seek it. He took you, then almost an infant, to his heart, has cherished you as his own, and now looks forward to the happiness of seeing you his son's wife; will you so cruelly disappoint him?"

" I will do whatever you ask me, dear mother," said Alice. " I will never see Walter again, if that will content you. I have already told him that I can never be to him more than I have always been—a sister. Yet I can not help loving him."

" Cannot help loving a man whose very birth is attended with shame," said Mrs. Weston; "whose passions are ungovernable, who has already treated with the basest ingratitude his kindest friends? Have you so little pride? I will not reproach you, my darling; promise me you will never see Walter again, after to-morrow, without my know ledge. I can trust you. Oh! give up forever the thought of being his wife, if ever you have entertained it. Time will show you the justice of my fears, and time will bring back your old feelings for Arthur, and we shall be happy again."

"I will make you the promise," said Alice, "and I will keep it; but I will not deceive Arthur. Ungrateful as I may appear, he shall know all. He will then love some one more worthy of him than I am."

"Let us leave the future in the hands of an unerring
Q
God, my Alice. Each one must bear her burden, I would gladly bear yours; but it may not be. Forget all this for a while; let me sleep by you to-night."

Alice could not but be soothed by the gentle tone, and dear caress. Oh, blessed tie! uniting mother and child. Earth cannot, and Heaven will not break it.

CHAPTER VIII. .

As absurd would it be for one of the small unsettled stars, for whose pla'ce and wanderings we care not, to usurp the track of the Queen of night or of the God of day, as for an unpretending writer to go over ground that has been trodden by the master minds of the age. It was in the olden time that Cooper described a dinner party in all its formal, but hospitable perfection. Washington was a guest there, too, though an unacknowledged one; we can not introduce him at Exeter, yet I could bring forward there, more than one who knew him well, valuing him not only as a member of society and a hero, but as the man chosen by God for a great purpose. Besides, I would

introduce to my readers, some of the residents of L .

I would let them into the very heart of Virginia life; and, although I cannot arrogate to it any claims for superiority over other conditions of society, among people of the same class in life, yet, at least, I will not allow an infe riority. As variety is the spice of society, I will show them, that here are many men of many minds.

Mark, was a famous waiter, almost equal to Bacchus, who was head man, on such occasions. They were in their elements at a dinner party, and the sideboard, and tables, on such an occasion, were in their holiday attire. A strong arm, a hard brush, and plenty of beeswax, banished all appearance of use, and the old servants thought that every article in the room looked as bright and handsome as on the occasion of their young mistress' first presiding at her table. The blinds of the windows looking south, were partly open; the branches of the Temon-tree, and the tendrils of the white-jessamine, as-

sisted in shading the apartment, making it fragrant too. The bird-cages were hung among the branches of the flowers, and the little prisoners sang as if they had, at last, found a way of escape to -their native woods; old-fash ioned silver glittered on the sideboard, the large china punch-bowl maintaining its position in the centre.

William had gone to the drawing-room to announce the important intelligence, "Dinner is ready!" and Bacchus looked around the room for the last time, to see that every thing was, as it should be, snuffing up the rich fumes of the soup as it escaped from the sides of the silver-covered tureen. He- perceived that one of the salt-cellars was rather near the corner of the table, and had only time to rearrange it, when William threw open the doors. The company entered, and with some delay and formality took their places. We need not wait until the Rev. Mr. Aldie says grace, though that would not detain us long; for the Rev. Mr. Aldie, besides being very hungry, has a great deal of tact, and believes in short prayers ; nor will we delay to witness the breaking down of the strongholds of precision and ultra propriety, that almost always solemnizes the commencement of an entertainment; but the old Madeira having been passed around, we will listen to the conversation that is going on from different parts of the table.

"We have outlived, sir," said Mr. Chapman, addressing a northern gentleman present, "we have outlived the first and greatest era of our country. Its infancy was its greatest era. The spirit of Washington still breathes among us. One or two of us here have conversed with him, sat at his table, taken him by the hand. It is too soon for the great principles that animated his whole career to have passed from our memory. I am not a very old man, gentlemen and ladies, yet it seems to me a great while since the day of Washington's funeral. My father called me and my brothers to him, and while our mother was fastening a band of black crape around our hats, « My boys,' said he, ‹you have seen the best days of this re public.' It is so, for as much as the United States has increased in size, and power, and wealth, since then, dif ferent interests are dividing her."

" Was Washington a cheerful man ?" asked an English gentleman who was present, " I have heard that he never laughed. Is it so ?"

Miss Janet, who was considered a kind of oracle when personal memories of Washington were concerned, an swered after a moment's pause, " I have seen him smile often, I never saw him laugh but once. He rode over, one afternoon, to see a relative with whom I was staying; it was a dark, cloudy day, in November; a brisk wood fire was very agreeable. After some little conversation on ordinary topics, the gentlemen discussed the politics of the times, Washington saying little, but listening attentively to others.

" The door opened suddenly, and a son of my relative entered, in a noisy bustling manner. Passing the gentle men with a nod, he turned his back to the fire, putting his hands behind him. «Father,' said he, scarcely wait ing until the sentence that General Washington was utter ing, was finished, «what do you think ? Uncle Jack and I shot a duck in the head!' He deserved a reproof for his forwardness; but Washington joined the rest in a laugh, no doubt amused at the estimation in which the youth held himself and Uncle Jack. The two together, killed a duck, and the boy was boasting of it in the pre sence of the greatest man the world ever produced. The poor fellow left the room, and for a time his sporting talents were joked about more than he liked."

After the ladies retired, Mr. Selden proposed the health of the amiable George Washington.

" Good heavens ! sir," said Mr. Chapman, the veins in his temples swelling, and his whole frame glowing with vexation, « what is that you say ? Did ever any one hear of a soldier being amiable ? No, sir, I will give you a toast that was drank just before the death of the greatest and best of men. I picked up an old newspaper, and laid it aside in my secretary. In it I read a toast worth giving. Fill high, gentlemen—' The man who forgets the services of George Washington, may he be forgotten by his country and his God."

Mr. Selden, who possessed in a remarkable degree the amiableness that he had ascribed to another, swallowed the wine and approved the toast. Mr. Chapman was some time recovering his composure.

"You intend to leave Virginia very soon, Mr. Lee," said Mr. Kent, addressing Walter.

"Very soon, sir," Walter replied.

"Where shall you go first ?" asked Mr. Kent.

"I have not decided on any course of travel," said Walter. "I shall, perhaps, wander toward Germany."

"We will drink your health, then," said Mr. Westori.

" A pleasant tour, Walter, and a safe return."

* # * # *

"You are from Connecticut, I believe, Mr. Perkins?" said Mr. Barbour, " but as you are not an Abolitionist, I suppose it will not be uncourteous to discuss the subject before you. I have in my memorandum book a copy of a law of your State, which was in existence at one time, and which refers to what we have been conversing about. It supports the Fugitive Slave Law, in prospect. At that time you New Englanders held not only negro, but Indian slaves. Let me read this, gentleman. «Be it enacted by the Governor, Council, and Representatives, in General Court assembled, and by the authority of the same, that whatsoever negro, mulatto, or Indian servant or servants, shall be wandering out of the bounds of the town or place to which they belong, without a ticket or pass, in writing, under the hand of some Assistant or Justice of the Peace,

or under the hand of the master or owner of such negro, mulatto, or Indian servant or servants, shall be deemed and accounted as runaways, and may be treated as such. And every person inhabiting in this colony, finding or meeting with any such negro, mulatto, or Indian servant or servants not having a ticket as aforesaid, is hereby em powered to seize and secure him or them, and bring him or them before the next authority, to be examined and re turned to his or their master or owner, who shall satisfy the charge accruing thereby.

" < And all ferrymen within the colony are hereby re quested not to suffer any Indian, mulatto, or negro ser vant without certificate as aforesaid, to pass over their respective ferries by assisting them, directly or indirectly, on the penalty of paying a fine of twenty shillings for every such offence, to the owner of such servants.' In the same act," continued Mr. Barbour, "a free person who receives any property, large or small, from a slave, without an order from his master, must either make full restitution or be openly whipped with so many stripes, (not exceeding twenty.)"

"Now, gentlemen," said Mr. Chapman, who was an im petuous old gentleman, " don't you see those Yankees were close enough in taking care of their own slaves, and if they could have raised sugar and cotton, or had deemed it to their advantage to be slaveholders to this day, they'd have had a Fugitive Slave Law long before this. A Daniel would have come to judgment sooner even than the immortal Daniel "Webster."

"Wait a moment, my dear sir," said Mr. Barbour. " Another paragraph of the same act provides, ' that if any negro, mulatto, or Indian servant or slave, shall be found abroad from home, in the night season, after nine o'clock, without a special order from his or their master or mistress, it shall be lawful for any person or persons to apprehend and secure such negro, mulatto, or Indian ser-

vant or slave, so offending, and him, her, or them, bring before the next assistant or justice of the peace, which au thority shall have full power to pass sentence upon such servant or slave, and order him, her, or them, to be publicly whipped on the naked body, not exceeding ten stripes, &c."

"Pretty tight laws you had, sir," said Mr. Chapman, addressing Mr. Perkins. " A woman could be picked up and whipped, at the report of any body, o-n the naked body. Why, sir, if we had such laws here, it would be whipping all the time, (provided so infamous a law could be carried into execution.) There is one thing certain, you made the most of slavery while you had it."

"But we have repented of all our misdeeds," said Mr. Perkins, good-humouredly.

"Yes," said Mr. Chapman, "like the boy that stole a penny, and when he found it wouldn't buy the jack-knife he wanted, he repented, and carried it to the owner."

" But you must remember the times, my dear sir," said Mr. Perkins.

"I do, I do, sir," said Mr. Chapman. "The very time that you had come for freedom yourself, you kidnapped the noble sons of the soil, and made menials of them. I wonder the ground did not cry out against you. Now we have been left with the curse of slavery upon us, (for it is in some respects a curse on the negro and the white man,) and God may see fit to remove it from us. But why don't the Abolitionists buy our slaves, and send them to Liberia?"

"That would be against their principles," said Mr. Perkins.

"Excuse me, sir," said Mr. Chapman, "but d—n their principles; it is against their pockets. Why don't those who write Abolition books, give the profits to purchase some of these poor wretches who are whipped to death, and starved to death, and given to the flies to eat up, and burned alive; then I would believe in their principles, or at least in their sincerity. But now the fear is for their pockets. I am a poor man. I own a few slaves, and I will sell them to any Northern man or woman at half-price for what I could get from a trader, and they may send them to Liberia. Lord! sir, they'd as soon think of buying the d—l himself. You must excuse my strong language, but this subject irritates me. Not long ago, I was in the upper part of the State of New York, looking about me, for I do look about me wherever I am. One morning I got up early, and walked toward the new railroad that they were constructing in the neighborhood. I chanced to get to the spot just in time to see a little fracas between a stout, burly Irishman, and the superintendent of the party.

"'I thought, be Jasus,' said the Irishman, just as I approached near enough to hear what was going on, 'that a man could see himself righted in a free country.'

"'Go to your work,' said the superintendent, 'and if you say another word about it, I'll knock you over.'

"'Is it you'll knock me over, you will,' began the Irishman.

"He was over in a moment. The superintendent, sir, gave him a blow between the eyes, with a fist that was hard as iron. The man staggered, and fell. I helped him up, sir; and I reckon he thought matters might be worse still, for he slowly walked off.

"'D—d free country,' he muttered to me, in a kind of confidential tone. 'I thought they only knocked niggers over in Ameriky. Be me soul, but I'll go back to Ireland.'

"I could not help expressing my astonishment to the superintendent, repeating the Irishman's words, 'I thought only niggers could be knocked over in this country.'

"'Niggers!' said the superintendent, 'I guess if you had to deal with Irishmen, you'd find yourself obliged to knock 'em down.'

"'But don't the laws protect them?' I asked.

! why railroads have to be made, and have to be made the right way. I aint afraid of the laws. I think no more of knocking an Irishman over, sir, than I do of eating my dinner. One is as necessary as the other.'

"Now," continued Mr. Chapman, "if an Abolitionist sees a slave knocked over, he runs home to tell his mammy; it's enough to bring fire and brimstone, and hail, and earthquakes on the whole country. A man must have a black skin or his sorrows can never reach the hearts of these gentlemen. They had better look about at home. There is wrong enough there to make a fuss about."

"Well," said the Englishman, "you had both better come back to the mother country. The beautiful words, so often quoted, of Curran, may invite you: 'No matter with what solemnities he may have been devoted upon the altar of slavery, the moment he touches the sacred soil of Britain, the altar and the God sink together in the dust, and he stands redeemed, regenerated, and disenthralled, by the irresistible genius of universal emancipation."

" Thank you, sir, for your invitation," said Mr. Chapman, "but I'll stay in Virginia. The old State is good enough for me. I have been to England, and I saw some of your redeemed, regenerated, disenthralled people—I saw features on women's faces that haunted me afterward in my dreams. I saw children with shrivelled, attenuated limbs, and countenances that were old in misery and vice —such men, women, and children* as Dickens and Charlotte Elizabeth tell about. My little grand-daughter was recovering from a severe illness, not long ago, and I found her weeping in her old nurse's arms. < 0! grandpa, said she, as I inquired the cause of her distress, < I have been reading « The Little Pin-headers." ' I wept over it too, for it was true. No, sir; if I must see slavery, let me see it in its best form, as it exists in our Southern country."

"You are right, sir, I fear," said the Englishman.

" Well," said Mr. Perkins, "I am glad I am not a slave holder, for one reason; I am sure I should never get to heaven. I should be knocking brains out from morning till night, that is if there are brains under all that mass of wool. Why, they are so slow, and inactive—I should be stumbling over them all the time; though from the specimens I have seen in your house, sir, I should say they made most agreeable servants."

"My servants are very faithful," said Mr. Weston, "they have had great pains taken with them. I rarely have any complaints from the overseer."

"Your overseers,—that is the worst feature in slavery," said Mr. Perkins.

" Why, sir," said Mr. Chapman, ready for another argument, "you have your superintendents at the North—and they can knock their people down whenever the^ see fit."

"I beg your pardon, sir," said Mr. Perkins. "I had forgotten that."

« Stay a little while with us," said Mr. Chapman, as Mr. Weston rose to lead the way to the drawing-room. « You will not find us so bad as you think. We may roast a negro now and then, when we have a barbecue, but that will be our way of showing you hospitality. You must remember we are only 'poor heathenish Southerners,' according to the best received opinions of some who live with

you in New England."

* ******

"Alice," said Mrs. Weston, at a late hour in the evening, when the last of the guests were taking their departure, "Walter would like to see you in the library; but, my love, I wish you would spare yourself and him the useless pain of parting."

"I must see him, dear mother, do not refuse me; it is for the last time—pray, let me go."

"If you choose," and Alice glided away as her mother was interrupted by the leave-taking of some of their visi-

tors. The forms, the courtesies of life had no claims upon her now—she was enduring her first sorrow; the foundation of youth's slight fabric of happiness was yielding beneath her touch. The dread "nevermore," that Edgar Poe could not drive from his heart and sight, was oppressing her. She sought him before whom her young heart had bowed, not the less devotedly and humbly that it was silently and secretly. It was to be a bitter parting, not as when she watched to the last Arthur Weston, who was dear to her as ever was brother to a sister, for they had the promise and hope of meeting again; but now there was no tear in her eye, no trembling in her frame, and no hope in her heart. From the utmost depth of her soul arose the prophetic voice, "Thou shalt see him no more."

"Alice," said Walter, taking her hand between both of his, and gazing at her face, as pale and sad as his own, "it is your mother's wish that from this time we should be strangers to each other, even loving as we do; that our paths on earth should separate, never to meet again. Is it your wish too?"

"We must part; you know it, Walter," said Alice, musingly, looking out upon, but not seeing the calm river, and the stars that gazed upon its waves, and all the solemn beauty with which night had invested herself.

"But you love me, Alice; and will you see me go from you forever, without hope? Will you yourself speak the word that sends me forth a wanderer upon the earth?" said Walter.

"What can I do?" said Alice.

"Choose, Alice, your own destiny, and fix mine."

"Walter, I cannot leave my mother; I would die a thousand times rather than bring such sorrow upon her who has known so much. My uncle, too—my more than father—oh! Walter, I have sinned, and I suffer."

"You are wise, Alice; you have chosen well; you cling to mother, and home, and friends; I have none of these ties; there is not upon earth a being so utterly friendless as I am."

"Dear Walter, you have friends, and you can make them; you have wealth, talent, and many gifts from God. Go forth into the "world and use them. Let your noble heart take courage; and in assisting others and making them happy, you will soon be happy yourself."

Walter looked at her with surprise: such words were unlike her, whom he had been accustomed to consider a loving and lovely child. But a bitter smile passed over his countenance, and in a stern voice he said, "And you, Alice, what are you to do?"

"God alone knows," said Alice, forced into a consideration of her own sorrow, and resting against a lounge near which she had been standing. She wept bitterly. Waiter did not attempt to restrain her, but stood as if contemplating a grief that he could not wish to control. Alice again spoke, "It must come, dear Walter, first or last, and we may as well speak the farewell which must be spoken—but I could endure my part, if I had the hope that you will be happy. Will you promise me you will try to be?"

"No, Alice, I cannot promise you that; if happiness were in our own power, I would not be looking on you, whom I have loved all my life, for the last time.

"But I will hope," he continued, "you may be fortunate enough to forget and be happy."

"Children," said Miss Janet—for she had gently approached them—" do you know when and where happiness is to be found? When we have done all that God has given us to do here; and in the heaven, above those stars that are now looking down upon you. Look upon Alice, Walter, with the hope of meeting again; and until then, let the remembrance of her beauty and her love be ever about you. Let her hear of you as one who deserves the pure affection of her young and trusting heart. You have lived as brother and sister; part as suck, and may the blessing of God be upon both of you forever."

Walter took Alice in his arms, and kissed her cheek; all sternness and pride had gone from his handsome face, but there was such a look of hopeless sorrow there, as we would not willingly behold on the countenance of one so young.

Cousin Janet led him away, and with words of solemn, deep affection, bade him farewell—words that came again, for a time, unheeded and unwelcomed—words that at the last brought hope and peace to a fainting heart.

Cousin Janet returned to Alice, whose face lay hidden within her hands: "Alice, darling," she said, "look up— God is here; forget your own grief, and think of one who suffered, and who feels for all who, like Him, must bear the burden of mortality. Think of your many blessings, and how grateful you should feel for them; think of your mother, who for years wept as~ you, I trust, may never weep; think of your kind uncle, who would die to save you an hour's pain. Trust the future, with all its fears, to God, and peace will come with the very effort to attain it."

" Oh, Cousin Janet," said Alice, « if Walter were not so lonely; he knows not where he is going, nor what he is going to do."

"It is true," said Cousin Janet, weeping too; "but we can hope, and trust, and pray. And now, my love, let us join your mother in her room; it is a sad parting for her, too, for Walter is dear to us all."

Reader! have so many years passed away, that thou hast forgotten the bitterness of thy first sorrow, or is it yet to come ? Thinkest thou there is a way of escape— none, unless thou art young, and Death interpose,- saving thee from all sadness, and writing on thy grave, " Do not weep for me, thou knowest not how much of sorrow this early tomb has saved me."

When were thy first thoughts of death ? I do not mean the sight of the coffin, the pall, or any of its sad accompaniments, but the time when the mind first arrested itself with the melancholy convictions of mortality. There was a holiday for me in my young days, to which I looked forward as the Mohammedan to his Paradise ; this was a visit to a country-place, where I revelled in the breath of the woodbines and sweetbriers, and where I sat under tall and spreading trees, and wondered why towns and cities were ever built. The great willows swept the windows of the chamber where I slept, and faces with faded eyes looked upon me from their old frames, by the moonlight, as I fell asleep, after the day's enjoyment. I never tired of wandering through the gardens, where were -roses and sweet-williams, hyacinths and honeysuckles, and flowers of every shape and hue. This was the fairy spot of my recollection, for even childhood has its cares, and there were memories of little griefs, which time has never chased away. There I used to meet two children, who often roamed through the near woods with me. I do not remember their ages nor their names ; they were younger though than I. They might not have been beautiful, but I recollect the bright eyes, and that downy velvet hue that is only found on the soft cheek of infancy.

Summer came; and when I went again, I found the clematis sweeping the garden walks, and the lilies-of-the-valley bending under the weight of their own beauty. So we walked along, I and an old servant, stopping to enter an arbor, or to raise the head of a drooping plant, or to pluck a sweet-scented shrub, and place it in my bosom. " Where are the little girls ?" I asked. " Have they come again, too?"

" Yes, they are here," she said, as we approached two little mounds, covered over with the dark-green myrtle and its purple flowers.

«What is here?"

« Child, here are the little ones you asked for."

Oh! those little myrtle-covered graves, how wonderingly I gazed upon them. There was no thought of death mingled with my meditation ; there was, of quiet and repose, but not of death. I had seen no sickness, no suffering, and I only wondered why those fair children had laid down under the myrtle. I fancied them with the fringed eyelids drooping over the cheeks, and the velvet hue still there. How much did I know of death ? As little as of life!

Time passed with me, and I saw the sorrows of others. Sometimes I thought of the myrtle-covered graves, and the children that slept beneath. Oh ! how quiet they must be, they utter no cry, they shed no tears.

Time passed, and an angel slept in my bosom, close to my heart. Need I say that I was happy when she nestled there? that her voice was music to my soul, and her smile the very presence of beauty? Need I say it w r as joy when she called me, Mother? Then I lived for the present; all the sorrow that I had seen around me, was forgotten.

God called that angel to her native heaven, and I wept. Now was the mystery of the myrtle-covered graves open before my sight. I had seen the going forth of a little life that was part of. my own, I remembered the hard sighs that convulsed that infant breast. I knew that the grave was meant to hide from us, silence and pallor, desolation and decay. I was in the world, no longer a garden of flowers, where I sought from under the myrtle for the bright eyes and the velvet cheeks. I was in the world, and death was there too; it was by my side. I gave my darling to the earth, and felt for myself the bitterness of tears.

Thus must it ever be—by actual suffering must the young be persuaded of the struggle that is before them— well is it when there is one to say, « God is here."

CHAPTER IX.

WE must bring Uncle Bacchus's wife before our read ers. She is a tall, dignified, bright mulatto woman, named Phillis; it is with the qualities of her heart and mind, rather than her appearance, that we have to do. Bayard Taylor, writing from Nubia, in Upper Egypt, says:— " Those friends of the African race, who point to Egypt as a proof of what that race has done, are wholly mistaken. The only negro features represented in Egyptian sculpture are those of the slaves and captives taken in the Ethiopian wars of the Pharaohs. The temples and pyramids through out Nubia, as far as Abyssinia, all bear the hieroglyphics of these monarchs. There is no evidence in all the valley of the Nile that the negro race ever attained a higher de gree of civilization than is at present exhibited in Congo and Ashantee. I mention this, not from any feeling hos tile to that race, but simply to controvert an opinion very prevalent in some parts of the United States."

It seemed impossible to know Phillis without feeling for her sentiments of the highest respect. The blood of the freeman and the slave mingled in her veins; her well-regulated mind slowly advanced to a conclusion; but once made, she rarely changed it.

Phillis would have been truly happy to have obtained her own freedom, and that of her husband and children: she scorned the idea of running away, or of obtaining it otherwise than as a gift from her owner. She was a firm believer in the Bible, and of^n pondered on the words of the angel, "Return and submit thyself to thy mistress." She had on one occasion accompanied her master and Mrs. Weston to the North, where she was soon found out by some of that disinterested class of individuals called Abo-litionists. In reply to the question, "Are you free?" there was but a moment's hesitation; her pride of heart gave way to her inherent love of truth, "I'll tell no lie," she answered; "I am a slave!"

"Why do you not take your freedom?" was the rejoin der. " You are in a free state; they cannot force you to the South, if you will take the offers we make you, and leave your master."

"You are Abolitionists, I 'spose?" asked Phillis.

"We are," they said, "and we will help you off."

"I want none of your help," said Phillis. "My husband and children are at home; but if they wasn't, I am an honest woman, and am not in the habit of taking any thing. I'll never take my freedom. If my master would give it to me, and the rest of us, I should be thankful. I am not going to begin stealing, and I fifty years of age."

An eye-witness described the straightening of her tall figure, and the indignant flashing of her eye, also the discomfited looks of her northern friends.

I have somewhere read of a fable of Iceland. According to it, lost souls are to be parched in the burning heat of Hecla, and then cast for ever to cool in its never-thawing snows. Although Phillis could not have quoted this, her opinions would have applied it. For some reason, it was evident to her mind (for she had been well instructed in the Bible) that slavery was from the first ordained as a curse. It might, to her high spirit, have been like burning in the bosom of Hecla; but taking refuge among Abolitionists was, from the many instances that had come to her knowledge, like cooling in its never-thawing snows.

At the time that we introduced her to the reader, she was the mother of twelve, children. Some were quite young, but a number of them were grown, and all of them, with the exception of one, (the namesake of his father,) inherited their mother's energy of character. She had accustomed them to constant industry, and unqualified obedience to her directions; and for this reason, no one had found it necessary to interfere in their management.

Pride was a large ingredient in Phillis's composition. Although her husband presented one of the blackest visages the sun ever shone upon, Phillis appeared to hold in small esteem the ordinary servants on the plantation. She was constantly chiding her children for using their expressions, and tried to keep them in the house with white people as much as possible, that they might acquire good manners. It was quite a grief to her that Bacchus had not a more genteel dialect than the one he used. She had a great deal of family pride; there was a difference in her mind between family servants and those employed in field labor. For "the quality" she had the highest respect; for "poor white people" only a feeling of pity. She had some noble qualities, and some great weaknesses; but as a slave! we present her to the reader, and she must be viewed as such.

Miss Janet was, in her eyes, perfection. Her children were all the better for her kind instructions. Her youngest child, Lydia, a girl of six or seven years old, followed the old lady everywhere, carrying her key and knitting-basket, looking for her spectacles, and maintaining short conversations in a confidential tone.

/ One of Phillis's chiefest virtues was, that she had been able to bring Bacchus into subjection, with the exception of his love for an occasional spree, f Spoiled by an indulgent master, his conceit and wilfulness had made him unpopular with the servants, though his high tone of speaking, and a certain pretension in his manner and dress, was not without its effect. He was a sort of paj/rjarch among waiters and carriage-drivers; could tell anecdotes of dinners where Washington was a guest; and had been, familiar with certain titled people from abroad, whose shoes he had had the honor of polishing. The only person in whose presence he restrained his braggadocio style was Phillis.

Her utter contempt for nonsense was too evident. Bacchus was the same size as his master, and often fell heir to his cast-off clothes. A blue dress-coat and buff vest that he thus inherited, had a great effect upon him, bodily and spiritually. Not only did he swagger more when arrayed in them, but his prayers and singing were doubly effective. He secretly prided himself on a likeness to Mr. Weston, but this must have been from a confusion of mind into which he was thrown, by constantly associating himself with Mr. Weston's coats and pantaloons.

He once said to Phillis, " You might know master was a born gentleman by de way his clothes fits. Dey don't hang about him, but dey 'pears as if dey had grow'd about Trim by degrees ; and if you notice, dey fits me in de same way. Pity I can't wear his shoes, dey's so soft, and dey don't creak. I hates boots and shoes all time creakin, its so like poor white folks when they get dressed up on Sun day. I wonders often Miss Anna don't send me none of master's old ruffled shirts. 'Spose she thinks a servant oughtn't to wear 'em. I was a wishin last Sunday, when I gin in my 'sperience in meetin, that I had one of master's old ruffled shirts on. I know I could a 'scoursed them nig gers powerful. Its a hard thing to wear a ruffled shirt. Dey sticks out and pushes up to people's chins—I mean people dat aint born to wear 'em. Master wears 'em as if he was born in 'em, and I could too. I wish you'd put Miss Janet up to gittin one or two for me. Miss Janet's mighty 'bliging for an ole maid; 'pears as if she liked to see even cats happy. When an ole maid don't hate cats, there aint nothin to be feared from 5 em."

Phillis ruled her husband in most things, but she in dulged him in all his whims that were innocent. She de termined he should have, not an old ruffled shirt, but a new one. She reported the case to Miss Janet, who set two of her girls to work, and by Saturday night the shirt was made and done up, and plaited. Bacchus was to be plea-

santly surprised by it next morning appearing on the top of his chest.

It happened that on this identical Sunday, Bacchus had (as the best of men will sometimes) got up wrong foot fore most, and not having taken the trouble to go back to bed, and get up again, putting the right foot out first, he con tinued in the same unhappy state of mind. He made, as was his wont, a hasty toilet before breakfast. He wore an old shirt, and a pair of pantaloons that did not reach much above his hips. One of his slippers had no instep; the other was without a heel. His grizzly beard made him look like a wild man of the woods ; a certain sardonic ex pression of countenance* contributed to this effect. He planted his chair on its remaining hind leg at the cabin door, and commenced a systematic strain of grumbling be fore he was fairly seated in it.

"I believe in my soul," Phillis heard him say, "dat ole Aunt Peggy al'ars gits up WTong on a Sabbath mornin. Will any one hear her coughin ? My narves is racked a listenin to her. I don't see what she wants to live for, and she most a hundred. I believe its purpose to bother me, Sabbath mornins. Here, Phillis, who's this bin here, diggin up my sweet-williams I planted?—cuss dese chil dren—"

" The children had nothing to do with it," said Phillis. " Master wanted some roots to give to Mr. Kent and he asked me for 'em. I dug 'em up and they're all the bet ter for being thinned out."

" I wish master 'd mind his own business, and not be pryin and pilferin 'bout other people's gardens; givin my flowers to that yallow-headed Abolitioner. I'll speak my mind to him about it, any how."

"You'd better," said Phillis, drily.

"I will so," said Bacchus; "I'd rather he'd a burned *em up. Kent's so cussed mean, I don't b'lieve he'd 'low his flowers ground to grow in if he could help hisself. If

Miss Nannie 'd let him, he'd string them niggers of hers up, and wallop their gizzards out of 'em. I hate these Abolitioners. I knows 'em,—I knows their pedigree."

"Much you know about 'em," said Phillis, who was shaking the dew drops off her «morning glory."

"I knows enuff of 'em—I reckon Miss Nannie do, about dis time. De ole gentleman did right, any how, when he lef 'em all to her—if he hadn't, dat feller would a sold 'em all off to Georgia 'fore this, and a runn'd off wid de money."

"Well," said Phillis, "you'd better mind your own affairs ; come in and eat your breakfast, if you want any, for I aint going to keep it standin there all day, drawing the flies."

Bacchus kicked his slippers off and stumbled into a chair beside the table. "I'll swar," said he, after a glance at the fried ham and eggs, "if ever a man had to eat sich cookin as dis. Why didn't you fry 'em a little more?" Phillis not minding him, he condescended to eat them all, and to do justice to the meal in general.

"The old fool," thought Phillis, amused and provoked; "talkin of master's pilferin—never mind, I've put his ruffled shirt out, and he'll get in a good humor when he sees it, I reckon."

Having finished his breakfast, Bacchus put an enormous piece of tobacco in his mouth, and commenced sharpening a small-sized scythe, that he called a razor. In doing so, he made a noise like a high-pressure steamboat, now and then breathing on it, and going in a severe fit of coughing with every extra exertion. On his table was a broken piece of looking-glass, on the quicksilver side of which, Arthur had, when a child, drawn a horse. Into this Bacchus gave a look, preparatory to commencing operations. Then, after due time spent in lathering, he hewed down at each shave, an amount of black tow that was inconceivable. After he had done, he gathered up his traps, and stowed them away in the corner of his chest.

Phillis sat outside the door, smoking; looking in at the window, occasionally, to observe the effect of the first sight of the new shirt. She saw him turn toward the little red painted bureau, on which she had laid out his clean clothes, starting with surprise and pleasure, when his eye first took in the delightful vision. Cortez, when he stood conqueror of Mexico, did not feel the glow of satisfaction that thrilled through Bacchus's heart as he gently patted the plaited ruffles and examined the wristbands, which were stitched with the utmost neatness. He got weak in the knees with pleasure, and sat down on the chest in the corner, to support with more ease this sudden accession of happiness, while his wife was reaping a harvest of gratification at the success of her efforts toward his peace of mind. All at once she saw a change pass over his visage. Bacchus recollected that it would not do for him so suddenly to get into a good humor; besides, he reflected it was no more than Phillis's duty to make him ruffled shirts, and she ought to have been so doing for the last twenty years. These considerations induced him not to show much pleasure on the occasion, but to pretend he was not at all satisfied with the style and workmanship of the article in question.

"Why, lord a massy," said he, "Phillis, what do you call dis here? faint a shirt? at fust I thought 'twas one of Miss Janet's short night gowns you'd been a doing up for her."

Phillis smoked on, looking inquiringly into the distant hills.

« Phillis, you don't mean me to wear dis here to meetin ? T'aint fit. Dese wristbands is made out o' cotton, and I b'lieves in my soul Aunt Peggy done dis stitchin widout any spectacles."

Phillis knocked the ashes out of her pipe, and puffed on.

"Look here, Phillis," said Bacchus, going to the door as fast as the uncertain condition of his pantaloons would allow him, " did you 'spose I was sich a fool as to wear dis to meetin to-day?"

"Yes, I did," said Phillis.

" Why, t'aint fit for a nigger to hoe corn in, its as big as a hay-stack."

" Have you tried it on ?" asked Phillis.

" T'aint no use," said Bacchus, "I can tell by de looks."

"I'm sorry you don't like it," said Phillis.

"Like it," said Bacchus, contemptuously, "why, if it twasn't for the trouble of going to my chist, I'd wear one of my old ones. Cuss de ruffles, I wish you'd cut 'em off."

Bacchus went in, and in due time made his appearance in full dress. He wore the blue coat and buff vest, and a pair of white pantaloons, made after the old style. His shoes were as bright as his eyes, and his hat dusted until it only wanted an entire new nap to make it as good as new. His hair was combed in a sort of mound in front, and the tout ensemble was astounding. He passed Phillis in a dignified way, as if she were a valuable cat that he would not like to tread upon.

Phillis looked after him with a most determined expression of face. If she had been made out of stone she could not have seemed more resolved. She got up, however, soon after, and went in to arrange matters after her lord and master.

Bacchus purposely passed Aunt Peggy's cabin, making her a stylish bow. Peggy had taken off her handkerchief, to air her head, her hair standing off every which way, appearing determined to take her up somewhere, the point of destination being a matter of no consequence. She chuckled audibly as she saw Bacchus.

"Look at dat ole fool now, wid dat ruffled shirt on; he's gwine to bust dis blessed mornin. Look at de way he's got his wool combed up. I b'lieves in my soul he's got somebody buried up thar. He's a raal ole peacock. Dat's de way! 'Kase I'm ole and wuthless, no matter 'bout me; and dat ole nigger 'lowed to make a fool of his-self, dressin up drunk in a ruffled shirt. No matter, I'll be dead and out of der way, fore long."

Bacchus prayed with great effect this morning, calling himself and the whole congregation the most dreadful names, with the utmost satisfaction. He made a short address too, warning the servants against sin in general, and a love of finery in particular. On his return he beamed forth upon Phillis like one of her own "morning glories." The rest of the day he was brimful of jokes and religion.

The next Sunday came around. Phillis smoked outside while Bacchus made his toilet.

"Phillis," said the old fellow, blandly, coming to the door, "I don't see my ruffled shirt out here."

"High!" said Phillis, "I laid your shirt with the rest; but I'll look. Here it is," said she, pleasantly, "jest where I put it."

"Why, whar's the ruffles?"

"I cut 'em off," said Phillis; "you asked me to."

Bacchus got weak in the knees again, and had to sit down on the old chest. Not a word escaped his lips; a deep sigh burst from the pent-up boiler of his remorse. With an agonized countenance he seized a piece of rag which he had used as a shaving towel, and wiped away a repentant tear. His soul was subdued within him. He went to meeting, but declined officiating in any capacity, pleading a pain in his stomach as an excuse. At dinner he found it impossible to finish the remaining quarter of a very tough old rooster Phillis had stuffed and roasted for him. At sundown he ate a small-sized hoe-cake and a tin pan of bonnyclabber; then observing "That he believed he was put into dis world for nothing but to have trouble," he took to his bed.

Phillis saw that he would be more docile for the rest of his life; for a moment, the thought of restoring the shirt to its original splendor occurred to her, but she chased it away as if it had been a fox, and took the greatest satisfaction in "having given the old fool a lesson that would last him all the days of his life."

"To you, generous and noble-minded men and women of the South, I appeal*, (I quote the words of a late writer on Abolitionism, when I say,) Is man ever a creature to be trusted with wholly irresponsible power ? Can anybody fail to make the inference, what the practical result will be ?"* Although she is here speaking of slavery politically, can you not apply it to matrimony in this miserable country of ours ? Can we not remodel our husbands, place them under our thumbs, and shut up the escape valves of their grumbling forever? To be sure, St. Paul exhorts " wives to be obedient to their own husbands," and "servants to be obedient to their own masters," but St. Paul was not an Abolitionist. He did not take into consideration the necessities of the free-soil party, and woman's rights. This is the era of mental and bodily emancipation. Take advantage of it, wives and negroes ! But, alas for the former ! there is no society formed for their benefit; their day of deliverance has not yet dawned, and until its first gleamings arise in the east, they must wear their chains. Except when some strong-minded female steps forth from the degraded ranks, and asserts her position, whether by giving loose to that unruly member the tongue, or by a piece of management which will give "an old fool a lesson that will last him all the days of his life."

* Uncle Tom's Cabin.

CHAPTER X.

PHILLIS was at her ironing early in the morning, for she liked to hurry it over before the heat of the day. Her cabin doors were open, and her flowers, which had been watered by a slight rain that fell about day break, looked fresh and beautiful. Her house could be hardly called a cabin, for it was very much superior to the others on the plantation, though they were all comfortable. Phillis was regarded by the Weston family as the most valuable servant they owned—and, apart from her services, there were strong reasons why they were attached to her. She had nursed Mrs. Weston in her last illness, and as her death occurred immediately after Arthur's birth, she nourished him as her own child, and loved him quite as well. Her comfort and wishes were always objects of the greatest consideration to the family, and this was proved whenever occasion allowed. Her neatly white-washed cottage was enclosed by a wooden fence in good condition—her little garden laid out with great taste, if we except the rows of stiffly-trimmed box which Phillis took pride in. A large willow tree shaded one side of it; and on the other, gaudy sunflowers reared their heads, and the white and Persian lilacs, contrasted with them. All kinds of small flowers and roses adorned the front of the house, and you might as well have sought for a diamond over the whole place, as a weed. The back of the lot was arranged for the accommodation of her pigs and chickens ; and two enormous peacocks, that were fond of sunning themselves by the front door, were the handsomest ornaments about the place.

The room in which Phillis ironed, was not encumbered with much furniture. Her ironing-table occupied a large part of its centre, and in the ample fireplace was blazing a fire great enough to cook a repast for a moderate number of giants. Behind the back door stood a common pine bedstead, with an enormous bed upon it. How any bedstead held such a bed was remarkable; for Phillis believed there was a virtue in feathers even in the hottest weather, and she would rather have gone to roost on the nearest tree than to have slept on any thing else. The quilt was of a domestic blue and white, her own manufacture, and the cases to the pillows were very white and smooth. A little, common trundle bedstead was underneath, and on it was the bedding which was used for the younger children at night. The older ones slept in the servants' wing in the house, Phillis making use of two enormous chests, which were Bacchus's, and her wardrobes, for sleeping purposes for a couple more. To the right of the bed, was the small chest of drawers, over which was suspended Bacchus's many-sided piece of shaving glass, and underneath it a pine box containing his shaving weapons. Several chairs, in a disabled state, found places about the room, and Phillis's clothes-horse stood with open arms, ready to receive the white and well-ironed linen that was destined to hang upon it. On each side of the fireplace was a small dresser, with plates and jars of all sizes and varieties, and over each were suspended some branches of trees, inviting the flies to rest upon them. There was no cooking done in this room, there being a small shed for that purpose, back of the house; not a spot of grease dimmed the whiteness of the floors, and order reigned su preme, marvellous to relate ! where a descendant of Afiic's daughters presided.

Lydia had gone as usual to Miss Janet, and several of the other children were busy about the yard, feeding the chickens, sweeping up, and employed in various ways ; the only one who ever felt inclined to be lazy, and who was in

10*

body and mind the counterpart of his father, being seated on the door step, declaring he had a pain in his foot.

The adjoining room was the place in which Phillis's soul delighted, the door of it being at all times locked, and the key lost in the depths of her capacious pocket. From this place of retirement it emerged when any of the family honored her with their company, especially when attended by visitors; and after their departure, traces of their feet were carefully sought with keen and anxious eyes, and quickly obliterated with broom and duster.

This, her sanctum sanctorum, was a roomy apartment with three windows, each shaded by white cotton curtains. On the floor was a home-made carpet; no hand was em ployed in its manufacture save its owner's, from the time she commenced tearing the rags in strips, to the final blow given to the last tack that confined it to the floor. A very high post bedstead, over which were suspended white cotton curtains, gave an air of grandeur to one side of the room. No one had slept in it for ten years, though it was made with faultless precision. The quilt over it contained pieces of every calico and gingham dress that had been worn in the Weston family since the Revolution, and in the centre had been transferred from a remnant of curtain calico, an eagle with outstretched wings. The pillow cases were finished off with tape trimming, Alice's work, at Cousin Janet's suggestion. Over an old fashioned-mahogany bureau hung an oval looking glass, which was carefully covered from the flies. An easy chair stood by the window at the foot of the bed, which had, like most of the other ancient looking pieces of furniture, occupied a con spicuous place in Mr. Weston's house. Six chairs planted with unyielding stiffness against the walls seemed to grow out of the carpet; and the very high fender enclosed a pair of andirons that any body with tolerable eyesight could have seen their faces in.

Over the mantel piece were suspended two pictures. One

was a likeness of Mr. Weston, cut in paper over a black surface, with both hands behind him, and his right foot foremost; the other was a picture of the Shepherds in Pilgrim's Progress, gazing through a spy-glass at the Celestial city. Alice's first sampler, framed in a black frame, hung on one side of the room, and over it was a small sword which used to swing by Arthur's side, when receiving lessons in military science from Bacchus, who, in his own opinion, was another Bonaparte. Into this room Phillis's children gazed with wondering eyes; and those among the plantation servants who had been honored with a sight of it, declared it superior, in every respect, to their master's drawing room; holding in especial reverence a small table, covered with white, which supported the weight of Phillis's family Bible, where were registered in Arthur's and Alice's handwriting, the births of all her twelve descendants, as well as the ceremony which united her to their illustrious father.

Phillis was ironing away with a good heart, when she was interrupted by a summons to attend her master in the library. She obeyed it with very little delay, and found Mr. Weston seated in his arm-chair, looking over a note which he held in his hand.

"Come in, Phillis," he said, in a kind but grave manner. "I want to speak with you for a few moments; and as I have always found you truthful, I have no doubt you will be perfectly so on the present occasion."

"What is it, master?" Phillis said, respectfully.

"I received a note, yesterday, from Mr. Dawson, about his servant Jim, who ran away three weeks ago. He charges me with having permitted my servants to shelter him for the night, on my plantation; having certain information, that he was seen leaving it the morning after the severe storm we had about that time. If you know any thing of it, Phillis, I require you to tell it to me; I hardly think any of the other servants had opportunities of doing so, and yet I cannot believe that you would so far forget yourself as to do what is not only wrong, but calculated to involve me in serious difficulties with my neighbors."

"I hope you will not be angry with me, master?" said Phillis, "but I can't tell a lie; I let Jim stay in my room that night, and I've been mightily troubled about it; I was afeard you would be angry with me, if you heard of it, and yet, master, I could not help it when it happened."

« Could not help it! Phillis," said Mr. Weston. "What do you mean by that? Why did you not inform me of it, that I might have sent him off?"

"I couldn't find it in my heart, sir," said Phillis, the tears coming in her fine eyes. « The poor creature come in when the storm was at its worst. I had no candle lit, for the lightning was so bright that I hadn't no call for any other light. Bacchus was out in it all, and I was thinking he would be brought in dead drunk, or dead in earnest, when all at once Jim burst open the door, and asked me to let him stay there. I know'd he had run away, and at first I told him to go off, and not be gitting me into trouble; but, master, while I was sending him off such a streak of lightning come in, and such a crash of thunder, that I thought the Almighty had heard me turn him out, and would call me to account for it, when Jim and me should stand before him at the Judgment Day. I told Jim he had better go back to his master, that he wouldn't have any comfort, always hiding himself, and afeard to show his face, but he declared he would die first; and so as I couldn't persuade him to go home agin, I couldn't help myself, for I thought it would be a sin and shame, to turn a beast out in such a storm as that. As soon as the day began to break, and before, too, I woke him up, and told him never to come to my cabin again, no matter what happened. And so, master, I've told you the whole truth, and I am sure you couldn't have turned the poor wretch out to perish in that storm, no matter what would have come of it after."

Phillis had gained confidence as she proceeded, and Mr. Weston heard her without interruption.

"I can hardly blame you," he then said, "for what you have done; but, Phillis, it must never be repeated. Jim is a great rascal, and if I were his master I would be glad to be rid of him, but my plantation must not shelter run away slaves. I am responsible for what my servants do. I should be inclined to hold other gentlemen responsible for the conduct of theirs. The laws of Virginia require the rights of the master to be respected, and though I shan't make a constable of myself, still I will not allow any such thing to be repeated. Did Bacchus know it?"

"No, indeed, sir; he hates Jim, and no good, may be, would have come of his knowing it; besides, he was asleep long after Jim went off, and there was too much whiskey in him to depend on what he'd have to say."

"That will do, Phillis; and see that such a thing never happens again," said Mr. Weston.

Phillis went back to her ironing, assured her master was not angry with her. Yet she sighed as she thought of his saying, «see that such a thing never happens again." " If it had been a clear night," she thought within herself, "he shouldn't have stayed there. But it was the Lord himself that sent the storm, and I can't see that he never sends another. Anyway its done, and can't be helped;" and Phillis busied herself with her work and her children.

I have not given Phillis's cottage as a specimen of the cabins of the negroes of the South. It is described from the house of a favorite servant. Yet are their cabins generally, healthy and airy. Interest, as well as a wish for the comfort and happiness of the slave, dictates an atten tion to his wants and feelings. " Slavery," says Voltaire, "is as ancient as war; war as human nature." It is to be wished that truth had some such intimate connection with

human nature. Who, for instance, could read without an indignant thought, the following description from the pen of Mrs. Stowe: " They (their cabins) were rude shells, destitute of any pieces of furniture, except a heap of straw, foul with dirt, spread confusedly over the floor." "The small village was alive with no inviting sounds; hoarse, guttural voices, contending at the handmills, w r here their morsel of hard corn was yet to be ground into meal to fit it for the cake that was to constitute their only supper." But such statements need no denial; the very appearance of the slaves themselves show their want of truth. Look at their sound and healthy limbs, hear the odd, but sweet and musical song that arrests the traveler as he goes on his way; listen to the ready jest which is ever on his lips, and see if the slavery which God has permitted in all ages to exist, is as is here described; and judge if our fair Southern land is tenanted by such fiends as they are repre sented to be, by those who are trying to make still worse the condition of a mass of God's creatures, born to a life of toil, but comparative freedom from care. If it be His will that men should be born free and equal, that w T ill is not revealed in the Bible from the time of the patriarchs to the present day. There are directions there for the master and the slave. When the period of emancipation advances, other signs of the times will herald it-, besides the uncalled-for interference, and the gross misrepresenta tions, of the men and women of the North.

Sidney Smith said of a man, who was a great talker, that a few flashes of silence would make a great improve ment in him. So of the Abolition cause, a few flashes of truth would make it decidedly more respectable.

CHAPTER XL

"COME, Alice," said Mr. Barbour, "I hear, not the trump of war, but the soul-inspiring scrape of the banjo. I notice the servants always choose the warmest nights to dance in. Let us go out and see them."

"We'll go to the arbor," said Alice; "where we will be near enough to see Uncle Bacchus's professional airs. Ole Bull can't exceed him in that respect."

"Nor equal him," said Mr. Barbour. "Bacchus is a musician by nature; his time is perfect; his soul is absorbed in his twangs and flourishes."

" I must come, too," said Mr. Weston. "You are afraid of the night air, Cousin Janet?"

"Never mind me," said Cousin Janet; "I'll sit here and fan myself."

"And as I prefer music, especially the banjo, at a dis tance, I will stay too," said Mrs. Weston.

Aunt Phillis was smoking outside her door, her mind divided between speculations as to what had become of Jim, and observations on the servants, as they were col lecting from every direction, to join in the dancing or to find a good seat to look on.

The first sound of the banjo aroused Bacchus the younger from his dreams. He bounded from his bed on the chest, regardless of the figure he cut in his very slight dishabille, and proceeded to the front door, set, as his mother would have said, on having his own way.

" Oh, mammy,' ' he said, " dare's de banjo."

" What you doin here ?" said Phillis. " Go long to bed this minute, 'fore I take a switch to you."

" Oh, mammy," said the boy, regardless of the threat in his enthusiastic state of mind, " jist listen, daddy's gwine to play < Did you ever see the devil ?"

" Will any body listen to the boy ? If you don't go to bed"

" Oh, mammy, please lem me go. Dare's Jake, he's gwine to dance. Massa said I'd beat Jake dancin one o' dese days."

" High," said Phillis; " where's the sore foot you had this morning ?"

"Its done got well. It got well a little while ago, while I was asleep."

"Bound for you; go long," said Phillis.

Bacchus was about to go, without the slightest addition to his toilet.

"Come back here," said Phillis, "you real cornfield nigger ; you goin there naked ?"

The boy turned back, and thrust his legs in a pair of pants, with twine for suspenders. His motions were much delayed, by his nervous state of agitation, the consequence of the music which was now going on in earnest.

He got off finally, not without a parting admonition from his mother.

"Look here," said she, "if you don't behave yourself, I'll skin you."

Allusion to this mysterious mode of punishment had the effect of sobering the boy's mind in a very slight degree. No sooner was he out of his mother's sight than his former vivacity returned.

His father, meanwhile, had turned down a barrel, and was seated on it. Every attitude, every motion of his body, told that his soul, forgetful of earth and earthly things, had withdrawn to the regions of sound. He kicked his slippers off keeping time, and his head dodged about with every turn of the quick tune. A stranger, not un derstanding the state of mind into which a negro gets after

playing " The devil among the tailors," would have supposed he was afflicted with St. Vitus's dance. The mistake would soon have been perceived, for two of the boys having tired themselves out with manoeuvres of every kind, were obliged to sit down to get some breath, and Bacchus fell into a sentimental mood, after a little tuning up.

It was uncertain in what strain he would finally go off. First came a bar that sounded like Auld Lang Syne, then a note or two of Days of Absence, then a turn of a Me thodist hymn, at last he went decidedly into " Nelly was a lady." The tune of this William had learned from Alice singing it to the piano. He begged her to teach him the words. She did so, telling him of the chorus part, in which many were to unite. Bacchus prepared an accom paniment ; a number of them sang it together. "William sang the solos. He had a remarkably good voice and fine taste; he therefore did justice to the sweet song. When the full but subdued chorus burst upon the ear, every heart felt the power of the simple strain; the master with his educated mind and cultivated taste, and the slave with the complete power of enjoyment with which the Creator has endowed him.

Hardly had the cadence of the last note died away, when "Shout, shout, the devil's about," was heard from a stentorian voice. Above the peals of laughter with wTich the words were received, rose Jake's voice, " Come on, ole fiddler, play somefin a nigger kin kick up his heels to; what's de use of singing after dat fashion; dis aint no meetin."

" What'll you have, Jake ?" said Bacchus.

"What'll I have? Why, I never dances to but one tune," and Jake started the first line of "Oh, plantation gals, can't you look at a body," while Bacchus was giving a prelude of scrapes and twangs. Jake made a circle of somersets, and come down on his head, with his heels in the air, going through flourishes that would have astonished an uninitiated observer. As it was, Jake's audience were in

a high condition of enjoyment. They were in a constant state of expectation as to where he would turn up, or what would be the nature of the next caper. Now, he cut the pigeon-wing for a length of time that made the spectators hold their breath; then he would, so to speak, stand on his hands, and with his feet give a push to the barrel where Uncle Bacchus was sitting, and nearly roll the old man un derneath. One moment he is dancing with every limb, making the most curious contortions of his face, rolling out his tongue, turning his eyes wrong side out. Suddenly, he stretches himself on the grass, snoring to a degree that might be heard at almost any distance. Starting up, he snaps his fingers, twirls round, first on one foot, and then on the other, till feeling the time approaching when he must give up, he strikes up again:

" Shout, shout, the devil's about; Shut the door and keep him out,"

leaps frog over two or three of the servants' shoulders, disappearing from among them in an immoderate state of conceit and perspiration.

Bacchus is forced at this crisis to put down the banjo and wipe his face with his sleeve, breathing very hard. He was thinking he wouldn't get near so tired if he had a little of the " Oh, be joyful" to keep up his spirits, but such aspirations were utterly hopeless at the present time : getting tipsy while his master, and Mr. Barbour, and Alice were looking at him, was quite out of the question. He made a merit of keeping sober, too, on the ground of setting a good example to the young servants. He con soled himself with a double-sized piece of tobacco, and rested after his efforts. His promising son danced Juba at Mr. Weston's particular request, and was rewarded by great applause.

A little courting scene was going on at this time, not far distant. Esther, Phillis's third daughter, was a neat,

genteel-looking servant, entirely above associating with « common niggers," as she styled those who, being con stantly employed about the field, had not the advantage of being called upon in the house, and were thus very de ficient in manners and appearance from those who were so much under the eye of the family. Esther, like her mother, was a great Methodist. Reading well, she was familiar with the Bible, and had committed to memory a vast number of hymns. These, she and her sister, with William, often sung in the kitchen, or at her mother's cabin. Miss Janet declared it reminded her of the em ployment of the saints in heaven, more than any church music she had ever heard; especially when they sang, " There is a land of pure delight."

That heart must be steeled against the sweet influences of the Christian religion, which listens not with an earnest pleasure to the voice of the slave, singing the songs of Zion. No matter how kind his master, or how great and varied his comforts, he is a slave! His soul cannot, on earth, be animated to attain aught save the enjoyment of the passing hour. Why need he recall the past ? The present does not differ from it—toil, toil, however miti gated by the voice of kindness. Need he essay to pene trate the future ? it is still toil, softened though it be by the consideration which is universally shown to the feel ings and weaknesses of old age. Yet has the Creator, who placed him in this state, mercifully provided for it. The slave has not the hopes of the master, but he is with out many of his cares. He may not strive after wealth, yet he is always provided with comfort, Ambition, with its longings for fame, and riches, and power, never stimu lates his breast; that breast is safe from its disappointments. His enjoyments, though few, equal his expectations. His occupations, though servile, resemble the mass of those around him. His eye can see the beauties of nature; his ear drinks in her harmonies; his soul content itself with what is passing in the limited world around him. Yet, he is a slave ! And if he is ever elevated above his condition, it is when praising the God of the white man and the black; when, with uplifted voice, he sings the songs of the redeemed; when, looking forward to the invitation which he hopes to receive, " Come in, thou servant of the Lord."

Christian of the South, remember who it was that bore thy Saviour's cross, when, toiling, and weary, and fainting beneath it, he trod the hill of Calvary. Not one of the rich, learned, or great; not one of thine ancestors, though thou mayest boast of their wealth, and learning, and heroic acts—it was a black man who relieved him of his heavy burden ; Simon of Cyrene was his name.

Christian of the North, canst thou emancipate the Southern slave ? Canst thou change his employments, and elevate his condition? Impossible. Beware then, lest thou add to his burden, and tighten his bonds, and deprive him of the simple enjoyments which are now allowed him.

* * * * *

Esther, seated on the steps of a small porch attached to the side of the house, was mentally treating with great contempt the amusements of the other servants. She had her mother's disposition, and disliked any thing like noisy mirth, having an idea it was not genteel; seeing so little of it in her master's family. She was an active, cheerful girl, but free from any thing like levity in her manner.

She had a most devoted admirer in the neighborhood; no less a personage than Mrs. Kent's coachman. His name was Robert, after Mrs. Kent's father. Assuming the family name, he was known as Robert Carter. . Phillis called him a harmless goose of a fellow, and this gives the best idea of his character. He understood all about horses, and nothing else, if we except the passion of love, which was the constant subject of his conversation. He had made up his mind to court Esther, and with that in view he dressed himself in full livery, as if he were going to take his mistress an airing. He asks Mrs. Kent's permission to be married, though he had not the slightest reason to suppose Esther would accept him, with a confidence and self-exultation that man in general is apt to feel when he has determined to bestow himself upon some fortunate fair one. He went his way, passing the dancers without any notice, and going straight to that part of the house where he supposed he should find Esther.

Esther received him with politeness, but with some reserve ; not having a chair to offer him, and not intending him to take a seat on the steps beside her, she stood up, and leaned against the porch.

They talked a little of the weather, and the health of the different members of their respective families, during which, Robert took the opportunity to say, " His master, (Mr. Kent) had a bilious attack, and he wished to the Lord, he'd never get better of it." Finally, he undid one of the buttons of his coat, which was getting too small for him, and drawing a long breath, proceeded to lay himself (figuratively) at Esther's feet.

He did not come to the point at once, but drove round it, as if there might be some impediment in the way, which, though it could not possibly upset the whole affair, might make a little unnecessary delay. Esther thought he was only talking nonsense, as usual, but when he waxed warm, and energetic in his professions, she interrupted him with, « Look here, Robert, you're out of your head, aint you?"

"No deed, Miss Esther, but I'm dying in love with you."

"The best thing you can do, is to take yourself home," said Esther. "I hope you're sober."

"I was never soberer in my life," said Robert, "but the fact is, Miss Esther, I'm tired of a bachelor's life; 'pears as if it wasn't respectable, and so I'm thinking of settling down."

"You want settling down, for true," said Esther.

"I'm mighty happy to hear you say so," said Robert, "and if you'll only mention what time it 'll be agreeable to you to make me the happiest man in Virginny, I'e speak to Uncle Watty Harkins about performing the ceremony, without you prefer a white minister to tie the knot."

"Robert," said Esther, "you're a born fool; do you mean to say you want me to marry you?"

"Certainly, Esther; I shouldn't pay you no attentions, if I didn't mean to act like a gentleman by you."

"Well, I can tell you," said Esther, "I wouldn't marry you, to save your life."

"You ain't in earnest, Esther?"

"Indeed Iam," said Esther, "so you better not be coming here on any such fool's errand again."

"Why, Esther," said Robert, reproachfully, "after my walking home from meeting with you, and thinking and dreaming about you, as I have for this long time, aint you going to marry me?"

"No, I aint," said Esther.

"Then I'll bid you good night; and look here, Esther, to-morrow, mistress will lose one of her most valuable servants, for I shall hang myself."

Esther went up the steps, and shut the door on him, internally marvelling at the impudence of men in general; Robert, with a strong inclination to shed tears, turned his steps homeward. He told Mrs. Kent, the next morning, that he had come to the conclusion not to be married for some time yet, women were so troublesome, and there was no knowing how things would turn out. Mrs. Kent saw he was much dejected, and concluded there were sour grapes in the question.

After due consideration, Robert determined not to commit suicide; he did something equally desperate. He married Mrs. Kent's maid, an ugly, thick-lipped girl, who had hitherto been his especial aversion. He could not though, entirely erase Esther's image from his heart—always feeling a tendency to choke, when he heard her voice in meeting.

Esther told her mother of the offer she had had, and Phillis quite agreed with her, in thinking Robert was crazy. She charged "Esther to know when she was well off, and not to bring trouble upon herself by getting married, or any such foolishness as that."

CHAPTER XII.

"I TELL you what, Abel," said Arthur Weston, "the more I think about you Northern people, the harder it is for me to come to a conclusion as to what you are made of."

"Can't you experiment upon us, Arthur; test us chemically?"

"Don't believe you could be tested," said Arthur, "you are such a slippery set. Now here is a book I have been looking over, called Annals of Salem, by Joseph B. Felt, published in 1827. On the 109th page it says: < Captain Pierce, of the ship Desire, belonging to this port, was com missioned to transport fifteen boys and one hundred women, of the captive Pequods, to Bermuda, and sell them as slaves. He was obliged, however, to make for Providence Island. There he disposed of the Indians. He returned from Tor-tugas the 26th of February following, with a cargo of cotton, tobacco, salt, and negroes.' In the edition of 1849, this interesting fact is omitted. Now, was not that trading in human bodies and souls in earnest? First they got all they could for those poor captive Pequods, and they

traded the amount again for negroes, and some et ceteras. You are the very people to make a fuss about your neighbours, having been so excessively righteous yourselves. No wonder that the author left it out in a succeeding edition. I am surprised he ever put it in at all."

"It seems more like peddling with the poor devils than any thing else," said Abel. "But you must remember the spirit of the age, Arthur, as Mr. Hubbard calls it?"

"Yes," said Arthur, "I forgot that; but I wonder if Mr. Hubbard excuses the conduct of England to her colonies in consideration of the spirit of the age— that allowed taxation and all of her other forms of oppression, I suppose. It is a kind of charity that covers a multitude of sins. But I was saying," continued Arthur, "that I could not make you out. While they were carrying on two kinds of slave trade, they were discussing in Boston the propriety of women's wearing veils, having lectures about it. Let me read to you. <• Mr. Cotton, though while in England of an opposite opinion on this subject, maintained that in countries where veils were to be a sign of submission, they might be properly disused. But Mr. Endicott took different ground, and endeavored to retain it by general argument from St. Paul. Mr. Williams sided with his parishioner. Through his and others' influence, veils were worn abundantly. At the time they were the most fashionable, Mr. Cotton came to preach for Mr. Skelton. His subject was upon wearing veils. He endeavored to prove that this was a custom not to be tolerated. The consequence was, that the ladies became converts to his faith in this particular, and for a long time left off an article of dress, which indicated too great a degree of submission to the lords of creation.' Did you ever hear of such a set of old meddlers, lecturing and preaching about women's dressing. I suppose the men wore petticoats at that time themselves."

"If they did," said Abel, "I am very glad they have

turned them over to the other sex since, as they are worn in the number which the present fashion requires. I should think they would be very uncomfortable. But, Arthur, I heard such a good story the other day, about Lawyer Page. He fights bravely with his tongue for other people's rights, but he darcn't say his soul's his own before his wife. Well, when that affair came out about Morton's whipping his wife, as he was going to the Court house, Page said to old Captain Caldwell, 'Do you know, captain, that before all the facts were out in this case about Morton, they actually had it in every direction that it was I who had whipped my wife.' ' Now Page,' said the old captain, < you know that's no such thing; for every body in New Haven is well aware that when there was any flogging going on in the matrimonial line, in your house, it was you that came off the worst.' Page did not say a word."

"I am glad I am not yoked with one of your New Haven belles, if turning a Jerry Sneak is to be the consequence," said Arthur.

"This marrying is a terrible necessity, Arthur," said Abel. "I don't know how I'll be supported under it when my time comes; but after all, I think the women get the worst of it. There were not two prettier girls in New Haven than my sisters. Julia, who has been married some eight or nine years, was really beautiful, and so animated and cheerful; now she has that wife-like look of care, forever on her countenance. Her husband is always reproaching her that that little dare devil of a son of hers does not keep his clothes clean. The other evening I was at their house, and they were having a little matrimonial discussion about it. It seems little Charlie had been picked up out of the mud in the afternoon, and brought in in such a condition, that it was sometime before he could be identified. After being immersed in a bathing tub it was ascertained that he had not a clean suit of

clothes; so the young gentleman was confined to his chamber for the rest of the evening, in a night gown. This my brother-in-law considered a great hardship, and they were talking the matter over when I went in.

"' Why don't you make the boy clothes enough, Julia?' said he.

" < I am forever making and forever mending,' said Julia; <but it is impossible to keep that young one clean. He had twelve pairs of pantaloons in the wash last week, and the girl was sick, and I had to iron them myself. I guess if you had all the trouble I have with him, you would put him to bed and make him stay there a week.'

" 'I tell you what it is, good people,' said I, 'when I go courting I intend to ask the lady in the first place if she likes to make boys' clothes. If she says No, I shan't have her, no matter what other recommendations she may

" (She'll be sure to give you the mitten for your impu dence^ said Julia. Then, there is my pretty sister Har riet, quilting quilts, trimming nightcaps, and spoiling her bright eyes making her wedding-clothes; after a while she'll be undergoing some of the troubles of the married state, which will lengthen her face. The men get the best of it, decidedly; for they have not all the petty annoyances a woman must encounter. What do you think about it, Arthur?"

"I hardly know," said Arthur. "I have been in love ever since I could tell my right hand from my left. I have hardly ever looked forward to marriage; my time has been so much occupied here, that when I get a few moments for reflection, my thoughts go back to Alice, and the happy years I have passed with her, rather than to anticipations of any kind. I suppose I shall find out, though, and then you may profit by my experience."

"You will have a sad experience with those niggers of yours, I am afraid, Arthur," said Abel. "Our people are

determined never to let them alone. I wonder you do not employ white hands upon the plantation, and have done with any trouble about the matter."

" What would be done with the slaves in the mean time ?" said Arthur.

"Set 'em free," said Abel; "colonize, or hang 'em all."

"The latter is the more practicable suggestion," said Arthur. "As to setting them free, they could not remain in Virginia afterward if I were willing to do so: there is a law against it. Colonizing them would be equally diffi cult, for the most of them would refuse to go to Africa; and if I have not the right to hold them slaves, I certainly have not a right to force them into another country. Some of them would be willing and glad to come to the North, but some would object. My father set a house-servant free; he was absent a year, and returned voluntarily to his old condition. Mark had got some Abolition notions in his head, and my father told him he might have his free papers, and go: I have told you the result. The fact is, Abel, you Yankees don't stand very well with our slaves. They seem to consider you a race of pedlars, who come down upon them in small bodies for their sins, to wheedle away all their little hoardings. My father has several times brought servants to New York, but they have never run away from him. I think Virginia would do well with out her colored people, because her climate is moderate, and white labor could be substituted. But it is not so with the more Southern States. I would like to see a Louisiana sun shining upon your New England States for a while—how quickly you would fit out an expedition for Africa. It is the mere accident of climate that makes your States free ones."

"I suppose so," said Abel. "A great many of your slaves run away through the year, don't they?"

"No, indeed," said Arthur; " comparatively, very few. Just before I came to New Haven, I went to pass a few weeks at a plantation belonging to a family with whom we were intimate. One of the sons and I went on the river, two of the servants rowing us. 1 said to one of them, a large fat negro, <What's your name, uncle?' <Meschach, sir,' he said. 'Meschach,' said I; 'why, you ought to have two brothers, one named Shadrach and the other Abed nego.' «So I had, sir.' < Well, what has become of them ?' said I. < Shadrach, he's dead,' he answered. l And where is Abednego?' said I. 'He's gone, too,' he replied, in a low voice. My friend gave me a look, and told me after wards that Abednego had ran away, and that his family considered it a disgrace, and never spoke of him. I heard of a negro boy who absconded, and when he was found, and being brought home, an old washerwoman watched him as he went up the street. 'La,' said she, 'who'd a thought he'd a beginned to act bad so young,' But let us leave off Abolition and take a walk. Our cigars are out, and we will resume the subject to-morrow afternoon, when we light some more."

******

"Now," said Abel, "having a couple of particularly good cigars, where did we leave off?"

"Its too warm for argument," said Arthur, watching the curling of the gray smoke as it ascended.

"We need not argue," said Abel; "I want to catechize you."

"Begin."

" Do you think that the African slave-trade can be de fended?"

"No, assuredly not."

"Well," said Abel, "how can you defend your right to hold slaves as property in the United States?"

"Abel," said Arthur, "when a Yankee begins to ques tion there is no reason to suppose he ever intends to stop. I shall answer your queries from the views of Governor Hammond, of Carolina. They are at least worthy of con-sideration. What right have you New England people to the farms you are now holding?"

" The right of owning them," said Abel.

" From whom did you get them ?" asked Arthur.

" Our fathers."

"And how did they get them?"

"From the Red men, their original owners."

"Well," said Arthur, "we all know how these transac tions were conducted all over the country. We wanted the lands of the Red men, and we took them. Sometimes they were purchased, sometimes they were wrested; always, the Red men were treated with injustice. They were driven off, slaughtered, and taken as slaves. Now, God as clearly gave these lands to the Red men as he gave life and free dom to the African. Both have been unjustly taken away."

"But," said Abel, "we hold property in land, you in the bodies and souls of men."

" Granted," said Arthur ; " but we have as good a right to our property as you to yours—we each inherit it from our fathers. You must know that slaves were recognized as property under the constitution. John Q. Adams, speak ing of the protection extended to the peculiar interests of the South, makes these remarks: «Protected by the ad vantage of representation on this floor, protected by the stipulation in the constitution for the recovery of fugitive slaves, protected by the guarantee in the constitution to the owners of this species of property, against domestic violence.' It was considered in England as any other kind of commerce; so that you cannot deny our right to con sider them as property now, as well as then."

"But can you advocate the enslaving of your fellow man?" said Abel."

"No," said Arthur, "if you put the question in that manner; but if you come to the point, and ask me if I can conscientiously hold in bondage slaves in the South, I say yes, without the slightest hesitation. I'll tell you why.

12

You must agree with me, if the Bible allow slavery there is no sin it. Now, the Bible does allow it. You must read those letters of Governor Hammond to Clarkson, the English Abolitionist. The tenth commandment, your mother taught you, no doubt: ' thou shalt not covet thy neighbor's house, thou shalt not covet thy neighbor's wife, nor his man-servant, nor his maid-servant, nor his ox, nor his ass, nor any thing that is thy neighbor's.' These are the words of God, and as such, should be obeyed strictly. In the most solemn manner, the man-servant and the maid servant are considered the property of thy neighbor. Generally the word is rendered slave. This command in cludes all classes of servants ; there is the Hebrew-brother, who shall go out in the seventh year, and the hired-servant, and those 'purchased from the heathen round about,' who were to be bondmen forever. In Leviticus, speaking of t&e 'bondmen of the heathen which shall be round about,' God says, 'And ye shall take them for an inheritance, for your children after you, to inherit them for a possession; they shall be your bondmen forever.' I consider that God permitted slavery when he made laws for the master and the slave, therefore I am justified in holding slaves. In the times of our Saviour, when slavery existed in its worst form, it was regarded as one of the conditions of human society; it is evident Abolition was not shadowed forth by Christ or his apostles. 'Do unto all men as ye would have them do unto you,' is a general command, inducing charity and kindness among all classes of men; and does not authorize interference with the established customs of society. If, according to this precept of Christ, I am obliged to manumit my slaves, you are equally forced to purchase them. If I were a slave, I would have my master free me; if you were a slave, and your owner would not give you freedom, you would have some rich man to buy you. From the early ages of the world, there existed the poor and the rich, the master and the slave.

"It would be far better for the Southern slaves, if our institution, as regards them, were left to 'gradual mitiga tion and decay, which time may bring about. The course of the Abolitionists, while it does nothing to destroy this institution, greatly adds to its hardships.' Tell me that < man-stealing' is a sin, and I will agree with you, and will insist that the Abolitionists are guilty of it. In my opin ion, those who consider slavery a sin, challenge the truth of the Bible.

"Besides, Abel," continued Arthur, "what right have you to interfere ? Your Northern States abolished slavery when it was their interest to do so: let us do the same. In the meantime, consider the condition of these dirty vagabonds, these free blacks, who are begging from me every time I go into the street. I met one the other day, who had a most lamentable state of things to report. He had rheumatism, and a cough, and he spit blood, and he had no tobacco, and he was hungry, and he had the toothache. I gave him twenty-five cents as a sort of panacea, and ad vised him to travel South and get a good master. He took the money, but not the advice."

"But, Arthur, the danger of insurrection; I should think it would interfere greatly with your comfort."

"We do not fear it," said Arthur. "Mobs of any kind are rare in the Southern country. We are not (in spite of the bad qualities ascribed to us by the Abolitionists) a fussy people.

"Sometimes, when an Abolitionist comes along, we have a little fun with him, the negroes enjoying it exceedingly. Slaveholders, as a general thing, desire to live a peaceful, quiet life; yet they are not willing to have their rights wrested from them."

"One great disadvantage in a slaveholding community is, that you are apt to be surrrounded by uneducated peo ple," said Abel.

" We do not educate our slaves," said Arthur; " but you do not presume to say that we do not cultivate our minds as assiduously as you do yours. Our statesmen are not inferior to yours in natural ability, nor in the improvement of it. We have far more time to improve ourselves than you, as a general thing- When you have an opportunity of judging, you will not hesitate to say, that our women can bear to be compared with yours in every respect, in their intellect, and refinement of manners and conversation. Our slaves are not left ignorant, like brutes, as has been charged upon us. Where a master feels a religious responsi bility, h^ must and does cause to be given, all necessary knowledge to those who are dependent upon him. I must say, that though we have fewer sects at the South, we have more genuine religion. You will think I am prejudiced. Joining the church here is, in a great measure, a form. I have formed this opinion from my own observation. With us there must be a proper disregard of the customs of the world; a profession of religion implying a good deal more than a mere profession. Look at the thousand new and absurd opinions that have agitated New England, while they never have been advanced with us. There is Unita-rianism, that faith that would undermine the perfect struc ture of the Christian religion; that says Christ is a man, when the Scriptures style him < Wonderful, Counsellor, The Mighty God, The Everlasting Father, The Prince of Peace.' Why, it is hardly tolerated at the South. Have you any right to claim for yourself superior holiness? None whatever.

" There never was any thing so perfectly false (I cannot help referring to it again,) as that religion is discouraged among our slaves. It is precisely the contrary. Most of them have the same opportunities of attending worship as their owners. They generally prefer the Methodist and Baptist denominations; they worship with the whites, or they have exclusive occasions for themselves, which they prefer. They meet on the plantations for prayer, for singing, or for any religious purpose, when they choose ; the ladies on the plantations instruct them in the Bible, and how to read it. Many of them are taught to write.

Religion seems to be a necessary qualification of the fe male mind—I think this, because I have been so fortunate in those of our own family. My mother died soon after my birth; her friends often dwell on the early piety so beautfully developed in her character. We have a rela tive, an old maid, who lives with us; she forgets her own existence, laboring always for the good of others. My aunt is a noble Christian woman, and Alice has not breathed such an atmosphere in vain. We have a servant woman named Phillis, her price is far above rubies. Her industry, her honesty, her attachment to our family, ex ceeds every thing. I wish Abolitionists would imitate one of her virtues—humility. I know of no poetry more beautiful than the hymns she sang to me in my infancy; her whole life has been a recommendation of the religion of the Bible. I wish my chance of Heaven were half as good as hers. She is a slave here, but she is destined to be a saint hereafter."

CHAPTER XIII.

THE evening is drawing on again at Exeter, and Alice and her mother are in a little sitting room that opens on the porch. Mrs. Weston is fanning her daughter, who has been suffering during the day from headache. Miss Janet is there, too, and for a rare occurrence, is idle; looking from the window at the tall peaks of the Blue Ridge upon which she has gazed for many a year. Little Lydia stands by her side, her round eyes peering into Miss Janet's face, w r ondering what would happen, that she should be unem ployed. They are awaiting Mr. Weston's return from an afternoon ride, to meet at the last and most sociable meal of the day.

"Miss Janet," said Lydia, " aint Miss Alice white?"

"Very pale," said Miss Janet, looking at Alice; then, with a sigh, turning to the mountains again.

"What makes her so white ?" asked Lydia, in an under tone.

" She has had a headache all day. Be quiet, child," said Miss Janet.

After a moment, Lydia said, " I wish I could have de headache all de time."

" What do you say such a foolish thing as that for, Lydia?"

" 'Kase I'd like to be white, like Miss Alice." Miss Janet did not reply. Again Lydia spoke, " If I was to stay all time in de house, and never go in de sun, would I git w r hite ?"

" No—no—foolish child ; what gives you such ideas ?"

There was another pause. Mrs. Weston fanned Alice, who, with closed eyes, laid languidly on the lounge.

"Miss Janet," said Lydia, speaking very softly, "who made de lightning-bugs ?"

" God made them," said Miss Janet.

"Did God make de nanny-goats, too?"

"You know that God made every thing," said Miss Janet. " I have often told you so."

"He didn't make mammy's house, ma'am; I seed de men makin it."

" No; man makes houses, but God made all the beauti ful things in nature. He made man, and trees, and rivers, and such things as man could not make."

Lydia looked up at the sky. The sun had set, and the moon was coming forth, a few stars glistened there. Long, fleecy clouds extended over the arch of heaven, and some passing ones for a moment obscured the brightness that gilded the beautiful scene.

"Miss Janet," said Lydia, "its mighty pretty there; but 'spose it was to fall."

"What was to fall?"

" De sky, ma'am-."

" It cannot fall. God holds it in its place."

Another interval and Lydia said: "Miss Janet, 'spose God was to die, den de sky would broke down."

"What put such a dreadful thought into your head, child?" said Miss Janet. God cannot die."

"Yes, ma'am, he kin," said Lydia.

"No, he cannot. Have I not often told you that God is a spirit ? He created all things, but he never was made; he cannot die."

Lydia said inquiringly, "Wasn't Jesus Christ God, ma'am?"

"Yes, he was the Son of God, and he was God."

" Well, ma'am, he died onct, dat time de Jews crucified him—dat time de ground shook, and de dead people got up—dat time he was nailed to de cross. So, ma'am, if God died onct, couldn't he die agin ?"

Miss Janet, arousing herself from her reverie, looked at the child. There she stood, her eyes fixed upon the sky, her soul engaged in solving this mysterious question. Her ^ little hands hung listlessly by her side; there was no beauty in her face; the black skin, the projecting lips, the heavy features, designated her as belonging to a degraded race. Yet the soul was looking forth from its despised tenement, and eagerly essaying to grasp things beyond its reach.

"Could he die agin, Miss Janet?" asked Lydia.

Poor child! thought Miss Janet, how the soul pinioned and borne down, longs to burst its chains, and to soar through the glorious realms of light and knowledge. I thought but now that there was no more for me to do here; that tired of the rugged ascent, I stood as it were on the tops of those mountains, gazing in spirit on the celestial city, and still not called to enter in. Now, I see there is work for me to do. Thou art a slave, Lydia; yet God has called thee to the freedom of the children that he loves; thou art black, yet will thy soul be washed white in the blood of the Lamb; thou art poor, yet shalt thou be made rich through Him who, when on earth, was poor indeed. Jesus, forgive me! I murmured that I still was obliged to linger. Oh! make me the honored instrument of good to this child, and when thou callest me hence, how gladly will I obey the summons.

"Lydia," she said, "the Son of God died for us all, for you and for me, but he was then in the form of man. He died that we might live; he never will die again. He rose from the dead, and is in heaven, at the right hand of God. He loves you, because you think about him."

"He don't love me like he do Miss Alice, 'kase she's so white," said Lydia.

"He loves all who love him," said Miss Janet, "whether they are black or white. Be a good child, and he will surely love you. Be kind and obliging to everybody; be industrious and diligent in all you have to do; obey your mother and father, and your master. Be truthful and honest. God hates a liar, and a deceitful person. He will not take care of you and love you, unless you speak the truth. Sometimes you try to deceive me. God will not be your friend if you deceive any one. And now go to your mother, she will put you to bed."

Lydia made a curtsey, and said, "Good-night, ma'am." She went to Mrs. Weston, and bade her good-night too. Then turning toward Alice, she gazed wonderingly at her pale face.

"Is you got de headache now, Miss Alice?"

"Not much," said Alice, gently.

"Good night, miss," said Lydia, with another curtesy, and she softly left the room. "Oh, mammy," she said, as she entered her mother's cabin, "Miss Janet say, if I'm a good child, God will love me much as he loves Miss Alice, if I is black. Miss Alice is so white to-night; you never see'd her look as white as she do to-night." * * * * * *

Mr. Weston alighted from his horse, and hurried to the sitting-room, "Have you waited tea for me?" he said. "Why did you do so? Alice, darling, is your head better?"

"A great deal, uncle," said Alice. "Have you had a pleasant ride?"

"Yes; but my child, you look very sick. What can be the matter with you? Anna, did you send for the doctor?"

"No—Alice objected so."

"But you must send for him—I am sure she is seriously ill."

"There is nothing the matter with me, but a headache," said Alice. "After tea, I will go to bed, and will be well in the morning."

"God grant you may, my sweet one. What has come over you?"

"Tea is ready," said Cousin Janet. "Let us go in to it, and then have prayers, and all go to bed early. ' Why Cousin Weston, you are getting quite dissipated in your old age; coming home to tea at this hour; I suppose I shall begin such practices next."

Miss Janet's suggestion of retiring early, was followed. Phillis came in to see how Alice's head was, and recommended brown paper and vinegar. She made no comment on her appearance, but did not wonder that Lydia was struck with the expression of her countenance. There was an uneasiness that was foreign to it; not merely had the glow of health departed, there was something in its place, strange there. It was like the storm passing over the beautiful lake; the outline of rock, and tree, and surface, is to be seen, but its tranquil beauty is gone; and darkness and gloom are resting where has been the home of light, and love, and beauty.

Alice undressed and went to bed; her mother raised all the windows, put out the candle, and laid down beside her. Hoping that she would fall asleep, she did not converse, but Alice after a few minutes, called her.

"What is it, Alice?"

"Did you hear what Cousin Janet said to Lydia, to night, mother? God hates those who deceive."

" Why think of that now, my love ?"

" Because it refers to me. She did not mean it for me, but it came home to my heart."

"To your heart? That has always been truth and candor itself. Try and banish such thoughts. If you were well, fancies like these would not affect you."

"They are not fancies, they are realities," said Alice. She sighed and continued, " Am I not deceiving the kind protector and friend of my childhood ? Oh, mother, if he knew all, how little would he love me! And Arthur, can it be right for me to be engaged to him, and to deceive him, too?"

" Dear Alice, how often have we talked about this, and I hoped you were satisfied as to the propriety of being silent on the subject at present. Your uncle's health is very feeble ; he is subject to sudden and alarming attacks of sickness, and easily thrown into a state of agitation that endangers his life. Would you run such a risk ? What a grief would it be to him to know that the hopes of years were to be destroyed, and by one whom he had nursed in his own bosom as a child. Poor Arthur, too ! away from home so long—trusting you with such confidence, looking forward with delight to the time of his return, could you bear thus to dash his dearest prospects to the earth ?"

" But he must know it, mother. I could not marry him with a lie in my right hand."

"It will not be so, Alice; you cannot help loving Ar-" thiir, above all men, when you are with him; so noble, so generous, so gifted with all that is calculated to inspire affection, you will wonder your heart has ever wavered."

"But it has," said Alice; " and he must know all."

" Of course," said Mrs. Weston; " nothing would justify your having any reserve with him, but this is not the time for explanation. If I believed that you really and truly loved Walter, so as to make it impossible for you to forget him and return Arthur's affection ; if I thought you would not one day regard Arthur as he deserves, I would not wish you to remain silent for a day. It would be an injustice, and a sin, to do so. Yet I feel assured that there is no such danger.

"A woman, Alice, rarely marries her first love, and it is well that it is so. Her feelings, rather than her judgment, are then enlisted, and both should be exercised when so fearful a thing as marriage is concerned. You have been a great deal with Walter, and have always regarded him tenderly, more so of late, because the feelings strengthen with time, and Walter's situation is such as to enlist all your sympathies; his fascinating appearance

and interesting qualities have charmed your affections. You see him casting from him the best friends he has ever had, because he feels condemned of ingratitude in their society. He is going forth on the voyage of life, alone; you weep as any sister would, to see him thus. I do not blame him for loving you; but I do censure him in the highest degree, for endeavoring to win more than a sister's regard from you, in return; it was selfish and dishonorable. More than all, I blame myself for not foreseeing this. You said yesterday, you could not bear the thought of being separated from Arthur. You do not know your own heart, many a woman does not, until time has been her teacher; let it be yours. Cousin Janet has thus advised you; be guided by us, and leave this thing to rest for a while; you will have reason to rejoice at having done so. Would you leave me for Walter, Alice?"

" No, mother. How could you ask me ?"

" Then trust me; I would not answer for your uncle's safety were we to speak to him on this subject. How cruel to pain him, when a few months may restore us to the hopes and happiness which have been ours! Do what is right, and leave the future to God."

" But how can I write to Arthur, when I know I am not treating him as I would wish him to treat me?"

"Write as you always have; your letters have never been very sentimental. Arthur says you write on all subjects but the one nearest his heart. If you had loved him as I thought you did, you never would have allowed another to usurp his place. But we cannot help the past. Now, dear child, compose yourself; I am fatigued, but cannot sleep until you do."

Alice, restless for a while, at last fell asleep, but it was not the rest that brings refreshment and repose. Her mother watched her, as with her hand now pressed on her brow, now thrown on the pillow, she slept. Her mind, overtaxed, tried even in sleep to release itself of its burden. The wish to please, and the effort to do right, was too much for her sensitive frame. It was like the traveler unaccustomed to fatigue and change, forced to commence a journey, unassured of his way, and ignorant of his destination.

Her mother watched her—a deep hue was settled under her eyelashes, the veins in her temple were fearfully distinct, and a small crimson spot rested on her cheek. She watched her, by the moonlight that glanced over every part of the room. She listened to her heavy breathing, and lightly touched her dry and crimson lips. She stroked the long luxuriant curls, that appeared to her darker than they ever had before. She closed the nearest window, lest there should be something borne on the breath of night, to disturb the rest of the beloved one. But, mother ! it will not do; the curse of God is still abroad in the world, the curse on sin. It falls, like a blighting dew, on the loveliest and dearest to our hearts. It is by our side and in our path. It is among the gay, the rich, the proud, and the gifted of the earth; among the poor, the despised, the desolate and forsaken. It darkens the way of the monarch and the cottager, of the maiden and the mother, of the master and the slave. Alas ! since it poisoned the flowers in Eden, and turned the children of God from its fair walks, it is abroad in the world—the curse of God on sin.

There is a blessing, too, within the reach of all. He who bore the curse, secured the blessing. Son of God! teach us to be like thee; give us of thy spirit, that we may soften to each other the inevitable ills of life. Prepare us for that condition to which we may aspire; for that assembly wiiere will be united the redeemed of all the earth, where will rejoice forever in thy presence those of all ages and climes, who looked up from the shadow of the curse, to the blessing which thou didst obtain, with thy latest sigh, on Calvary!

13

CHAPTER XIV.

AFTER Phillis left Mrs. Western's room, she was on her way to her cabin, when she noticed Aunt Peggy sitting alone at the door. She was rather a homebody; yet she reproached herself with having neglected poor old Peggy, when she saw her looking so desolate and dejected. She thought to pay her a visit, and bidding her good evening, sat down on the door-step. ." Time old people were in bed, Aunt Peggy," said she; "what are you settin up for, all by yourself?"

"Who's I got to set up wid me?" said Aunt Peggy.

"Why don't you go to bed, then?" asked Phillis.

"Can't sleep^ can't sleep," said Aunt Peggy; "aint slep none dese two, three nights; lays awake lookin at de moon; sees people a lookin in de winder at me, people as I aint seen since I come from Guinea; hears strange noises I aint never heard in dis country, aint never hearn sence I come from Guinea."

"All notions," said Phillis. "If you go to sleep, you'll forget them all."

" Can't go to sleep," said Aunt Peggy; "somefin in me won't sleep; somefin I never felt afore. It's in my bones; mebbe Death's somewhere in the neighborhood."

"I reckon you're sick, Aunt Peggy," said Phillis; "why didn't you let me know you wasn't well?"

"Aint sick, I tell you," said Aunt Peggy, angrily; "nothin the matter wid me. 'Spose you think there's nothin bad about, 'cep what comes to me."

Phillis was astonished at her words and manner, and looked at her intently. Most of the servants on the

plantation stood in awe of Aunt Peggy. Her having been brought from Africa, and the many wonders she had seen there; her gloomy, fitful temper; her tall frame, and long, skinny hands and arms; her haughty countenance, and mass of bushy, white hair. Phillis did not wonder most people were afraid of her. Besides, Peggy was thought to have the power of foresight in her old age. The serv ants considered her a sort of witch, and deprecated her displeasure. Phillis had too much sense for this; yet there was one thing that she had often wondered at; that was, that Aunt Peggy cared nothing about religion. When employed in the family, she had been obliged to go some times to church: since she had been old, and left to follow her own wishes, she had never gone. Miss Janet fre quently read the Bible, and explained it to her. Alice, seated on a low stool by the old woman's side, read to her scenes in the life of Christ, upon which servants love to dwell. But as far as they could judge, there were no good impressions left on her mind. She never objected, but she gave them no encouragement. This Phillis had often thought of; and now as she sat with her, it occurred to her with overwhelming force. "Death's about some where," said Aunt Peggy. "I can't see him, but I feels him. There's somefin here belongs to him; he wants it, and he's gwine to have it."

"'Pears to me," said Phillis, "Death's always about. Its well to be ready for him when he 'comes ; 'specially we old people."

"Always ole people," said Aunt Peggy, "you want to make out that Death's always arter ole people. No such thing. Look at the churchyard, yonder. See any little graves thar ? Plenty. Death's always arter babies ; 'pears like he loves 'em best of all."

"Yes," said Phillis, "young people die as well as old, but 'taint no harm to be ready. You know, Aunt Peggy, we aint never ready till our sins is repented of, and our

souls is washed in the blood of Jesus. People ought to think of that, old and young, but they don't."

" Death loves young people," said Aunt Peggy; " always arter 'em. See how he took young Mr. William Jones, thar, in town, and he healthy and strong, wid his young bride; and his father and mother old like me. See how he took little George Mason, not long ago, that Uncle Geoffrey used to bring home wid him from town, setting on de horse, before him Didn't touch his ole grandmother ; she's here yet. Tell you, Death loves 'em wid de red cheeks and bright eyes."

Phillis did not reply, and the old woman talked on as if to herself.

" Thinks thar's nothin bad but what comes to niggers; aint I had nuff trouble widout Death. I aint forgot de time I was hauled away from home. Cuss him, 'twas a black man done it; he told me he'd smash my brains out if I made a sound. Dragged along till I come to de river ; thar he sold me. I was pushed in long wid all de rest of 'em, crying and howlin—gwine away for good and all. Thar we was, chained and squeezed together; dead or live, all one. Tied me to a woman, and den untied me to fling her into de sea—dead all night, and I tied to her. Come long, cross de great sea; more died, more flung to de sharks. No wonder it thundered and lightened, and de waves splashed in, and de captain prayed. Lord above! de captain prayed, when he was stealin and murderin of his fellow-creeturs. We didn't go down, we got safe across. Some went here, some went thar, and I come long wid de rest to Virginny. Ever sence, workin and slavin; ever sence, sweatin and drivin; workin all day, workin all night."

"You never worked a bit in the night time, Aunt Peggy," said Phillis ; " and you know it."

"Worked all time," said Aunt Peggy, "niggers aint made for nothin else. Now, kase Death's somewhar, wantin somefin, thinks it must be me."

"I didn't say 'twas you,. Aunt Peggy," said Phillis.

" Wants somefin," said Aunt Peggy. « Tell you what, Phillis," and she laughed, "wants Miss Alice."

" What's come over you?" said Phillis, looking at her, terrified. " There's nothing the matter with Miss Alice but a headache."

"Headache!" said Aunt Peggy, "that's all?" and she laughed again. "Think I didn't see her yesterday? Whars the red cheeks ?—white about her lips, black about her eyes ; jist like Mistis when she was gwine fast, and de young baby on her arm. Death wants Miss Alice—aint arter me."

" Aint you ashamed to talk so about Miss Alice, when she's always coming to you, bringing you something, and trying to do something for you?" said Phillis. "You might as well sit here and talk bad of one of the angels above."

"Aint talking bad of her," said Aunt Peggy; "aint wishin her no harm. If there is any angels she's as good as any of 'em; but it's her Death's arter, not me; look here at my arms—stronger than yourn—" and she held out her sinewy, tough arm, grasping her cane, to go in the house.

Phillis saw she was not wanted there, and looking in to be assured that Nancy (Aunt Peggy's grand-daughter, who lived with her to take care of her,) was there, went home and thought to go to bed. But she found no disposition to sleep within her. Accustomed, as she was, to Aunt Peggy's fault finding, and her strange way of talking, she was particularly impressed with it to-night. 'Twas so strange, Phillis thought, that she should have talked about being stolen away from Guinea, and things that happened almost a hundred years ago. Then her saying, so often that, "Death was about." Phillis was no more nerv-

13*

ous than her iron tea-kettle, but now she could not feel right. She sat down by the door, and tried to compose herself. Every one on the plantation was quiet; it seemed to her the night got brighter and brighter, and the heavens more crowded with stars than she had ever seen them. She looked at her children to see if they all were well, and then gave a glance at old Bacchus, who was snoring loud enough to wake the dead. She shook him heartily and told him to hush his clatter, but she might as well have told a twenty-four pounder to go off without making a noise. Then she sat down again and looked at Alice's window, and could not avoid seeing Aunt Peggy's house when she turned in that direction; thus she was reminded of her saying, "Death was about and arter somefin." Wondering what had come over her, she shut the door and laid down without undressing herself.

She slept heavily for several hours, and waked with the thought of Aunt Peggy's strange talk pressing upon her. She determined not to go to bed again, but opened the door and fixed the old rush-bottomed chair within it. Bacchus, always a very early riser, except on Sunday, was still asleep; having had some sharp twinges of the rheumatism the day before, Phillis hoped he might sleep them off; her own mind was still burdened with an unaccountable weight. She was glad to see the dawning of " another blue day."

Before her towered, in their majestic glory, Miss Janet's favorite mountains, yet were the peaks alone distinctly visible; the twilight only strong enough to disclose the mass of heavy fog that enveloped them. The stars had nearly all disappeared, those that lingered were sadly paling away. How solemn was the stillness ! She thought of the words of Jacob, "Surely God is here !"— the clouds were flying swiftly beneath the arch of Heaven, as if from God's presence. Many thoughts were suggested to her by the grandeur of the scene, for my reader must remember, that an admiration of the glories of nature is not unfrequently a characteristic of an uneducated mind. Many verses of Scripture occurred to her, " From the rising of the sun unto the going down of the same, the Lord's name be praised. The Lord is high above all nations, and his glory above the heavens. Who is like unto the Lord our God, who dwelleth on high? Who humbleth himself to behold the things that are in Heaven, and in the earth." The soul of the slave-woman rejoiced in the Lord, her Maker and her Redeemer.

Gradually a soft light arose above the mountains; the fog became transparent through its influence. A red hue gilded the top of the mist, and slowly descended toward it, as it sank away. All the shadows of the night were disappearing, at the command once given, " Let there be light," and re-obeyed at the birth of every day. Phillis's heart warmed with gratitude to God who had given to her a knowledge of himself. She thought of her many mercies, her health, her comforts, and the comparative happiness of each member of her family; of the kindness of her master and the ladies; all these considerations affected her as they never had before, for gratitude and love to God ever inspires us with love and kindness to our fellow creatures.

Her thoughts returned to Alice, but all superstitious dread was gone; Aunt Peggy's strange wanderings no longer oppressed her; her mind was in its usual healthy state. " The good Lord is above us all," she said, "and Miss Alice is one of his children." She saw the house door open, and William coming toward her on his way to the stable. It was without any agitation that she asked what was the matter? "Miss Alice is very sick," said William, "and I am going for the doctor."

"I am glad I happened to be here," said Phillis, " may be they want me."

"You better not go in now," said William, "for she's

asleep. Miss Anna told me to walk very easy, for she would not have her waked for all the world."

So Phillis, seeing Aunt Peggy's door open, thought she would step over and find out if the old lady had slept off her notions.

Aunt Peggy's cabin had two rooms, in one of which, she and her granddaughter slept, in the other Nancy cooked and washed, and occupied herself with various little matters. Nancy had been up a short time and was mixing some Indian bread for their breakfast. She looked surprised, at having so early a visitor.

" How is your grandmother, child ?" said Phillis ; "did she sleep well?"

« Mighty well," said Nancy. " She aint coughed at all as I heard, since she went to bed."

" Well, I'm glad to hear it," said Phillis, " for I thought she was going to be sick, she was so curious last night."

" She didn't complain, any way," said Nancy, going on with her breadmaking, so Phillis got up to go home. As she passed the door of the other room, she could but stop to look in at the hard, iron features of the old creature, as she lay in slumber. Her long black face contrasted most remarkably with the white pillow on which it was sup ported, her hair making her head look double its actual size, standing off from her ears and head. One long black arm lay extended, the hand holding to the side of the bed. Something impelled Phillis to approach. At first she thought of her grumbling disposition, her bitter resent ment for injuries, most of which were fanciful, her uncom promising dislike to the servants on the plantation. She almost got angry when she thought «the more you do for her, the more she complains." Then she recalled her talk the night before; of her being torn away from her mother, and sold off, tied to a dead woman, and the storm and the sharks; a feeling of the sincerest pity took the place of her first reflections, and well they did—for the

next idea—Phillis' knees knocked together, and her heart beat audibly, for what was before her ?

What but death! with all his grimness and despair, looking forth from the white balls that were only partially covered with the dark lids—showing his power in the cold hands whose unyielding grasp had closed in the struggle with him. Setting his seal on brow and lips, lengthening the extended form, that never would rouse itself from the position in which the mighty conqueror had left it, when he knew his victory was accomplished. What but -death, indeed! For the heart and the pulse were still forever, and the life that had once regulated their beatings, had gone back to the Giver of life.

The two slave women were alone together. She who had been, had gone with all her years, her wrongs, and her sins, to answer at the bar of her Maker. The fierce and bitter contest with life, the mysterious curse, the deal ings of a God with the children of men. Think of it, Oh! Christian! as you gaze upon her. The other slave woman is with the dead. She is trembling, as in the pre sence of God. She knows he is everywhere, even in the room of death. She is redeemed from the slavery of sin, and her regenerate soul looks forward to the rest that re-maineth to the people of God. She " submits herself to an earthly master," knowing that the dispensation of God has placed her in a state of servitude. Yet she trusts in a Heavenly Master with childlike faith, and says, " May I be ready when he comes and calls for me."

Phillis was perfectly self-possessed when she went back to the kitchen. "Nancy," she said, "didn't you think it was strange your grandmother slept so quiet, and laid so late this morning? She always gets up so early."'

"I didn't think nothin about it," said Nancy, "for I was 'sleep myself."

"Well there's no use putting it off," said Phillis. "I might as well tell you, first as last. She's dead."

"Dead, what do you mean?" said Nancy.

"I mean she's dead," said Phillis, "and cold, and very likely has been so, for most of the night. Don't be fright ened and make a noise, for Miss Alice is very sick, and you're so near the house."

Nancy went with her to the other room. A child would have known there was no mistake about death's being there, if the idea had been suggested to it. Nancy was in a moment satisfied that such was the case, but she shed very few tears. She was quite worn out taking care of the old woman, and the other servants were not willing to take their turns. They said they " couldn't abide the cross, ill-natured old thing."

Phillis went home for a few moments, and returned to perform the last offices. All was order and neatness under her superintendence; and they w r ho avoided the sight of Aunt Peggy when alive, stood with a solemn awe beside her and gazed, now that she was dead.

All but the children. Aunt Peggy was dead ! She who had been a kind of scarecrow in life, how terrible was the thought of her now! The severest threat to an unruly child was, "I will give you to Aunt Peggy, and let her keep you." But to think of Aunt Peggy in connection with darkness, and silence, and the grave, was dreadful indeed. All day the thought of her kept them awed and quiet; but as evening drew on, they crept close to their mothers' side, turning from every shadow, lest she should come forth from it. Little Lydia, deprived of Miss Janet's company in consequence of Alice's sickness, listened to the pervading subject of conversation all day, and at night dreamed that the old woman had carried her off to the top of the highest of the mountains that stood before them; and there she sat scowling upon her, and there, they were to be forever.

When the next afternoon had come, and the body was buried, and all had returned from the funeral, Phillis

locked up the vacant cabin. Nancy was to be employed in the house, and sleep in the servants' wing. Then Phil-lis realized that death had been there, and she remem bered once more, Aunt Peggy's words, "He's arter somefin, wants it, and he's gwine to have it; but it ain't me."

There is one thing concerning death in which we are apt to be sceptical, and that is, "Does he want me?"

CHAPTER XV.

AUNT Peggy's funeral was conducted quietly, but with that respect to the dead which is universal on Southern plantations. There was no hurry, no confusion. Two young women remained with the corpse during the night preceding the burial; the servants throughout the planta tion had holiday, that they might attend. At Mr. Wes-ton's request, the clergyman of the Episcopal church in L. read the service for the dead. He addressed the serv ants in a solemn and appropriate manner. Mr. Weston was one of the audience. Alice's sickness had become serious; Miss Janet and her mother were detained with her. The negroes sung one of their favorite hymns,

" Life is the time to serve the Lord,"

their fine voices blending in perfect harmony. Mr. Cald-well took for his text the 12th verse of the 2d chapter of Thessalonians, "That ye would walk worthy of God, who hath called you unto his kingdom and his glory."

He explained to them in the most affectionate and beau tiful manner, that they were called unto the kingdom and glory of Christ. He dwelt on the glories of that kingdom, as existing in the heart of the believer, inciting him to a faithful performance of the duties of life; as in the world,

promoting the happiness and welfare of all mankind, and completed in heaven, where will be the consummation of all the glorious things that the humble believer in Jesus has enjoyed by faith, while surrounded by the temptations, and enduring the trials of the world. He told them they were all called. Christ died for all; every human being that had heard of Jesus and his atonement, was called unto salvation. He dwelt on the efficacy of that atonement, on the solemn occasion when it was made, on the perfect peace and reconciliation of the believer. He spoke of the will of God, which had placed them in a condition of bond age to an earthly master; who had given them equal hopes of eternal redemption with that master. He reminded them that Christ had chosen his lot among the poor of this world; that he had refused all earthly honor and advantage. He charged them to profit by the present occasion, to bring home to their hearts the unwelcome truth that death was inevitable. He pointed to the coffin that contained the remains of one who had attained so great an age, as to make her an object of wonder in the neighborhood. Yet her time had come, like a thief in the night. There was no sickness, no sudden failing, nothing unusual in her appearance, to intimate the pre sence of death. God had given her a long time of health to prepare for the great change; he had given her every opportunity to repent, and he had called her to her ac count. He charged them to make their preparation now; closing, by bringing before their minds that great day when the Judge of the earth would summon before him every soul he had made. None could escape his all-pierc ing eye; the king and his subject, the rich and the poor, the strong and the weak, the learned and the ignorant, the Avhite and the colored, the master and his slave ! each to render his or her account for the deeds done in the body. The servants were extremely attentive, listening with breathless interest as he enlarged upon the awful events

of the Judgment. Many a tear fell, many a heart throbbed, many a soul stretched forth her wings toward the kingdom and glory which had been the clergyman's theme.

After he concluded, their attention was absorbed by the preparation to remove the body to its final resting place. The face was looked upon, then covered; the coffin lid screwed down; strong arms lifting and bearing it to the bier. Nancy and Isaac, her only relatives, were near the coffin, and Mr. Weston and the clergyman followed them. The rest formed in long procession. With measured step and appropriate thought they passed their cabins toward the place used for the interment of the slaves on the plantation.

They had gone a little way, when a full, rich female voice gently broke in upon the stillness; it was Phillis's. Though the first line was sung in a low tone, every one heard it.

"Alas ! and did my Saviour bleed!"

They joined in, following the remains of their fellow-servant, and commemorating the sufferings of one who became as a servant, that He might exalt all who trust in Him.

It might be there was little hope for the dead, but not less sufficient the Atonement on Calvary, not less true that for each and all " did he devote that sacred head;" that for pity which he felt for all,

" He hung upon the tree : Amazing pity, grace unknown I And love beyond degree!"

While the voices swept through the air, a tribute of lowly hearts ascended to God.

They had now reached the burial ground ; all was in readiness, and the men deposited their burden in the

14

earth. Deep and solemn thought was portrayed on every face ; music had softened their feelings, and the re flections suggested by the hymn prepared them for kind sentiments toward the dead, though no one had loved her in life. The first hard clod that rattled on the coffin, opened the fountain of their tears; she who had been the object of their aversion was gone from them forever; they could not now show her any kindness. How many a heart reproached itself with a sneering word, hasty anger, and disdainful laugh. But what was she now ? dust and ashes.

They wept as they saw her hidden from their eyes, turn ing from the grave with a better sense of their duties.

Reader, it is well for the soul to ponder on the great mystery, Death! Is there not a charm in it? The mystery of so many opposite memories, the strange union of adverse ideas. The young, the old, the gay,-the proud, the beautiful, the poor, and the sorrowful. Silence, dark ness, repose, happiness, woe, heaven and hell. Oh! they should come now with a startling solemnity upon us all, for while I write, the solemn tolling of the bells warns me of a nation's grief; it calls to millions—its sad reso nance is echoed in every heart.

HENRY CLAY is DEAD ! Well may the words pass from lip to lip in the thronged street. The child repeats it with a dim consciousness of some great woe; it knows not, to its full extent, the burden of the words it utters. The youth passes along the solemn sentence; there is a throb in his energetic heart, for he has seen the enfeebled form of the statesman as it glided among the multitude, and has heard his voice raised for his country's good; he is assured that the heart that has ceased to beat glowed with all that was great and noble.

The politician utters, too, the oft-repeated sound—Henry Clay is dead! Well may he bare his breast and say, for what is my voice raised where his has been heard? Is it for my country, or for my party and myself? Men of

business and mechanics in the land, they know that one who ever defended their interests is gone, and who shall take his place ? The mother—tears burst from her eyes, when looking into her child's face, she says, Henry Clay is dead! for a nation's freedom is woman's incalculable blessing. She thinks with grief and gratitude of him who never ceased to contend for that which gives to her, social and religious rights.

Henry Clay isd<3ad ! His body no longer animated with life; his spirit gone to God. How like a torrent thought rushes on, in swift review, of his wonderful and glorious career. His gifted youth, what if it were attended with the errors that almost invariably accompany genius like his! Has he in the wide world an enemy who can bring aught against him ? Look at his patriotism, his benevolence, his noble acts. Recall his energy, his calmness, his constant devotion to the interests of his country. Look, above all, at his patience, his humility, as the great scenes of life were receding from his view, and futurity was opening be fore him. Hear of the childlike submission with which he bowed to the Will that ordained for him a death-bed, pro tracted and painful. "Lead me," he said to a friend, "where I want to go, to the feet of Jesus."

Listen to the simplicity with which he commended his body to his friends, and his spirit, through faith in Jesus Christ, to his God. Regard him in all his varied relations of Christian, patriot, statesman, husband, father, master, and friend, and answer if the sigh that is now rending the heart of his country is not well merited.

Yes 1 reader, thoughts of death are useful to us all, whether it be by the grave of the poor and humble, or when listening to the tolling of the bell which announces to all that one who was mighty in the land has been sum moned to the judgment seat of God.

CHAPTER XVI.

MR. WESTON and Phillis returned to the sick-room from the funeral. Fever was doing its work with the fail-being, the beloved of many hearts, who was unconscious of aught that was passing around her. There was a startling light from the depths of her blue eyes ; their natural soft ness of expression gone. The crimson glow had flushed into a hectic ; the hot breath from her parted lips was drying away their moisture. The rich, mournful tones of her voice echoed in sad wailing through the chambers; it constantly and plaintively said Mother ! though that mother answered in vain to its appeal. The air circulated through the room, bearing the odor of the woods, but for her it had no reviving power; it could not stay the beatings of her pulse, nor relieve the oppression of her panting bosom. Oh! what beauty was about that bed of sickness. The perfect shape of every feature, the graceful turn of the head, the luxuriant auburn hair, the contour of her rounded limbs. There was no vacancy in her face. Alas! visions of sorrow were passing in her mind. A sad intelligence was expressed in every glance, but not to the objects about her. The soul, subdued by the suffering of its tenement, was wandering afar off, perchance endeavoring to dive into the future, perchance essaying to forget the past.

What says that vision of languishing and loveliness to the old man whose eyes are fixed in grief upon it? "Thou seest, O Christian! the uselessness of laying up thy treasures here. Where are now the hopes of half thy lifetime, where the consummation of all thy anxious plans? She who has been like an angel by thy side, how wearily throbs her young heart! Will she perpetuate the name of thy race? Will she close thine eyes with her loving hand? Will she drop upon thy breast a daughter's tear?"

What does the vision say to thee, oh! aged woman? "There is still more for thee to do, more for thee to suffer. It is not yet enough of this mortal strife! Thou mayest again see a fair flower crushed by the rude wind of death; perchance she may precede thee, to open for thine entrance the eternal gates!"

And what to thee, thou faithful servant?

"There are tears in thine eye, and for me. For me! Whom thou thoughtest above a touch of aught that could bring sorrow or pain. Thou seest, not alone on thy doomed* race rests a curse; the fierce anger of God, denounced against sin—the curse, falls upon his dearest children. I must, like you, abide by God's dealing with the children of men. But we shall be redeemed."

What to thee, oh, mother? Thou canst not read the interpretation—a cloud of darkness sweeps by thy soul's vision. Will it pass, or will it rest upon thee forever?

Yet the voice of God speaks to each one; faintly it may be to the mother, but even to her. There is a rainbow of hope in the deluge of her sorrow; she sees death in the multitude that passes her sight, but there is another there, one whose form is like unto the Son of God. She remembers how He wept over Lazarus, and raised him from the dead; oh! what comfort to place her case in his pitying bosom!

Many were the friends who wept, and hoped, and prayed with them. Full of grief were the affectionate servants, but most of all, Phillis.

It was useless to try and persuade her to take her usual rest, to remind her of her children, and her cares; to offer her the choice morsel to tempt her appetite, the refreshing drink she so much required. She wanted nothing but to weep with those who wept—nor rest, nor food, nor refreshing.

(It is universal, the consideration that is shown to the servants at the South, as regards their times of eating and of rest. Whatever may have occurred, whatever fatigue the different members of the family may feel obliged to undergo, a servant is rarely called upon for extra attendance. In the Northern country the whole labor of a family is frequently performed by one female, while five or six will do the same amount of work in the South. A servant at the South is rarely called upon at night; only in cases of absolute necessity. Negroes are naturally sleepy-headed—they like to sit up late at night,—in winter, over a large fire, nodding and bumping their heads against each other, or in summer, out of doors; but they take many a nap before they can get courage to undress and go regularly to bed. They may be much interested in a conversation going on, but it is no violation of their code of etiquette to smoke themselves to sleep while listening. Few of the most faithful servants can keep awake well enough to be of real service in cases of sickness. There is a feel ing among their owners, that they work hard during the day and should be allowed more rest than those who are

" not obliged to labor. " Do not disturb servants when they are eating," is the frequent charge of a Southern mother, "they have not a great many pleasures within their reach ; never do any thing that will lessen their comforts in the slightest degree." Mrs. West on, even in her own deep sorrow, was not unmindful of others ; she frequently tried to induce Phillis to go home, knowing that she must be much fatigued. " I cannot feel tired, Phillis ; a mother could not sleep with her only child as Alice is; I do not require the rest that you do."

«You needs it more, Miss Anna, though you don't think so now. I can take care of myself. Unless you drive me away, I shan't go until God's will be done, for life or death."

Miss Janet often laid down and slept for an hour or two, and returned refreshed to the sick chamber. Her voice retained its cheerfulness and kept Mrs. Weston's heart from failing. « Hope on, Anna," she would say, " as long as she breathes we must not give her up; how many have been thought entirely gone, and then revived. We must hope, and God will do the rest."

, This " hoping on" was one great cause of Cousin Janet's usefulness during a long life; religion and reason alike demand it of us. Many grand and noble actions have been done in the world, that never could have been ac complished without hoping on. When we become discour aged, how heavy the task before us; it is like drooping the eyes, and feebly putting forth the hands to find the way, when all appears to us darkness; but let the eye be lifted and the heart hope on, and there is found a glimmering of light which enables the trembling one to penetrate the gloom. Alice's symptoms had been so violent from the first, her disease had progressed so rapidly, that her con dition was almost hopeless; ere Mr. Weston thought of the propriety of informing Arthur of her condition. The first time it occurred to him, he felt convinced that he ought not to delay. He knew that Arthur never could be consoled, if Alice, his dearly loved, his affianced wife, should die without his having the consolation of a parting word or look. He asked Cousin Janet her opinion.

She recalled all that had passed previous to Alice's ill ness. As she looked into Mr. Weston's grieved and honest face, the question suggested itself,—Is it right thus, to keep him in ignorance ? She only wavered a moment. Already the traces of agitation caused by his niece's ill ness, were visible in his flushed face and nervous frame; what then might be the result of laying before him a sub ject in which his happiness was so nearly concerned? Besides, she felt convinced that even should Alice im prove, the suffering which had been one cause of her sick-

ness, might be renewed with double force if suggested by Arthur's presence.

" I know, my dear cousin," she said, " it will be a terri ble grief to Arthur, should Alice be taken from us, yet I think you had better not write. Dr. Lawton says, that a very short time must decide her case; and were the worst we fear to occur, Arthur could not reach here in time to see her with any satisfaction. If he lose her, it will pro bably be better for him to remember her in health and beauty."

Mr. Weston trembled, and burst into tears. " Try and not give way," said Miss Janet again; "we are doing all we can. We must hope and pray. I feel a great deal of hope. God is so merciful, he will not bring this stroke upon you in your old age, unless it is necessary. Why do you judge for him ? He is mighty to save. < The Lord on high, is mightier than the noise of many waters, yea, than the mighty waves of the sea.' Think of His mercy and power to save, and trust in Him."

In these most trying scenes of life, how little do we sympathize with the physician. How much oppressed he must feel, with the charge upon him. He is the adviser —to him is left the direction of the potions which may be the healing medicine or the deadly poison. He may se lect a remedy powerful to cure, he may prescribe one fatal to the invalid. How is he to draw the nice line of distinction ? he must consider the disease, the constitution, the probable causes of the attack. His reputation is at stake—his happiness—for many eyes are turned to him, to read an opinion he may not choose to give in words.

If he would be like the great Healer, he thinks not only of the bodily sufferings that he is anxious to assuage, but of the immortal soul on the verge of the great Interview, deciding its eternal destiny. He trembles to think, should he fail, it may be hurried to its account. If he be a friend, how do the ties of association add to his burden. Here is

one whom he has loved, whose voice he is accustomed to hear; shall he, through neglect or mismanagement, make a void in many hearts ? Shall he, from want of skill, bring weeping and desolation to a house where health and joy have been ? Alice was very dear to Dr. Lawton, she was the companion of his daughters; he had been accus tomed to regard her as one of them; he was untiring in his attendance, but from the first, had feared the result. Mrs. Weston had concealed nothing from him, she knew that he considered a physician bound in honour to know the affairs of a family only among themselves—she had no reserves, thus giving him every assistance in her power, in conducting the case. She detailed to him, explicitly, all that might have contributed to produce it.

"You know, my dear madam," the doctor said, "that at this season we have, even in our healthy country, severe fevers. Alice's is one of the usual nature; it could have been produced by natural causes. We cannot say, it may be that the circumstances you have been kind enough to confide to me, have had a bad effect upon her. The effort to do right, and the fear lest she should err, may have strained her sensitive mind. She must have felt much distress in parting with Walter, whom she has always loved as a brother. You have only done your duty. I should not like to see a daughter of mine interested in that young man. I fear he inherits his father's violent passions, yet his early training may bring the promised blessing. Alice has that sort of mind, that is always in fluenced by what is passing at the time ; remember what a child she was when Arthur left. There are no more broken hearts now-a-days—sometimes they bend a little, but they can be straightened again. If Alice gets well, you need not fear the future; though you know I disap prove of cousins marrying."

"Doctor," said Mrs. Weston, "I know you have not given her up!"

"I never give anybody up," said the doctor. "Who will say what God intends to do ? I trust she will strug gle through. Many a storm assails the fair ship on her first voyage over the seas> She may be sadly tossed about with the wind and waves; but may breast it gal lantly, and come back safe, after all. We must do what we can, and hope for the best." These words strength ened the mother's heart to watch and hope.

The doctor laid down to sleep for an hour or two in the afternoon. Cousin Janet, Mrs. Weston, and Phillis kept their watch in silence. The latter gently fanned AKce, who lay gazing, but unconscious; now looking in quiringly into her mother's face, now closing her eyes to every thing. There was no tossing or excitement about her, that was over. Her cheek was pale, and her eyes languid and faded. One would not have believed, to have looked upon her, how high the fever still raged. Sud denly she repeated the word that had often been on her lips—"Mother." Then, with an eifort to raise herself, she sank back upon her pillow, exhausted. A sorrowful look, like death, suffused itself over her countenance. Ah ! how throbbed those hearts ! Was the dreaded mes senger here ?

"Miss Anna," whispered Phillis, " she is not gone, her pulse is no lower; it is the same."

"Is it the same? are you sure?" said Mrs. Weston, who, for a few moments, had been unable to speak, or even to place her finger on the pulse.

« It is no worse, if you'll believe me," said Phillis ; "it may be a little better, but it is no worse."

" Had I not better wake the doctor ?" said Mrs. Weston, who hardly knew what to believe.

Miss Janet gently touched the wrist of the invalid.

" Do not wake him, my dear; Phillis is right in saying she is no worse; it was a fainting, which is passing away. See! she looks as usual. Give her the medicine, it is time; and leave her quiet, the doctor may be disturbed to-night."

The night had passed, and the morning was just visible, as symptoms of the same nature affected the patient. Dr. Lawton had seen her very late at night, and had requested them to awaken him should there be any change in her appearance or condition. Oh, how these anxious hearts feared and hoped through this night. What might it bring forth; joy or endless weeping?

This dread crisis past, and what would be the result ?

" Doctor," said Phillis, gently awaking him, " I'm sorry to disturb you. Miss Alice has had another little turn, and you'd better see her."

"How is her pulse?" said the doctor, quickly. "Is it failing ?"

" 'Pears to me not, sir ; but you can see."

They went to the room, and the doctor took Alice's small wrist, and lightly felt her pulse. Then did the mother watch his face, to see its writing. What was there ?

Nothing but deep attention. The wrist was gently laid down, and the doctor's hand passed lightly over the white arm. Softly it touched the forehead, and lay beneath the straying curl. There is no expression yet; but he takes the wrist again, and, laying one hand beneath it, he touches the pulse. Softly, like the first glance of moon light on the dark waters, a smile is seen on that kind face. There is something else besides the smile. Large tears dropped from the physician's eyes; tears that he did not think to wipe away. He stooped towards the fragile sufferer, and gently as the morning air breathes upon the drooping violet, he kissed her brow. "Alice, sweet one," he said, " God has given you to us again."

Where is that mother? Has she heard those cheering words? She hears them, and is gone; gone even from the side of her only one. The soul, when there is too much joy, longs for God. She must lay her rich burden

at the mercy-seat. Now, that mother kneels, but utters no word. The incense of her heart knows no language, and needs none; for God requires it not. The sacrifice of praise from a rejoicing heart, is a grateful offering that he accepts.

"Miss Anna," said Phillis, with trembling voice, but beaming eye, "go to bed now; days and nights you have been up. How can you stand it? The doctor says she is a great deal better, but she may be ill for a good while yet, and you will give out. I will stay with her if you will take a sleep."

"Sleep;" said Mrs. Weston. « No, no, faithful Phillis, not yet; joy is too new to me. God for ever bless you for your kindness to me and my child. You shall go home and sleep, and to-night, if she continue to do well, I will trust her with you, and take some rest myself."

Mr. Weston awoke to hear glad tidings. Again and again, through the long day, he repeated to himself his favorite Psalm, "Praise the Lord, oh my soul."

Miss Janet's joy, deep but silent, was visible in her happy countenance. Nor were these feelings confined to the family; every servant on the estate made his master's joy his own. They sorrowed with him when he sorrowed, but now that his drooping head was lifted up, many an honest face regarded him with humble congratulation, as kindly received as if it had come from the highest in the land.

CHAPTER XVII.

ALICE steadily, though slowly, improved; and Phillis again employed herself with her children and her work. Things had gone on very well, with one of her daughter's constant superintendence; but Bacchus had taken advantage of being less watched than usual, and had indulged a good deal, declaring to himself that without something to keep up his spirits he should die, thinking about Miss Alice. Phillis, lynx-eyed as she always was, saw that such had been the case.

It was about a week after Alice commenced to improve, that Phillis went to her house in the evening, after having taken charge of her for several hours, while Mrs. Weston slept. Alice was very restless at night, and Mrs. Weston generally prepared herself for it, by taking some repose previously; this prevented the necessity of any one else losing rest, which, now that Alice was entirely out of danger, she positively refused to permit. As Phillis went in the door, Lydia was on her knees, just finishing the little nightly prayer that Miss Janet had taught her. She got up, and as she was about to go to bed, saw her mother, and bade her good night.

"Good night, and go to bed like a good child. Miss Alice says you may come to see her again to-morrow," Phillis replied.

Lydia was happy as a queen with this promise. Aunt Phillis took her pipe, and her old station outside the door, to smoke. Bacchus had his old, crazy, broken-backed chair out there already, and he was evidently resolving something in his mind of great importance, for he propped the

15

chair far back on its one leg, and appeared to be taking the altitude of the mountains in the moon, an unfailing sign of a convulsion of some kind in the inner man.

"Phillis," said he, after a long silence, "do you know, it is my opinion that that old creature," pointing with his thumb to Aunt Peggy's house, "is so long used to grum-blin' and fussin', that she can't, to save her life, lie still in her grave."

"What makes you think so?" said Phillis.

"Bekase, I believes in my soul she's back thar this minute."

"People that drink, Bacchus, can't expect nothin' else than to be troubled with notions. I was in hopes Aunt Peggy's death would have made you afeered to go on sin ning. 'Stead of that, when we was all in such grief, and didn't know what was comin' upon us, you must go drink ing. You'd better a been praying, I tell you. But be sure your < sin will find you out' some day or other. The Lord above knows I pray for you many a time, when I'm hard at work. My heart is nigh breaking when I think where the drunkards will be, when the Lord makes up his jewels. They can't enter the kingdom of Heaven; there is no place for them there. Why can't you repent ? 'Spose you die in a drunken fit, how will I have the heart to work when I remember where you've got to; <where the worm never dieth, and the fire is not quenched."

Bacchus was rather taken aback by this sudden appeal, and he moved uneasily in his chair; but after a little re flection, and a good long look at the moon, he recovered his confidence.

"Phillis," said he, "do you b'lieve in sperrits?"

"No, I don't," said Phillis, drily, "of no kind."

Bacchus was at a loss again; but he pretended not to understand her, and giving a hitch to his uncertain chair, he got up some courage, and said, doggedly,

"Well, I do."

"I don't," said Phillis, positively, "of no kind."

Bacchus was quite discomposed again, but he said in an appealing voice to his wife, "Phillis, I couldn't stand it; when Miss Alice was so low, you was busy, and could be a doin somethin for her; but what could I do ? Here I sot all night a cryin, a thinkin about her and young master. I 'spected for true she was gwine to die; and my blessed grief! what would have come of us all. Master Arthur, he'd a come home, but what would be the use, and she dead and gone. Every which way I looked, I think I see Miss Alice going up to Heaven, a waving her hand good- by to us, and we all by ourselves, weepin and wailin. 'Deed, Phillis, I couldn't stand it; if I hadn't had a little whiskey I should a been dead and cold afore now."

" You'll be dead and cold afore long with it," said Phillis.

"I couldn't do nothing but cry, Phillis," said Bacchus, snuffing and blowing his nose; " and I thought I might be wanted for somethin, so I jest took a small drop to keep up my strength.'1

Phillis said nothing. She was rather a hard-hearted woman where whiskey was concerned; so she gave Bacchus no encouragement to go on excusing himself.

" I tell you why I believes in ghosts," said Bacchus, af ter a pause. "I've see'd one."

"When?" said Phillis.

"I was telling you that while Miss Alice was so ill," said Bacchus, "I used to set up most of de night. I don't know how I kep up, for you know niggers takes a sight of sleep, 'specially when they aint very young, like me. Well, I thought one time about Miss Alice, but more about old Aunt Peggy. You know she used to set outside de door thar, very late o' nights. It 'peared like 1 was 'spectin to see her lean on her stick, and come out every minute. Well, one night I was sure I hear somethin thar. I listened, and then somethin gin a kind o' screech, sounded like de little niggers when Aunt Peggy used to gin 'em a lick wid her

switch. Arter a while I see de curtain lifted up. I couldn't see what it was, but it lifted it up. I hearn some more noise, and I felt so strange like, that I shut de door to, and went to bed. Well, I seed dat, and heard it for two or three nights. I was gettin scared I tell you; for, Phil-lis, there's somethin awful in thinkin of people walking out of their graves, and can't get rest even thar. I couldn't help comin, every night, out here, 'bout twelve o'clock, for that's time sperrits, I mean ghosts, is so uneasy. One night, de very night Miss Alice got better, I hearn de screech an de fuss, and I seed de curtain go up, and pretty soon what do you think I saw. I'm tellin' you no lie, Phillis. I seed two great, red eyes, a glarin out de winder; a glarin right at me. If you believe me, I fell down out of dis very cheer, and when I got up, I gin one look at de winder, and thar was de red eyes glarin agin, so I fell head-fore most over de door step, tryin to get in quick, and then when I did get in, I locked de door. My soul, wasn't I skeered. I never looked no more. I seen nuff dat time."

" Your head was mighty foolish," said Phillis, "and you just thought you saw it."

" No such thing. I saw de red eyes—Aunt Peggy's red eyes."

"High!" said Phillis, "Aunt Peggy hadn't redeyes."

" Not when she was 'live ?" said Bacchus. " But thar's no knowin what kind of eyes sperrits gets, 'specially when they gets where it aint very comfortable."

"Well," said Phillis, "these things are above us. We've got our work to do, and the Lord he does his. I don't bother myself about ghosts. I'm trying to get to heaven, and I know I'll never get there if I don't get ready while I'm here. Aunt Peggy aint got no power to come back, unless God sends her; and if He sends her, its for some good reason. You better come in now, and kneel down, and ask God to give you strength to do what is right. We've got no strength but what He gives us."

" I wish you'd pray loud to-night," said Bacchus; "for I aint felt easy of late, and somehow I can't pray."

" Well, I can't do much, but I can ask God to give us grace to repent of our sins, and to serve him faithfully," said Phillis.

And they both kneeled down, and prayer went forth from an earnest heart; and who shall say that a more wel come offering ascended to His ear in that time of prayer, than the humble but believing petition of the slave !

Phillis was of a most matter-of-fact disposition, and pos sessed, as an accompaniment, an investigating turn of mind; so, before any one was stirring in her cottage, she dressed herself, and took from a nail a large-sized key, that was over the mantel-piece. She hung it to her little finger, and made straight for Aunt Peggy's deserted cabin. She granted herself a search-warrant, and determined to find some clue to Bacchus's marvellous story. Her heart did not fail her, even when she put the key in the lock, for she was resolved as a grenadier, and she would not have turned back if the veritable red ejes themselves had raised the cotton curtain, and looked defiance. The lock was somewhat out of repair, requiring a little coaxing be fore she could get the key in, and then it was some time be fore she succeeded in turning it; at last it yielded, and with one push the door flew open.

Now Phillis, anxious as she was to have the matter cleared up, did not care to have it done so instantaneously, for hardly had she taken one step in the house before she, in the most precipitous manner, backed two or three out of it.

At first she thought Aunt Peggy herself had flown at her, and she could hardly help calling for assistance, but making a great effort to recover her composure, she saw at a glance that it was Aunt Peggy's enormous black cat, who not only resembled her in color, but disposition. Ju piter, for that was the cat's name, did not make another

15*

grab, but stood \vith his back raised, glaring at her, while Phillis, breathing very short, sunk into Aunt Peggy's chair and wiped the cold perspiration from her face with her apron.

"Why, Jupiter," said Phillis, "is this you? How on earth did I happen to forget you. Your eyes is red, to be sure, and no wonder, you poor, half-starved creature. I must a locked you up here, the day after the funeral, and I never would a forgot you, if it hadn't been my mind was so taken up with Miss Alice. Why, you're thin as a snake,—wait a minute and I'll bring you something to eat."

Jupiter, who had lived exclusively on mice for a fortnight, was evidently subdued by the prospects of an early breakfast. The apology Phillis had made him seemed not to be without its effect, for when she came back, with a small tin pan of bread and milk, and a piece of bacon hanging to a fork, his back was not the least elevated, and he proceeded immediately to the hearth where the provender was deposited, and to use an inelegant Westernism, "walked into it;" Phillis meanwhile going home, perfectly satisfied with the result of her exploration. Bacchus's toilet was completed, he was just raising up from the exertion of putting on his slippers, when Phillis came in, laughing.

This was an unusual phenomenon, so early in the morning, and Bacchus was slightly uneasy at its portent, but he ventured to ask her what was the matter.

"Nothing," said Phillis, " only I've seen the ghost."

"Lord! what?"

"The ghost!" said Phillis, "and its got red eyes, too, sure enough."

"Phillis," said Bacchus, appealingly, "you aint much used to jokin, and I know you wouldn't tell an ontruth; what do you mean?"

"I mean," said Phillis, "that the very ghost you saw, and heard screeching, with the red eyes glarin at you through the window, I've seen this morning."

"Phillis," said Bacchus, sinking back in his chair, " 'taint possible! What was it a doin?"

"I can tell you what its doing now," said Phillis, "its eating bread and milk and a piece of bacon, as hard as it can. Its eyes is red, to be sure, but I reckon yours would be red or shut, one, if you'd a been nigh a fortnight locked up in an empty house, with now and then a mouse to eat. Why, Bacchus, how come it, you forgot old Jupiter? I was too busy to think about cats, but I wonder nobody else didn't think of the poor animal."

"Sure enough," said Bacchus, slowly recovering from his astonishment, "its old Jupiter—why I'd a sworn on the Bible 'twas Aunt Peggy's sperrit. Well, I do b'lieve! that old cat's lived all this time; well, he aint no cat any how—I always said he was a witch, and now I knows it, that same old Jupiter. But, Phillis, gal, I wouldn't say nothin at all about it—we'll have all dese low niggers laughin at us."

"What they going to laugh at me about?" said Phillis. " I didn't see no ghost."

"Well, its all de same," said Bacchus, "they'll laugh at me—and man and wife's one—'taint worth while to say nothin 'bout it, as I see."

" I shan't say nothing about it as long as you keep sober; but mind, you go pitching and tumbling about, and I aint under no kind of promise to keep your secret. And its the blessed truth, they'd laugh, sure enough, at you, if they did know it."

And the hint had such a good effect, that after a while, it was reported all over the plantation that Bacchus "had give up drinkin, for good and all."

CHAPTER XVIII.

IT was in answer to Arthur's letter, expressing great anxiety to hear from home, in consequence of so long a time having passed without his receiving his usual letters, that Mr. Weston wrote him of Alice's illness. She was then convalescing, but in so feeble and nervous a condition, that Dr. Lawton advised Arthur's remaining where he was—wishing his patient to be kept even from the excitement of seeing so dear a relative. Mr. Weston insisted upon Arthur's being contented with hearing constantly of her improvement, both from himself and Mrs. Weston. This, Arthur consented to do; but in truth he was not aware of the extent of the danger which had threatened Alice's life, and supposed it to have been an ordinary fever. With what pleasure did he look forward, in his leisure moments, to the time when it would be his privilege always to be near her; and to induce the tedious interval to pass more rapidly, he employed himself with his studies, as constantly as the season would allow. He had formed a sincere attachment to Abel Johnson, whose fine talents and many high qualities made him a delightful companion. Mr. Hubbard was a connection of young Johnson's, and felt privileged often to intrude himself upon them. It really was an intrusion, for he had at present a severe attack of the Abolition fever, and he could not talk upon any other subject. This was often very disagreeable to Arthur and his friend, but still it became a frequent subject of their discussion, when Mr. Hubbard was present, and when they were alone.

In the mean time, the warm season was passing away, and Alice did not recover her strength as her friends wished.

No place in the country could have been more delightful than Exeter was at that season; but still it seemed necessary to have a change of scene. September had come, and it was too late to make their arrangements to go to the North, and Alice added to this a great objection to so doing. A distant relation of Mr. Weston, a very young girl, named Ellen Graham, had been sent for, in hopes that her lively society would have a good effect on Alice's unequal spirits; and after much deliberation it was determined that the family, with the exception of Miss Janet, should pass the winter in Washington. Miss Janet could not be induced to go to that Vanity Fair, as she called it; and if proper arrangements for her comfort could not be made, the project would have to be given up. After many proposals, each one having an unanswerable difficulty, the old lady returned from town one day, with a very satisfied countenance, having persuaded Mrs. Williams, a widow, and her daughter, to pass the winter at Exeter with her. Mrs. Williams was a much valued friend of the Weston family, and as no objection could be found to this arrangement, the affair was settled. Alice, although the cause of the move, was the only person who was indifferent on the subject. Ellen Graham, young and gay as she was, would like to have entered into any excitement that would make her forget the past. She fancied it would be for her happiness, could the power of memory be destroyed. She had not sufficient of the experience of life to appreciate the old man's prayer, "Lord, keep my memory green."

Ellen at an early age, and an elder brother, were dependent, not for charity, but for kindness and love, on relatives who for a long time felt their guardianship a task. They were orphans; they bore each other company in the many little cares of childhood; and the boy, as is not unusual in such a case, always looked to his sister for counsel and protection, not from actual unkindness, but from coldness and unmerited reproof. They

never forgot their parting with their mother—the agony with which she held them to her bosom, bitterly reflecting they would have no such resting-place in the cold world, in which they were to struggle.

Yet they were not unkindly received at their future home. Their uncle and aunt, standing on the piazza, could not without tears see the delicate children in their deep mourning, accompanied only by their aged and respectable colored nurse, raise their eyes timidly, appealing to them for protection, as hand in hand they ascended the steps. It was a large and dreary-looking mansion, and many years had passed since the pictures of the stiff looking cavalier and his smiling lady, hanging in the hall, had looked down upon children at home there. The echoes of their own voices almost alarmed the children, when, after resting from their journey, they explored the scenes of their future haunts. On the glass of the large window in the hall, were the names of a maiden and her lover, descended from the cavaliers of Virginia. This writing was cut with a diamond, and the children knew not that the writing was their parents'. The little ones walked carefully over the polished floors; but there seemed nothing in all they saw to tell them they were welcome. They lifted the grand piano that maintained its station in one of the unoccupied rooms of the house; but the keys were yellow with age, and many of them soundless—when at last one of them answered to the touch of Ellen's little hand, it sent forth such a ghostly cry that the two children gazed at each other, not knowing whether to cry or to laugh.

Children are like politicians, not easily discouraged; and Ellen's "Come on, Willy," showed that she, by no means, despaired of finding something to amuse them. They lingered up stairs in their own apartment, William pointing to the moss-covered rock that lay at the foot of the garden.

« Willy, Willy, come! here is something," and Willy followed her through a long passage into a room, lighted only by the rays that found entrance through a broken shutter. " Only see this," she continued, laying her hand on a crib burdened with a small mattress and pillow; "here too," and she pointed to a little child's hat that hung over it, from which drooped three small plumes. " Whose can they be?"

" Come out o' here, children," said the nurse, who had been seeking them. " Your aunt told me not to let you come into this part of the house ; this was her nursery once, and her only child died here."

The children followed their nurse, and ever afterward the thought of death was connected with that part of the house. Often as they looked in their aunt's face they remembered the empty crib and the drooping plumes.

Time does not always fly with youth ; yet it passed along until Ellen had attained her sixteenth year, and William his eighteenth year. Ellen shared all her brother's studies, and their excellent tutor stored their minds with useful information. Their uncle superintended their education, with the determination that it should be a thorough one. William did not intend studying a profession ; his father's will allowed him to decide between this, or assuming, at an early age, the care of his large estate, with suitable advisers.

Ellen made excellent progress in all her studies. Her aunt was anxious she should learn music, and wished her to go to Richmond or to Alexandria for that purpose, but Ellen begged off; she thought of the old piano and its cracked keys, and desired not to be separated from her brother, professing her dislike to any music, but her old nurse's Methodist hymns.

William was tall and athletic for his age, passionate when roused by harshness or injustice, but otherwise affectionate in his disposition, idolizing his sister. His uncle looked at him with surprise when he saw him assume the

independence of manner, which sat well upon him; and his aunt sometimes checked herself, when about to reprove him for the omission of some unimportant form of politeness, which in her days of youth was essential. Ellen dwelt with delight upon the approaching time, when she would be mistress of her brother's establishment, and as important as she longed to be, on that account. Though she looked upon her uncle's house as a large cage, in which she had long fluttered a prisoner, she could not but feel an affection for it; her aunt and uncle often formal, and uselessly particular, were always substantially kind. It was a good, though not a cheerful home, and the young look for joy and gaiety, as do the flowers for birds and sunshine. Ellen was to be a ward of her uncle's until she was of age, but was to be permitted to reside with her brother, if she wished, from the time he assumed the management of his estate.

The young people laid many plans for housekeeping. William had not any love affair in progress, and as yet, his sister's image was stamped on all his projects for the future.

Two years before Ellen came to Exeter, William stood under his sister's window, asking her what he should bring her from C , the neighboring town. " Don't you want some needles," he said, "or a waist ribbon, or some candy? make haste, Ellen ; if I don't hurry, I can't come home to-night."

"I don't want any thing, Willie; but will you be sure to return to-night ? I never sleep well when you are away. Aunt and I are going on Tuesday to C ; wait, and we will stay all night then."

" Oh, no," said William, «I must go ; but you may de pend upon my being back: I always keep my promises. So good-by."

Ellen leaned from the window, watching her handsome brother as he rode down the avenue leading into the road.

He turned in his saddle, and bowed to her, just before he passed from her sight.

" Oh, mammy," she said to her attendant, for she had always thus affectionately addressed her; "did you ever see any one as handsome as Willie ?"

"Yes, child," she replied, "his father was, before him. You both look like your father; but Master Willie favors him more than you do. Shut down the window, Miss Ellen, don't you feel the wind ? A strong March wind aint good for nobody. Its bright enough overhead to-day, but the ground is mighty damp and chilly. There, you're sneezin ; didn't I tell you so?"

Late in the same day Ellen was seated at the window, watching her brother's return ; gaily watching, until the shadows of evening were resting on his favorite rocks. Then she watched anxiously until the rocks could no longer be seen; but never did he come again, though hope and expectation lingered about her heart until despair rested there in their place.

William was starting on horseback, after an early din ner at the tavern in C . As he put his foot in the stirrups, an old farmer, who had just driven his large co vered wagon to the door, called to him.

"You going home, Mr. William?" said he.

" Yes, I am; but why do you ask me ?"

"Why, how are you going to cross Willow's Creek?" asked the old man.

"On the bridge," said William, laughing; "did you think I was going to jump my horse across ?"

"No, but you can't cross the bridge," said the farmer, "for the bridge is broken down."

".Why, I crossed it early this morning," said William.

" So did I," said the farmer, "and, thank God, I and my team did not go down with it. But there's been a mighty freshet above, and Willow's Creek is something like my wife—she's an angel when she aint disturbed, but she's the devil himself when any thing puts her out. Now, you take my advice, and stay here to-night, or at any rate don't get yourself into danger."

"I must go home to-night," said William; "I have promised my sister to do so. I can ford the creek;" and he prepared again to start.

"Stop, young man," said the farmer, solemnly, "you mind the old saying, < Young people think old people fools, but old people know young people are fools.' I warn you not to try and ford that creek to-night; you might as well put your head in a lion's mouth. Havn't I been crossing it these fifty years? and aint I up to all its freaks and ways ? Sometimes it is as quiet as a weaned baby, but now it is foaming and lashing, as a tiger after prey. You'd better disappoint Miss Ellen for one night, than to bring a whole lifetime of trouble upon her. Don't be foolhardy, now ; your horse can't carry you safely over Willow's Creek this night."

"Never fear, farmer," said William. "I can take care of myself."

"May the Lord take care of you," said the farmer, as he followed the youth, dashing through the town on his spirited horse. «If it were not for this wagon-load, and there are so many to be clothed and fed at home, I would follow you, but I can't do it."

William rode rapidly homeward. The noonday being long passed, the skies were clouding over, and harsh spring winds were playing through the woods.

William enjoyed such rides. Healthy, and fearing nothing, he was a stranger to a feeling of loneliness. Alternately singing an old air, and then whistling with notes as clear and musical as a flute, he at last came in sight of the creek which had been so- tranquil when he crossed it in the morning. There was an old house near, where lived the people who received the toll. A man and his wife, with a large family of children, poor people's in-

heritance, had long made this place their home, and they were acquainted with all the persons who were in the habit of traveling this way.

William, whom they saw almost daily, was a great favo rite with the children. Not only did he pay his toll, but many a penny and sixpence to the small folks besides, and he was accustomed to receive a welcome.

Now the house was shut up. It had rained frequently and heavily during the month, and the bright morning, which had tempted the children out to play, was gone, and they had gathered in the old house to amuse themselves as they could.

The bridge had been partly carried away by the freshet. Some of the beams were still swinging and swaying them selves with restless motion. The creek was swollen to a torrent. The waters dashed against its sides, in their haste to go their way. The wind, too, howled mournfully, and the old trees bent to and fro, nodding their stately heads, and rustling their branches against each other.

"Oh, Mr. William, is it you?" said the woman, open ing the door. " Get off your horse, and come in and rest; you can't go home to-night."

"Yes, I can though," said William, «I have often forded the creek, and though I never saw it as it is now, yet I can get safely over it, I am sure."

"Don't talk of such things, for the Lord's sake," said Mrs. Jones. " Why, my husband could not ford the creek now, and you're a mere boy."

"No matter for that," said William. "I promised my sister to be at home to-night, and I must keep my word. See how narrow the creek is here! Good-by, I cannot wait any longer, it is getting dark."

"Don't try it, please don't, Mr. William," again said Mrs. Jones. All the children joined her, some entreating William, others crying out at the danger into which their favorite was rushing.

"Why, you cowards," cried William, "you make more noise than the creek itself. Here's something for ginger bread." None of the children offered to pick up the money which fell among them, but looked anxiously after William, to see what he was going to do.

"Mr. William," said Mrs. Jones, "come back; look at the water a roaring and tossing, and your horse is rest less already w r ith the noise. Don't throw your life away; think of your sister."

" I'm thinking of her, good Mrs. Jones. Never fear for me," said he, looking back at her with a smile, at the same time urging his horse toward the edge of the creek, where there was a gradual descent from the hill.

As Mrs. Jones had said, the horse had already become restless, he was impatiently moving his head, prancing and striking his hoofs against the hard ground. William re strained him, as he too quickly descended the path, and it may be the young man then hesitated, as he endeavored to check him, but it was too late. The very check ren dered him more impatient; springing aside from the path he dashed himself from rock to rock. William saw his danger, and with a steady hand endeavored to control the frightened animal. This unequal contest was soon de cided. The nearer the horse came to the water the more he was alarmed,—at last he sprang from the rock, and he and his rider disappeared.

"Oh, my God!" said Mrs. Jones, "he is gone. The poor boy; and there is no one to help him." She at first hid her eyes from the appalling scene, and then approached the creek and screamed as she saw the horse struggling and plunging, while William manfully tried to control him. Oh! how beat her heart, as with uplifted hands, and stayed breath, she watched for the issue—it is over now.

" Hush! hush! children," said their mother, pale as death, whose triumph she had just witnessed. "Oh! if your father had been here to have saved him—but who

could have saved him? None but thou, Almighty God!" and she kneeled to pray for, she knew not what.

"Too late, too late!" yet she knelt and alternately prayed and wept.

Again she gazed into the noisy w r aters — but there was nothing there, and then calling her frightened and weep ing children into the house, she determined to set forth alone, for assistance — for what ?

*

Oh ! how long was that night to Ellen, though she be lieved her brother remained at C - . She did not sleep till late, and sad the awakening. Voices in anxious whis pers fell upon her ear ; pale faces and weeping eyes, were everywhere around her — within, confusion ; and useless effort without. Her uncle wept as for an only son ; her aunt then felt how tenderly she had loved him, who was gone forever. The farmer, who had warned him at the tavern-door, smote his breast when he heard his sad fore bodings were realized. The young and the old, the rich and the poor, assembled for days about the banks of the creek, with the hopes of recovering the body, but the young rider and his horse were never seen again. Ah ! Ellen was an orphan now — father, mother, and friend had he been to her, the lost one. Often did she lay her head on the kind breast of their old nurse, and pray for death.

As far as was in their power, her uncle and aunt soothed her in her grief. But the only real comfort at such a time, is that from Heaven, and Ellen knew not that. How could she have reposed had she felt the protection of the Everlasting Arms !

But time, though it does not always heal, must assuage the intensity of grief; the first year passed after William's death, and Ellen felt a wish for other scenes than those where she had been accustomed to see him. She had now little to which she could look forward.

Her chief amusement was in retiring to the library, and reading old romances, with which its upper shelves were filled; this, under other circumstances, her aunt would have forbidden, but it was a relief to see Ellen interested in any thing, and she appeared not to observe her thus employing herself.

So Ellen gradually returned to the old ways; she studied a little, and assisted her industrious aunt in her numerous occupations. As of old, her aunt saw her restlessness of disposition, and Ellen felt rebellious and irritable. With what an unexpected delight, then, did she receive from her aunt's hands, the letters from Mrs. Weston, inviting her to come at once to Exeter, and then to accompany them to Washington. She, without any difficulty, obtained the necessary permission, and joyfully wrote to Mrs. Weston, how gladly she would accept the kind invitation.

CHAPTER XIX.

THERE was an ancient enmity between Jupiter and Bacchus. While the former was always quiet when Phillis came to see his mistress during her life, Bacchus never went near him without his displaying symptoms of the greatest irritation; his back was invariably raised, and his claws spread out ready for an attack on the slightest provocation. Phillis found it impossible to induce the cat to remain away from Aunt Peggy's house; he would stand on the door-step, and make the most appalling noises, fly into the windows, scratch against the panes, and if any children approached him to try and coax him away, he would fly at them, sending them off in a disabled condition. Phillis was obliged to go backward and forward putting him into the house and letting him out again. This was a good deal of trouble, and his savage mood continuing, the servants were unwilling to pass him, declaring he was a good deal worse than Aunt Peggy had ever been. Finally, a superstitious feeling got among them, that he was connected in some way with his dead mistress, and a thousand absurd stories were raised in consequence. Mr. Weston told Bacchus that he was so fierce that he might do some real mischief, so that he had better be caught and drowned. The catching was a matter of some moment, but Phillis seduced him into a bag by putting a piece of meat inside and then dexterously catching up the bag and drawing the string. It was impossible to hold him in, so Bacchus fastened the bag to the wheelbarrow, and after a good deal of difficulty, he got him down to the river under the bridge, and threw him in. He told Phillis when he got home, that he felt now for the first time as if

Aunt Peggy was really dead, and they all might hope for a little comfort. Twenty-four hours after, however, just as the moon was rising, Bacchus was taken completely by surprise, for Jupiter passed him with his back raised, and proceeded to the door of his old residence, commencing immediately a most vociferous demand to be admitted.

Bacchus was speechless for some moments, but at last made out to call Phillis, who came to the door to see what was the trouble. "Look thar," said he, "you want to make me b'lieve that aint ole Aunt Peggy's wraith— ground can't hold her, water can't hold him—why I drowned him deep—how you 'spose he got out of that bag?"

Phillis could not help laughing. "Well, I never did see the like—the cat has scratched through the bag and swam ashore."

" I b'lieves you," said Bacchus, " and if you had throw'd him into the fire, he wouldn't a got burned ; but I tell you, no cat's a gwine to get the better of me—I'll kill Jupiter, yet."

Phillis, not wanting the people aroused, got the key, and unlocked the door, Jupiter sprang in, and took up his old quarters on the hearth, where he was quiet for the night. In the morning she carried some bread and milk to him, and told Bacchus not to say any thing about his coming back to any one, and that after she came home from town, where she was going on business for Mrs. Weston, they would determine what they would do. But Bacchus secretly resolved to have the affair settled before Phillis should return, that the whole glory of having conquered an enemy should belong to him.

Phillis was going on a number of errands to L——,
and she expected to be detained all day, for she understood shopping to perfection, and she went charged with all sorts of commissions; besides, she had to stop to see one or two sick old colored ladies of her acquaintance, and she told Mrs. Weston she might as well make a day of it. Thus it was quite evening when she got home—found every thing had been well attended to, children in bed, but Bacchus among the missing, though he had promised her he would not leave the premises until her return.

Now, if there is a severe trial on this earth, it is for a wife (of any color) who rarely leaves home,—to return after a day of business and pleasure, having spent all the money she could lay her hands on, having dined with one friend and taken a dish of tea and gossiped with another—to return, hoping to see every thing as she expected, and to experience the bitter disappointment of finding her husband gone out in spite of the most solemn asseverations to the contrary. Who could expect a woman to preserve her composure under such circumstances?

Poor Phillis! she was in such spirits as she came home. How pretty the flowers look! She thought, after all, if I am a slave, the Lord is mighty good to me. I have a comfortable home, and a good set of children, and my old man has done so much better of late—Phillis felt really happy; and when she went in, and delivered all her parcels to the ladies, and was congratulated on her success in getting precisely the desired articles, her heart was as light as a feather. She thought she would go and see how all went on at home, and then come back to the kitchen and drink a cup of good tea, for the family had just got through with theirs.

What a disappointment, then, to find any thing going wrong. It was not that Bacchus's society was so entirely necessary to her, but the idea of his having started on another spree. The fear of his being brought home some time to her dead, came over her with unusual force, and she actually burst into tears. She had been so very happy a few minutes before, that she could not, with her usual calmness, make the best of every thing. She forgot all
about the pleasant day she had passed; lost her wish for a cup of tea; and passing even her pipe by, with a full heart she took her seat to rest at the door. For some time every thing seemed to go wrong with her. All at once she found out how tired she was. Her limbs ached, and her arm hurt her, where she had carried the basket. She had a great many troubles. She had to work hard. She had more children than anybody else to bother her; and when she thought of Bacchus she felt very angry. He might as well kill himself drinking, at once, for he was nothing but a care and disgrace to her—had always been so, and most likely would be so until they were both under the ground.

But this state of mind could not last long. A little quiet, rest, and thought, had a good effect. She soon began again to look at the bright side of things, and to be ashamed of her murmuring spirit. « Sure enough he has kept very sober of late, and I can't expect him to give it up entirely, all of a sudden. I must be patient, and go on praying for him." She thought with great pity of him, and her heart being thus subdued, her mind gradually turned to other things.

She looked at Aunt Peggy's house, and wondered if the old woman was better off in another world than she was in this; but she checked the forbidden speculation. And next she thought of Jupiter, and with this recollection came another remembrance of Bacchus and his antipathy both to the mistress and her cat. All at once she recalled Bacchus's determination to kill Jupiter, and the strange ferocity the animal evinced whenever Bacchus went near him; and she got up to take the key and survey the state of things at the deserted house. There was no key to be found; and concluding some one had been after Jupiter, she no longer delayed her intention of finding out what had occurred in that direction. She found the key in the door, but every thing was silent. With some caution she opened it, remembering Jupiter's last unexpected onset; when, looking round by the dim light, she perceived him seated opposite Aunt Peggy's big chest, evidently watch ing it. On hearing the door open, though, he got up and raised his back, on the defensive.

Phillis, having an indefinable feeling that Bacchus was somehow or other connected with the said elevation, looked carefully round the room, but saw nothing. Gradually the chest lid opened a little way, and a sepulchral voice, issuing from it, uttered in a low tone these words:

"Phillis, gal, is that you?"

The cat looked ready to spring, and the chest lid sud denly closed again. But while Phillis was recovering herself the lid was cautiously opened, and Bacchus's eyes glaring through the aperture. The words were repeated.

"Why, what on earth?" said the astonished woman: « Surely, is that you, Bacchus?"

"It is, surely," said Bacchus; "but put that devil of a tiger out of de room, if you don't want me to die dis minute."

Phillis's presence always had an imposing effect upon Jupiter; and as she opened the door to the other room, and called him in, he followed her without any hesitation.

She shut him in, and then hurried back to lift up the chest lid, to release her better half.

"Why, how," said she, as Bacchus, in a most cramped condition endeavored to raise himself, " did the lid fall on you?"

"No," groaned Bacchus. "Are you sure de middle door's shut. Let me git out o' dis place quick as possible, for since ole Peggy left, de ole boy hisself has taken up his 'bode here. 'Pears as if I never should git straight agin."

" Why, look at your face, Bacchus," said his wife. "Did Jupiter scratch you up that way."

" Didn't he though ? Wait till I gits out of reach of his claws, and I'll tell you about it;" and they both went out, Phillis locking the door to keep Jupiter quiet, that night at least. After having washed the blood off his face and hands, and surveyed himself with a dismal countenance in the looking-glass, Bacchus proceeded to give an account of his adventure.

After dinner he thought he would secure Jupiter, and have him effectually done for before Phillis came back. He mustered up all his courage, and unlocking the house, de termined to catch and tie him, then decide on a mode of death that would be effectual. He had heard some officers from Mexico describe the use of the lasso, and it occurred to him to entrap Jupiter in this scientific manner. But Jupiter was an old bird; he was not to be caught with chaff. Bacchus's lasso failed altogether, and very soon the cat became so enraged that Bacchus was obliged to take a three-legged stool, and act on the defensive. He held the stool before his face, and when Jupiter made a spring at him, he dodged against him with it. Two or three blows excited Jupiter's anger to frenzy, and after several ef forts he succeeded in clawing Bacchus's face in the most dreadful manner, so that it was with the greatest difficulty he could clear himself. Desperate with pain and fright, he looked for some way of escape. The door was shut, and Jupiter, who seemed to be preparing for another attack, was between him and it. He had but one resource, and that was to spring into Aunt Peggy's great chest, and close the lid to protect himself from another assault.

Occasionally, when nearly suffocated, he would raise the lid to breathe, but Jupiter immediately flew at him in such a furious manner, that he saw it would be at the risk of his life to attempt to escape, and he was obliged to bide his time. What his meditations were upon while in the chest, would be hard to decide; but when once more protected by the shadow of his own roof, he vowed Jupiter should die, and be cut in pieces before he was done with him.

Phillis went to Miss Janet, and gave her an account of the whole affair, with Bacchus's permission, and the kind old lady came to him with some healing ointment of her own manufacture, and anointed his wounds.

William was sent for; and the result of the discussion was, that he and his father should, early next morning, shoot the much dreaded cat effectually.

This resolution was carried into effect in the following manner. Phillis went a little in advance with a large bowl of bread and milk, and enticed Jupiter to the hearth. As he was very hungry, he did not perceive William entering with a very long gun in his hand, nor even Bacchus, his ancient enemy, with a piece of sticking-plaster down his nose and across his forehead.

William was quite a sportsman. He went through all the necessary formalities. Bacchus gave the word of command in a low voice: Make ready, take aim, fire—bang, and William discharged a shower of shot into Jupiter's back and sides. He gave one spring, and all was over, Bacchus looking on with intense delight.

As in the case of Aunt Peggy, now that his enemy was no more, Bacchus became very magnanimous. He said Jupiter had been a faithful old animal, though mighty queer sometimes, and he believed the death of Aunt Peggy had set him crazy, therefore he forgave him for the condition in which he had put his face, and should lay him by his mistress at the burial-ground. Lydia begged an old candle-box of Miss Janet, for a coffin, and assisted her father in the other funeral arrangements. With a secret satisfaction and a solemn air, Bacchus carried off the box, followed by a number of black children, that Lydia had invited to the funeral. They watched Bacchus with great attention while he completed his work, and the whole party returned under the impression that Aunt Peggy and Jupiter were perfectly satisfied with the morning's transactions.

CHAPTER XX.

THE time had come to leave home, and the "Westerns had but one more evening. Neither Mr. Weston nor Alice were well, and all hoped the change would benefit them. They were to travel in their own carriage, and the preparations were completed. The three ladies' maids were to go by the stage. Miss Janet had a number of things stowed away in the carriage, which she thought might be useful, not forgetting materials for a lunch, and a little of her own home-made lavender, in case of a headache. The pleasure of going was very much lessened by the necessity of leaving the dear old lady, who would not listen to their entreaties to accompany them. "You, with your smooth cheeks and bright eyes, may well think of passing a winter in Washington; but what should I do there ? Why, the people would say I had lost my senses. No, we three ladies will have a nice quiet time at Exeter, and I can go on with my quilting and patchwork. You see, Miss Alice, that you come back with red cheeks. The birds and the flowers will be glad to see you again when the spring comes."

"Ring the bell, Alice," said Mr. Weston. "I must know how Mr. Mason's little boy is. I sent Mark shortly after dinner; but here he is. Well, Mark, I hope the little fellow is getting well?"

"He is receased, sir," said Mark, solemnly.

"He is what?" said Mr. Weston. "Oh! ah! he is dead—I understand you. Well, I am truly sorry for it. When did he die?"

"Early this morning, sir," said Mark. "Have you any more orders to give, sir ? for as I am to be up mighty early in the morning, I was thinking of going to bed when you are done with me."

"Nothing more," said Mr. Weston; and Mark retired.

"Mark," continued Mr. Weston, "has the greatest propensity for using hard words. His receased means deceased. He was excessively angry with Bacchus the other day for interfering with him about the horses. 'Nobody,' said he, ' can stand that old fellow's airs. He's got so full of tomposity, that he makes himself disagreeable to every body.' By Tomposity, I suppose you all know he meant pomposity. Bacchus is elated at the idea of going with us. I hope I shall not have any trouble with him."

"Oh! no, uncle," said Alice; "he is a good old fellow, and looks so aristocratic with his gray hair and elegant bows. Ellen and I will have to take him as a beau when you are out. Aunt

Phillis says, that he has promised her not to drink a drop of any thing but water, and she seems to think that he has been so sober lately that he will keep his word."

"It is very doubtful," said Mr. Weston; "but the fact is he would be troublesome with his airs and his tomposity were I to leave him; so I have no choice."

"Dear Alice," said Ellen, fixing her large dark eyes on her; "how can I ever be grateful enough to you?"

"For what?" asked Alice.

« For getting sick, and requiring change of air, which is the first cause of my being here on my way to the great metropolis. Whoever likes a plantation life is welcome to it; but I am heartily sick of it. Indeed, Miss Janet, good as you are, you could not stand it at uncle's. Ten miles from a neighbor—-just consider it! Uncle disapproves of campmeetings and barbecues; and aunt is sewing from morning till night; while I am required to read the Spectator aloud. I have a mortal grudge against Addis on."

"But, my clear," said Miss Janet, "you must remember you are to return to your uncle's, and you must not learn to love the great world too much."

"Perhaps," said Mr. Barbour, who was much depressed at the approaching parting, "Miss Ellen may not mean to return to her uncle's. A young lady with good looks, and a heavy purse, will be found out in Washington. She will just suit a great many there—clerks with small salaries, army and navy men with expensive habits; and foreign attache's, who, being nothing in their own country, turn our young ladies' heads when they come here."

" So you think I am destined for no other fate than to pay a fortune-hunter's debts. Thank you, Mr. Barbour !"

" The fact is, Mr. Barbour wants you himself, Ellen, and he is afraid somebody will carry you off. He will pay us a visit this winter, I expect," said Mrs. Weston.

"Well," said Ellen laughingly, "I'd rather take up with him than to go back to my old life, now that I see you are all so happy here."

"But your aunt and uncle," said Miss Janet, "you must not feel unkindly toward them."

"No, indeed," said Ellen, "they are both good and kind in their way, but uncle is reserved, and often low-spirited. Aunt is always talking of the necessity of self-control, and the discipline of life. She is an accomplished teaze. Why, do you know," continued Ellen, laughingly, as she removed Miss Janet's hand from her mouth, the old lady thus playfully endeavoring to check her, "after I had accepted Mrs. Weston's kind invitation, and mammy and I were busy packing, aunt said I must not be too sanguine, disappointments were good for young people, and that something might occur which would prevent my going. I believe I should have died outright, if it had turned out so."

"And so," said Mr. Barbour, "to get rid of a dull home, you are determined to fly in the face of fate, and are going to Washington after a husband. Ah! Miss Ellen, beware of these young men that have nothing but their whiskers and their epaulettes. Let me tell you of a young friend of mine, who would marry the man of her choice, in spite of the interference of her friends, and one April morning in the honey moon they were seen break fasting under a persimmon tree. However, as you are a young lady of fortune, you will always be sure of coffee and hot rolls; your good father has made such a sensi ble will, that the principal never can be touched. How many fine fortunes would have been saved, if Southerners had taken such precautions long ago. You will have a fine time young ladies, you must keep an account of your conquests, and tell me of them when you come back."

" Its only Ellen who is going in search of love ad ventures, Mr. Barbour," said Alice.

"Make yourself easy, Mr. Barbour," said Ellen. "I mean to have a delightful time flirting, then come back to marry you, and settle down. Mammy says I can't help getting good, if I live near Miss Janet."

"Well, I will wait for you," said Mr. Barbour. "And now Alice, sing me a sweet old Scotch song. Sing, <'Twas within half a mile of Edinburgh town."

"I can't come quite so near it as that," said Alice, "but I will sing <' Twas within a mile.' ' She sang that, and then " Down the burn Davie." Then Miss Janet proposed «Auld lang syne,' in which they all joined; in singing the chorus, Mr. Barbour, as usual, got very much excited, and Alice a little tired, so that the music ceased and Alice took her seat by her uncle on the sofa.

" Miss Janet," said Mr. Barbour, " you look better than I have seen you for a long time."

« Thank you," said Miss Janet. " Mr. Washington asked me the other day if I were ever going to die. I suppose, like Charles II., I ought to apologize for being so long in dying ; but I am so comfortable and happy with my friends, that I do not think enough of the journey I soon must take to another world. How many comforts I have, and how

many kind friends ! I feel now that we are about to be separated, that I should thank you all for your goodness to me, lest in the Providence of God we should not meet again. Silver and gold have I none, but such as I have, my poor thanks are most gratefully offered."

" Oh! Cousin Janet," said Alice, with her eyes full of tears, " why will you not go with us; your talking so makes me dread to part with you."

" My darling, we must all try to get to Heaven, where there are no partings. I cannot be a great while with you; remember, I am eighty-five years old. But I will not grieve you. We will, I trust, all meet here in the spring. God is here, and He is in the great city; we are all safe beneath His care. Next summer He will bring Arthur home again."

"Partings should be as short as possible," said Mr. Barbour. " So I mean to shake hands with everybody, and be off. Young ladies, be generous ; do not carry havoc and desolation in your train; take care of your uncle, and come back again as soon as possible."

He then took a friendly leave of Mr. and Mrs. Weston, and mounted his horse to return home.

"What a nice old beau Mr. Barhour would make," said Ellen, « with his fine teeth and clear complexion. I wonder he never married."

"Upon my word !" said Miss Janet, "you will be won dering next, why I never married. But know, Miss Ellen, that Mr. Barbour once had a romantic love-affair—he was to have been married to a lovely girl, but death envied him his bride, and took her off—and he has remained true to her memory. It was a long time before he recovered his cheerfulness. For two years he was the inmate of an asylum."

"Poor old gentleman," said Ellen. "I do believe other people besides me have trouble^'

"Ah! when you look around you, even in the world, which you anticipate with so much pleasure, you will see

many a smiling face that tries to hide a sad and aching heart; a heart that has ached more painfully than yours."

"No," said Ellen, looking up from the ottoman at Miss Janet's feet, where she was seated; and then bursting into tears. " Oh! thoughtless and frivolous as I am, I shall never forget Mm. If you knew how I have wept and suf fered, you would not wonder I longed for any change that would make me forget."

"Dear child," said Miss Janet, laying her hand on that young head, "I did not mean to reprove you. When God brings sorrow on the young, they must bear it with resignation to his will. He delights in the happiness of his creatures, and it is not against his will that the young should enjoy the innocent pleasures of life. Then go you and Alice into the world, but be not of the world, and come back to your homes strengthened to love them more. Cousin Weston has the Bible opened, waiting for us."

* ***** *

In the mean time, Bacchus has received a good deal of wholesome advice from Phillis, while she was packing his trunk, and in return, he has made her many promises. He expresses the greatest sorrow at leaving her, declaring that nothing but the necessity of looking after his master induces him to do so, but he is secretly anticipating a successful and eventful campaign in Washington. All the servants are distressed at the prospect of the family being away for so long a time; even old Wolf, the house-dog, has repeatedly rubbed his cold nose against Alice's hand, and looked with the most doleful expression into her beautiful face; but dogs, like their masters, must submit to what is decreed, and Wolf, after prayers, went off peaceably with William to be tied up, lest he should attempt, as usual, to follow the carriage in the morning.

CHAPTER XXI.

You are very much mistaken in your estimate of the character of a Virginian, if you suppose he allows himself, or his horses, to be driven post-haste, when there is no urgent necessity for it. It is altogether different with a Yankee; there is no enjoyment for him from the time he starts on a journey until he reaches the end of it. He is bound to be in a hurry, for how knows he but there may be a bargain depending, and he may reach his destination in time to whittle successfully for it.

The Westons actually lingered by the way. There were last looks to be taken of home, and its neighborhood; there were partings to be given to many objects in nature, dear from association, as ancient friends. Now, the long line of blue hills stands in bold relief against the hazy sky—now, the hills fade away and are hid by thick masses of oak and evergreen. Here, the Potomac spreads her breast, a mirror to the heavens, toward its low banks, the broken clouds bending tranquilly to its surface. There, the river turns, and its high and broken shores are covered with rich and twining shrubbery, its branches bending from the high rocks into the water, while the misty hue of Indian summer deepens every tint.

Fair Alice raises her languid head, already invigorated by the delightful air and prospect. The slightest glow perceptible is making its way to her pale cheek, while the gay and talkative Ellen gazes awhile at the scenery around her, then leans back in the carriage, closes her brilliant eyes, and yields, oh! rare occurrence, to meditation.

Two days are passed in the journey, and our party, arrived safely at Willard's, found their comfortable apartments prepared for them, and their servants as glad of their arrival as if they had been separated a year, instead of a day.

And now, dear reader, I do not intend discussing Washington society. It must be a more skilful pen than mine that can throw a sun of light upon this chaos of fashionable life, and bring forth order and arrangement. We are only here for relaxation and change of air, and when our invalids feel their good effects, we must return with them to their quiet, but not unuseful life.

There were many preparations to be made, for our young ladies proposed to enter into the gayeties of the season. Ellen was to throw off her mourning, and her old nurse begged her and Alice "to buy a plenty of nice new clothes, for they might as well be out of the world as out of the fashion." They both agreed with her, for they were determined to be neither unnoticed nor unknown among the fair ones of the Union who were congregated at the capital.

Do not be astonished; there is already a tinge of red beneath the brown lashes on Alice's cheek. And as for her heart, oh! that was a great deal better, too; for it has been found by actual experiment, that diseases of the heart, if treated with care, are not fatal any more than any other complaints. Mrs. Weston grew happier every day; and as to Alice's uncle, he hardly ever took his eyes off her, declaring that there must be something marvellously strengthening in the atmosphere of our much abused city; while Alice, hearing that Walter Lee was mixing in all the gayeties of Richmond, already began to question her attachment to him, and thinking of Arthur's long-continued and devoted affection, trembled lest she should have cast away the love of his generous heart.

Mr. Weston often felt the time hang heavily upon him, though he saw many valued friends. He would not have exchanged the life of a country gentleman for all the honors that politics could offer to her favorite votary; and

for the ordinary amusements which charmed Alice and Ellen, even in advance, the time had come for him to say, "I have no pleasure in them." But thinking of Alice's health only, and, above all, anxious that her marriage with his son should be consummated during his lifetime, no sacrifice appeared to him too great to make.

The weather was still delightful, and as the soire'es, assemblies, and matine'es had not yet commenced, a party was formed to go to Mount Yernon. The day fixed upon was a brilliant one, in the latter part of November. A number of very agreeable persons boarding in the hotel were to accompany them. Bacchus was exceedingly well pleased at the prospect. "'Deed, Miss Alice," he said, "I is anxious to see de old gentleman's grave; he was a fine rider; the only man as ever I seed could beat master in de saddle." Mark objected to his carriage and horses being used over such rough roads, so a large omnibus was engaged to carry the whole party, Mark and Bacchus going as outriders, and a man in a little sort of a carry-all having charge of all the eatables, dishes, plates, &c., which would be required. The company were in good spirits, but they found traveling in the State of Virginia was not moving over beds of roses. Where are such roads to be found ? Except in crossing a corduroy road in the West, where can one hope to be so thoroughly shaken up ? I answer, no where! And have I not a right to insist, for my native State, upon all that truth will permit ? Am I not a daughter of the Old Dominion, a member of one of the F. F. V's ? Did not my grandfather ride races with General Washington? Did not my father wear crape on his hat at his funeral ? Let that man or woman inclined to deny me this privilege, go, as I have, in a four-horse omnibus to Mount Vernon. Let him rock and twist over gullies and mud-holes ; let him be tumbled and jostled about as I was, and I grant you he will give up the point.

Our party jogged along. At last the old gates were

in sight, and the ragged little negroes stood ready to open them. Here we should begin to be patriotic, but do not fear being troubled with a dissertation on this worn-out subject. I will not even observe that by the very gate that was opened for the Westons did the Father of his country enter; for it would be a reflection on the memory of that great and good man to suppose that he would have put his horse to the useless trouble of jumping the fence, when there was such a natural and easy way of accomplishing his entrance. Ellen, however, declared "that she firmly believed those remarkable-looking children that opened the gates, were the same that opened them for Washington; at any rate, their clothes were cut after the same pattern, if they were not the identical suits themselves." .. % '.

There was a gentleman from the North on the premises when they arrived. He joined the party, introduced himself, and gave information that he was taking, in plaster, the house, the tomb, and other objects of interest about the place, for the purpose of exhibiting them. He made himself both useful and agreeable, as he knew it was the best way of getting along without trouble, and he was very talkative and goodnatured. But some, as they approached the grave, observed that Mr. Weston, and one or two others, seemed to wish a certain quietness of deportment to evince respect for the hallowed spot, and the jest and noisy laugh were suddenly subdued. Had it been a magnificent building, whose proportions they were to admire and discuss; had a gate of fair marble stood open to admit the visitor; had even the flag of his country waved where he slept, they could not have felt so solemnized—but to stand before this simple building, that shelters his sarcophagus from the elements; to lean upon unadorned iron gates, which guarded the sacred spot from intrusion; to look up and count the little birds' nests in the plastered roof, and the numberless hornets that have made their homes there

too; to pluck the tendrils of the wild grapes that cluster here—this simple grandeur affected each one. He was again in life before them, steadily pursuing the great work for which he was sent, and now, reposing from his labor.

And then they passed on to the old, empty grave. It was decaying away, yawning with its open mouth as if asking for its honored tenement. Ellen gazed down, and sprang in, and ere the others could recover from their astonishment, or come forward to offer her assistance, she looked up in her beauty from the dark spot where she was standing.

" Let me get out alone," said she; "Ihave such a prize;" and she held in her hand a bird's nest, with its three little white eggs deposited therein.

" Oh ! Ellen," said Mrs. Weston, robbing a bird's nest. Put it back, my dear."

"No, indeed, Mrs. "Weston, do not ask me. Think of my finding it in Washington's grave. I mean to have it put on an alabaster stand, and a glass case over it, and consider it the most sacred gem I possess. There, Uncle Bacchus, keep it for me, and don't crush the eggs."

"I won't break 'em, Miss Ellen," said Bacchus, whose thoughts were apt to run on " sperrits." " I thought for certain you had see'd de old gentleman's ghost, and he had called you down in dat dark hole. But thar aint no danger of his comin back agin, I reckon. 'Pears as if it hadn't been long since I followed him to dis very grave."

"What!" said the Northern gentleman, "were niggers allowed to attend Washington's funeral?"

" Colored people was, sir," said Bacchus, in a dignified manner. "We aint much used to being called niggers, sir. We calls ourselves so sometimes, but gentlemen and ladies, sir, mostly calls us colored people, or servants. General Washington hisself, sir, always treated his servants with politeness. I was very well acquainted with them, and know'd all about the general's ways from them."

Mr. Weston could not but smile at the reproof Bacchus had given. He turned and apologized to the gentleman for his servant's talkativeness, saying he was an old and much indulged servant.

They turned away from that empty grave. The young girls round whom so many affections clustered; the fond and anxious mother; the aged and affectionate relative; the faithful and valued servant—turned away from that empty grave. When will stay the tumultuous beatings of their hearts ? When will they sleep in the shadow of the old church ? Each heart asked itself, When ?

Ere they left this hallowed spot, Mr. Weston addressed a gentleman who lingered with him. This gentleman was an Abolitionist, but he acknowledged to Mr. Weston that he had found a different state of things at the South from what he expected.

« Sir," said he to Mr. Weston, "there is a melancholy fascination in this hollow, deserted grave. It seems to be typical of the condition in which our country would be, should the spirit that animated Washington no longer be among us."

Mr. Weston smiled as he answered, " Perhaps it is good for you to be here, to stand by the grave of a slaveholder, and ask yourself « Would I dare here utter the calumnies that are constantly repeated by the fanatics of my party ?' On this spot, sir, the Abolitionist should commune with his own heart, and be still. Well was it said by one of your own statesmen, < My doctrines on the slavery ques tion are those of my ancestors, modified by themselves, as they were in an act of Confederation. In this one re spect they left society in the political condition in which they found it. A reform would have been fearful and calamitous. A political revolution with one class was morally impracticable. Consulting a wise humanity, they submitted to a condition in which Providence had placed them. They settled the question in the deep foundations

18

of the Constitution.' Would you then, sir, destroy the fabric, by undermining the Constitution ? Alas ! this would be the consequence, were it possible to carry out the views of the Abolition party."

* * * # # *

The beautiful words of Harrison G. Otis, delivered in Faneuil'Hall, Boston, Aug. 22d, 1835, would have been appropriate here, too. Speaking of the formation of Anti-slavery Societies, he said, " Suppose an article had been proposed to the Congress that framed the instrument of Confederation, proposing that the Northern States should be at liberty to form Anti-slavery Associations, and deluge the South with homilies upon slavery, how would it have been received ? The gentleman before me apostrophized the image of Washington. I will follow his example, and point to the portrait of his associate, Hancock, which is pendant by its side. Let us imagine an interview between them, in the company of friends, just after one had signed the commission for the other; and in ruminating on the lights and shadows of futurity, Hancock should have said, < I congratulate my country upon the choice she has made, and I foresee that the laurels you gained in the field of Braddock's defeat, will be twined with those which shall be earned by you in the war of Independence; yet such are the prejudices in my part of the Union against slavery, that although your name and services may screen you from opprobrium, during your life, your countrymen, when millions weep over your tomb, will bc branded by mine as man-stealers and murderers; and the stain of it conse quently annexed to your memory."

But, alas! the Abolitionist will not reflect. He lives in a whirlpool, whither he has been drawn by his own rashness. What to him is the love of country, or the memory of Washington ? John Randolph said, " I should have been a French Atheist had not my mother made me kneel beside her as she folded my little hands, and taught

me to say, < Our Father.' ' Remember this, mothers in America; and imprint upon the fair tablet of your young child's heart, a reverence for the early institutions of their country, and for the patriots who moulded them, that " God and my country" may be the motto of their lives.

CHAPTER XXII.

"ALICE," said Mrs. Weston, as they sat together one morning, before it was time to dress for dinner, "if you choose, I will read to you the last part of Cousin Janet's letter. You know, my daughter, of Walter's gay course in Richmond, and it is as I always feared. There is a tendency to recklessness and dissipation in Walter's dis position. With what a spirit of deep thankfulness you should review the last few months of your life ! I have sometimes feared I was unjust to Walter. My regret at the attachment for him which you felt at one time, became a personal dislike, which I acknowledge, I was wrong to yield to; but I think we both acted naturally, circum stanced as we were. Dear as you are to me, I would rather see you dead than the victim of an unhappy mar riage. Love is not blind, as many say. I believe the stronger one's love is, the more palpable the errors of its object. It was so with me, and it would be so with you. That you have conquered this attachment is the crowning blessing of my life, even should you choose never to con summate your engagement with Arthur. I will, at least, thank God that you are not the wife of a man whose vio lent passions, even as a child, could not be controlled, and who is destitute of a spark of religious principle. I will now read you what Cousin Janet says.

" 'I have received a long letter from Mr. C., the Episco pal clergyman in Richmond, in answer to mine, inquiring of Walter. All that I feared is true. Walter is not only gay, but dissipated. Mr. C. says he has called to see him repeatedly, and invited him to his house, and has done all that he could to interest him in those pleasures that are in nocent and ennobling; but, alas! it is difficult to lay aside the wine cup, when its intoxicating touch is familiar to the lips, and so of the other forbidden pleasures of life. To one of Walter's temperament there is two-fold danger. Walter is gambling, too, and bets high; he will, of course, be a prey to the more experienced ones, who will take ad vantage of his youth and generosity to rob him. For, is a professed gambler better than a common thief?

" 'It is needless for me to say, I have shed many tears over this letter. Tears are for the living, and I expect to shed them while I wear this garment of mortality. Can it be that in this case the wise- Creator will visit the sins of the father upon the child ? Are are all my tears and prayers to fail ? I cannot think so, while He reigns in heaven in the same body with which He suffered on earth. In the very hand that holds the sceptre is the print of the nails; under the royal crown that encircles His brow, can still be traced the marks of the thorns. He is surely, then, touched with a feeling of our infirmities, and He will in the end, bring home this child of my love and my adoption. I often say to myself, could I see Alice and Arthur and Walter happy, how happy should I be! I would be more than willing to depart; but there would be still a care for something in this worn-out and withered frame. It will be far better to be with Jesus, but He will keep me here as long as He has any thing for me to do. The dear girls! I am glad they are enjoying themselves, but I long to see them again. I hope they will not be carried away by the gay life they are leading. I shall be glad when they are at their home duties again.

" 'It will be well with Arthur and Alice; you know old maids are always the best informed on other people's love affairs. When Arthur left home Alice felt only a sisterly affection for him; when Walter went away it was really no more for him either, but her kind heart grieved when she saw him so situated: and sympathy, you know, is akin to lave. She must remember now the importance that at taches itself to an engagement of marriage, and not give Arthur any more rivals. She was off her guard before, as her feeling an affection for Arthur "was considered rather too much a matter of course; but she cannot fail at some future day to return his devoted affection. In the mean time, the young people are both, I trust, doing well. Ar thur, so long in another section of his own dear country, will be less apt to be unduly prejudiced in favor of his own; and Alice will only mingle in the gay world enough to see the vanity of its enjoyments. She will thus be pre pared to perform with fidelity the duties that belong to her position as the wife of a country gentleman. No wonder that my spectacles are dim and my old eyes aching after this long letter. Love to dear Cousin Weston, to the girls, to yourself, and all the servants.

"'From COUSIN JANET.'

"<Phillis says she has not enough to do to keep her employed. She has not been well this winter; her old cough has returned, and she is thinner than I ever saw her. Dr. L. has been to see her several times, and he is anxious for her to take care of herself. She bids me say to Bacchus that if he have broken his promise, she hopes he will be endowed with strength from above to keep it better in future. How much can we all learn from good Phillis!"

Alice made no observation as her mother folded the letter and laid it on her dressing table; but there lay not now on the altar of her heart a spark of affection for one, who for a time, she believed to be so passionately beloved. The fire of that love had indeed gone out, but there had lingered among its embers the form and color of its coals—these might have been rekindled, but that was past forever. The rude but kind candor that conveyed to her the knowledge of Walter's unworthiness had dissolved its very shape; the image was displaced from its shrine. Walter was indeed still beloved, but it was the aifection of a pure sister for an erring brother; it was only to one to whom her soul in its confiding trust and virtue could look up, that she might accord that trusting devotion and reverence a woman feels for the chosen companion of her life.

And this, I hear you say, my reader, is the awakening of a love dream so powerful as to undermine the health of the sleeper—so dark as to cast a terror and a gloom upon many who loved her; it is even so in life, and would you have it otherwise? Do you commend that morbid affection which clings to its object not only through sorrow, but sin? through sorrow—but not in sin. Nor is it possible for a pure-minded woman to love unworthily and continue pure.

This Alice felt, and she came forth from her struggle stronger and more holy; prizing above all earthly things the friends who had thus cleared for her her pathway, and turning with a sister's love, which was all indeed she had ever known, to that one who, far away, would yet win with his unchanging affection her heart to his own.

Walter Lee's case was an illustration of the fact that many young men are led into dissipation simply from the want of proper occupation. There was in him no love of vice for itself; but disappointed in securing Alice's consent to his addresses, and feeling self-condemned in the effort to win her affections from Arthur, he sought forgetfulness in dissipation and excitement. He fancied he would find happiness in the ball-room, the theatre, the midnight revel, and at the gambling table. Have you not met in the changing society of a large city, one whose refined and gentle manners told of the society of a mother, a sister, or of some female friend whose memory, like an angel's wing, was still hovering around him? Have you not pitied him when you reflected that he was alone, far away from such good influences? Have you not longed to say to him, I wish I could be to you what she has been, and warn you of the rocks and quicksands against which you may be shipwrecked.

There were many who felt thus towards "Walter; his strikingly handsome face and figure, his grace and intelligence, with a slight reserve that gave a charm to his manner. To few was his history familar; the world knew of his name, and to the world he was an object of importance, for gold stamps its owner with a letter of credit through life.

Walter launched into every extravagance that presented itself. He was flattered, and invited to balls and parties; smiles met him at every step, and the allurements of the world dazzled him, as they had many a previous victim. Sometimes, the thought of Alice in .her purity and truth passed like a sunbeam over his heart; but its light was soon gone. She was not for him; and why should he not seek, as others had done, to drown all care? Then the thought of Cousin

Janet, good and holy Cousin Janet, with her Bible in her hand, and its sacred precepts on her lips, would weigh like a mountain on his soul; but he had staked all for pleasure, and he could riot lose the race.

It is not pleasant to go down, step after step, to the dark dungeon of vice. We will not follow Walter to the revel, nor the gaming-table. We will close our ears to the blasphemous oaths of his companions, to the imprecations on his own lips. The career of folly and of sin was destined to be closed; and rather would we draw a veil over its every scene. Step by step, he trod the path of sin, until at last, urged by worldly and false friends to a quarrel, commenced on the slightest grounds, he challenged one who had really never offended him; the challenge was accepted, and then Walter Lee was a murderer!

He gazed upon the youthful, noble countenance; he felt again and again the quiet pulse, weeping when he saw the useless efforts to bring back life.

He was a murderer, in the sight of God and man! for he had been taught that He who gave life, alone had the power to take it away. He knew that God would require of him his brother's blood. He knew, too, that though the false code of honor in society would acquit him, yet he would be branded, even as Cain. He could see the finger of scorn pointed towards him; he could hear men, good men, say, "There is Walter Lee, who killed a man in a duel!"

Ah! Cousin Janet, not in vain were your earnest teachings. Not in vain had you sung by his pillow, in boyhood, of Jesus, who loved all, even his enemies. Not in vain had you planted the good seed in the ground, and watered it. Not in vain are you now kneeling by your bedside, imploring God not to forsake forever the child of your prayers. Go to your rest in peace, for God will yet bring him home, after all his wanderings; for Walter Lee, far away, is waking and restless; oppressed with horror at his crime, flying from law and justice, flying from the terrors of a burdened conscience—he is a murderer!

Like Cain, he is a wanderer. He gazes into the depths of the dark sea he is crossing; but there is no answering abyss in his heart, where he can lose the memory of his deed. He cannot count the wretched nights of watching, and of thought. Time brings no relief, change no solace. When the soul in its flight to eternity turns away from God, how droop her wings! She has no star to guide her upward course; but she wanders through a strange land, where all is darkness and grief.

He traversed many a beautiful country; he witnessed scenes of grandeur; he stood before the works of genius and of art; he listened to music, sweet like angels' songs; but has he peace? Young reader, there is no peace without God. Now in this world, there is many a brow bending beneath the weight of its flowers. Could we trace the stories written on many hearts, how would they tell of sorrow! How many would say, in the crowded and noisy revel, "I have come here to forget; but memory will never die!"

CHAPTER XXIII.

ALICE and Ellen, accompanied by Mrs. Weston, and some gentlemen from their section of the country, were to attend a private ball, expected to be one of the most brilliant of the season. Mr. Weston, not feeling well, retired early, preferring to listen to the young ladies' account of the evening, after his breakfast and newspaper the next morning. When they were ready to go, they came into Mr. Weston's parlor to obtain his commendation on their taste. Mrs. Weston was there awaiting them; and her own appearance was too striking to be passed over without notice. She was still really a handsome woman, and her beauty was greatly enhanced by her excellent taste in dress. Her arms, still round and white, were not uncovered. The rich lace sleeves, and the scarf of the same material that was thrown over her handsome neck and shoulders, was far more becoming than if she had assumed the bare arms and neck which was appropriate to her daughter. Her thick dark hair was simply put back from her temples, as she always wore it, contrasting beautifully with the delicate white flowers there. Her brocade silk, fitting closely to her still graceful figure, and the magnificent diamond pin that she wore in her bosom; the perfect fitness of every part of her apparel gave a dignity arid beauty to her appearance, that might have induced many a gay lady who mixes, winter after winter, in the amuse-

ments of our city, to go and do likewise. When youth is gone forever, it is better to glide gracefully into middle age; and if half the time and thought that is expended on the choice of gay colors and costly material, were passed in properly arranging what is suitable to age and appearance, the fashionable assemblies of the present day would not afford such spectacles, as cannot fail both to pain and amuse.

Mr. Weston turned to the door as it opened, expecting the girls to enter; and a little impatient, too, as it was already half-past ten o'clock. The gentlemen had been punctual to their appointed hour of ten, but declared that three quarters of an hour was an unusually short time to be kept waiting by ladies. Ellen came first, her tall but well-proportioned figure arrayed in a rose-colored silk of the most costly material. She wore a necklace and bracelet of pearl, and a string of the same encircled her beautifully-arranged hair. The rich color that mantled in her cheeks deepened still more, as she acknowledged the salutation of the gentlemen; but Alice, who entered immediately after her, went at once to her uncle, and putting her hand in his, looked the inquiry, "Are you pleased with me?" No wonder the old man held her hand for a moment, deprived of the power of answering her. She stood before him glowing with health again, the coral lips parted with a smile, awaiting some word of approval. The deep-blue eyes, the ivory skin, the delicately-flushed cheeks, the oval face, the auburn curls that fell over brow and temple, and hung over the rounded and beautiful shoulders; the perfect arm, displayed in its full beauty by the short plain sleeve; the simple dress of white; the whole figure, so fair and interesting, with no ornaments to dim its youthful charms; but one flower, a lily, drooping over her bosom. The tears gathered in his large eyes, and drawing her gently towards him, he kissed her lips. " Alice, my beloved," he said, "sweetest of God's earthly gifts,

you cannot be always as fair and young as you are now; but may God keep your heart as pure and childlike, until he take you to the Heaven which is your destiny." Before any one could reply, he had bowed to the rest of the company and left the room; and even Alice, accustomed as she was to his partial affection, felt solemnized at the unusual earnestness with which he had addressed her; but Mrs. Weston hurried them off to the scene of fashion and splendor which they had been anticipating.

* * * *

Mr. Weston was about to retire, when Bacchus suddenly entered the room, preceded by a slight knock. He was very much excited, and evidently had information of great importance to communicate.

"Master," said he, without waiting to get breath, "they're all got took."

"What is the matter, Bacchus?"

"Nothing, sir, only they're all cotched, every mother's son of 'em."

" Of whom are you speaking ?"

" Of them poor misguided niggers, sir, de Aboli-tioners got away; but they're all cotched now, and I'm sorry 'nuff for 'em. Some's gwine to be sold, and some's gwine to be put in jail; and they're all in the worst kind of trouble."

" Well, Bacchus, it serves them right; they knew they were not free, and that it was their duty to work in the condition in which God had placed them. They have no body to blame but themselves."

" 'Deed they is—'scuse me for contradictin you—but there's them as is to blame a heap. Them Abolitioners, sir, is the cause of it. They wouldn't let the poor devils rest until they 'duced them to go off. They 'lowed, they would get 'em off, and no danger of their being took agin. They had the imperance, sir, to 'suade those poor deluded niggers that they were born free, when they knowed they

were born slaves. I hadn't no idea, sir, they was sich liars ; but I've been up to de place whar the servants is, and its heart-breaking to hear 'em talk. Thar's Simon, that strapping big young man, as drives Mrs. Seymour's carriage; they got him off. He's a crying up thar, like a baby a month old. He's been a hidin and a dodgin for a week—he's nigh starved. And now he's cotched, and gwine to be sold. He's a raal spilt nigger: his master dressed him like a gentleman, and he had nothin to do all day but to drive de carriage; and he told me hisself, when he was out late at night wid de young ladies, at par ties, he never was woke in de mornin, but was 'lowed to sleep it out, and had a good hot breakfast when he did wake. Well, they got him off. They made out he'd go to the great Norrurd, and set up a trade, or be a gentleman, may be; and like as not they told him he stood a good chance of being President one of dese days. They got him off from his good home, and now he's done for. He's gwine to be sold South to-morrow. He's a beggin young Mr. Seymour up thar not to sell him, and makin promises, but its no use ; he's goin South. I bin hearin every word he said to his young master. «Oh, Master George,' says he, < let me off dis time. I didn't want to go till the Aboli-tioners told me you had no right to me, kase God had made me free ; and you, they said, was no better than a thief, keepin me a slave agin natur and the Bible too."

" 'But, Simon,' said young Mr. Seymour, <you stole a suit of my new clothes when you went off; and you got money, too, from Mrs. Barrett, saying I had sent you for it. How came you to do that?'

"' I will 'fess it all, sir,' said Simon, «and God knows I'm speakin truth. I took de suit of clothes. The Abolitioner, he said I'd be a gentleman when I got North, and I must have somethin ready to put on, to look like one. So he said you'd always had the use of me, and twasn't no harm for me to take de suit, for I was 'titled to it for my sarvices. He

axed me if any body owed my mistis money, as I know'd of. I told him, yes, Mrs. Barrett did, and mistis often sent me after it without any order, for she know'd I'd bring it straight to her. Now, my boy, said the Abolitioner, dis money is yourn—its your wages. You've got a better right to it than ever your mistis had. You can't start on a journey without money; so you go to dis lady and tell her you was sent for money by your mistis, and you keep de money for your own use. Here's de money,' said he, < Master George, take it to mistis, and tell her de truth.'

" < Damn the rascals,' says young Mr. Seymour, < they're not content with man-stealing, but they're stealing money and clothes, and every thing they can lay their hands upon. So nmch for your Abolition friends, Simon,' says he. < I wish you joy of them. They've brought you to a.pretty pass, and lost you as good a home as ever a servant had.'

" < Oh, master,' said Simon, 'won't you take me back ? Indeed I will be faithful.'

" i Can't trust you, Simon,' said Mr. Seymour ; < besides, none of your fellow-servants want you back. You have no relations. My mother bought you, when you was a little boy, because she knew your mother; and after she died you were knocked about by the other servants.

My sister taught you how to read the Bible, and you have been a member of the Methodist church. If you was a poor ignorant fellow, that didn't know what was right, I would take you back; but you've done this wid your eyes open. Our servants say they wants no runaways to live ^ 'long o' them. Now, if you can get any of your Abolition friends to buy you, and take you North, and make a gen tleman of you, I'll sell you to them; but they wouldn't give a fip to keep you from starving. I am sorry its so, but I can't take you back.' He said these very words, sir. He felt mighty bad, sir; he talked husky, but he went out. Simon called after him, but he didn't even look back; so I know Simon's goin for true."

19

"I am really sorry for the servants, Bacchus," said Mr. Weston, " but they won't take warning. I'm told that since Abolitionists have come to live in .Washington, and have been going among the colored people, that it is almost im possible to employ an honest servant; it is on this account that the Irish are so much employed. Some years ago the families had no trouble with their domestics, but Abo lition has ruined them. What a wretched looking class they are, too ! lazy and dirty; these are the consequences of taking bad advice."

"Well, master," said Bacchus,"'I wish to de Lord we could take 'em all to Virginny, and give 'em a good coat of tar and feathers; thar's all them feathers poor Aunt Peggy had in them barrels. We aint got no call for 'em at home. I wish we could put 'em to some use. I wouldn't like no better fun than to spread de tar on neat, and den stick de feathers on close and thick."

"Well, Bacchus," said Mr.Weston, "its near bedtime, and I am not well; so I will retire."

" Certainly, master; you must 'scuse me, I'm afeard I've kep you up; I felt mightily for them poor creaturs, thar. Lor', master, I aint nigh so weakly as you, and think I nussed you, and used to toat you on my back when you was a little boy. You was mighty fat, I tell you—I used to think my back would bust, sometimes, but I'm pretty strong yet. Tears like I could toat you now, if I was to try."

^ "Not to-night, thank you, Bacchus. Though if any thing should occur to make it necessary, I will call you," said Mr. Weston.

Bacchus slept in a kind of closet bedroom off his mas ter's, and he went in accordingly, but after a few moments returned, finding Mr. Weston in bed.

"Will you have any thing, sir?"

"Nothing, to-night."

"Well, master, I was thinkin to say one thing more,

and 'tis, if dese Abolitioners, dat has so much larnin, if they only had some of the Bible larnin my wife has, how / much good 'twould do 'em. My wife says, < God put her 1 here a slave, and she's a gwine to wait for Him to set her free; if he aint ready to do so till he calls her to Heaven, she's willin to wait.' Lord, sir, my wife, she sets at de feet of Jesus, and larns her Bible. I reckon de Aboli tioners aint willin to do that; they don't want to get so low down; 'pears as if they aint willin to go about doin good like Jesus did, but they must be puttin up poor slaves to sin and. sorrow. Well, they've got to go to their ac count, any how."

Bacchus finally retired, but it was with difficulty he composed himself to sleep. He was still mentally dis cussing that great subject, Abolition, which, like a mighty tempest, was shaking the whole country. All at once it occurred to him "that it wouldn't do no good to worry about it," so he settled himself to sleep. A bright idea crossed his mind as he closed his eyes upon the embers that were fading on the hearth in his master's room ; in another moment he was reposing, in utter oblivion of all things, whether concerning his own affairs or those of the world in general.

The next morning, just as Mr. Weston had finished his paper, Bacchus came in with a pair of boots, shining as tonishingly. "I believe," said Mr. Weston, "I won't put them on yet, our ladies have not come down to breakfast, and its hardly time, for it is but half-past nine o'clock; I think it must have been morning when they came home."

"Yes sir," said Bacchus; "they aint awake yet, Aunt Mar thy tells me."

"Well, let them sleep. I have breakfasted, and I will sit here and enjoy this good fire, until they come."

Bacchus lingered, and looked as if he could not enjoy any thing that morning.

"Any thing the matter, Bacchus?" said Mr. Weston.

"Well," said Bacchus, "nothin more I 'spose than what I had a right to expect of 'em. Simon's got to go. I done all I could for him, but it aint nothin, after all."

"What could you do?" said Mr. Weston.

"Well, master, I was nigh asleep last night, when all at once I thought 'bout dis here Abolition gentleman, Mr. Baker, that boards long wid us. Now, thinks I, he is a mighty nice kind of man, talks a heap 'bout God and the Gospel, and 'bout our duty to our fellow-creaturs. I know'd he had a sight of money, for his white servant told me he was a great man in Boston, had a grand house thar, his wife rode in elegant carriages, and his children has the best of every thing. So, I says to myself, he aint like the rest of 'em, he don't approve of stealing, and lying, and the like o' that; if he thinks the Southern gentlemen oughter set all their niggers free, why he oughter be willin to lose just a little for one man; so I went straight to his room to ask him to buy Simon."

"That was very wrong, Bacchus," said Mr. Weston, sternly. "Don't you know your duty better than to be in terfering in the concerns of these people? I am exces sively mortified. What will this gentleman think of me?"

"Nothin', master," said Bacchus. "Don't be oneasy. I told him I come to ax him a favor on my own 'sponsibility, and that you didn't know nothin' about it. Well, he axed me if I wanted a chaw of tobacco. <No sir,' says I, 'but I wants to ax a lktle advice.' < I will give you that with pleasure,' says he.

"'Mr. Baker,' says I, 'I understands you think God made us all, white and colored, free and equal; and I knows you feels great pity for de poor slaves that toils and frets in de sun, all their lives like beasts, and lays down and dies like beasts, clean forgot like 'em too. I heard you say so to a gentleman at de door; I thought it was mighty kind of you to consider so much 'bout them of a different color from your own. I heard you say it was de duty of de gentlemen of de South to set their slaves free, if it did make 'em poor, kase Jesus Christ, he made hisself poor to set us all free. Warn't dat what you said, sir?'

"'Exactly,' says he. <I didn't know you had such a good memory.'

"<Now, Mr. Baker,' says I, <you're a Christian your self, or you couldn't talk dat way. I know Christians must like to make other people happy; they're bound to, for their Master, Christ, did. Well, sir, all de poor creturs dat de Abolitionists got off is cotched--they're gwine to be sold, and thar's one young man thar, that had a good home and a good mistis, and him they 'suaded off, and now he's gwine to be sold South, whar he'll toil and sweat in de hot sun. Now, Mr. Baker, if de Southern gentlemen's duty's so plain to you, that they oughter make themselves poor, to make their slaves free and happy, surely you'll buy this one poor man who is frettin' hisself to death* It won't make you poor to buy jist this one; his master says he'll sell him to any Abolitioner who'll take him to the great Norrurd, and have him teached. Buy him, sir, for de Lord's sake—de poor fellow will be so happy; jist spend a little of your money to make dat one

poor cretur happy. God gave it all to you, sir, and he aint gave none to de poor slaves, not even gave him his freedom. You set dis one poor feller free, and when you come to die, it will make you feel so good to think about it; when you come to judgment, maybe Christ may say, " You made dis poor man free, and now you may come into de kingdom and set down wid me forever.' Oh ! sir, says I, buy him, de Lord will pay you back, you won't lose a copper by him."

" Well," said Mr. Weston, " what did he say ?"

"Why, sir," said Bacchus, "he got up and stood by de fire, and warmed hisself, and says he, < Ole felur, if I'd a had de teaching of you, I'd a lamed you to mind your owi\ business. I'll let you know I didn't come to Washington to buy niggers.' <• Here,' says he, to dat white nigger that waits on him, < Next time dis feller wants me, tell him to go 'bout his business.'

" <Good mornin' sir,' says I, <I shan't trouble you agin. May de Lord send better friends to de slaves than de like of you.' '

"Well, Bacchus," said Mr. Weston, "you did very wrong, and I hope you will not again take such a liberty with any person. You see for yourself what an Aboli tionist is. I wish those poor runaways had had some such experience, it would have saved them from the trouble they are now in."

"Yes, indeed,master. I've been down thar agin, to-day. I went right early; thar's an ole woman thar that tried to run away. She's gwine too, and she leaves her husband here. She aint a cryin, though, her heart's too full for tears. Oh! master," said Bacchus, sighing deeply, «I think if you'd seed her, you'd do more than the Aboli- tioners."

****

In the afternoon Mr. Weston usually walked out. He did not dine with the ladies at their late hour, as his com plaint, dyspepsia, made it necessary for him to live lightly and regularly. Bacchus attended him in his walks, and many a person turned back to look upon the fine-looking old gentleman with his gold-headed cane, and his servant, whose appearance was as agreeable as his own. Bacchus was constantly on the lookout for his master, but he managed to see all that was going on too, and to make many criticisms on the appearance and conduct of those he met in his rambles.

Bacchus followed his master, and found that he was wending his steps to the place where the arrested run aways were confined. This was very agreeable to him, for his heart was quite softened towards the poor prisoners, and he had an idea that his master's very presence might carry a blessing with it. "Bacchus," said Mr. Weston, as they were going in, you need not point out the servants to me. I will observe for myself, and I do not wish to be conspicuous."

There were a great many lounging about, and looking round there. Some were considering the scene as merely curious; some were blaming the slaves; some their mas ters, some the Abolitionists. There was confusion and constant going in and out. But though the countenances of the runaways expressed different emotions, it was evi dent that one feeling had settled in each breast, and that was, there was no hope that any thing would occur to re lieve them from their undesirable position.

Mr. Weston easily recognized Simon, from Bacchus's description. He had a boyish expression of disappoint ment and irritation on his countenance, and had evi dently been recently weeping. There were several men, one or tw r o of them with bad faces, and one, a light mulatto, had a fine open countenance, and appeared to be making an effort not to show his excessive disappointment. In the corner sat the woman, on a low bench—her head was bent forward on her lap, and she was swaying her body slightly, keeping motion with her foot.

"What is the woman's name, Bacchus?" asked Mr. Weston in a low tone.

" I axed her dis mornin, sir. Its Sarah—Sarah Mills."

Mr. Weston walked up nearer to her, and was regarding her, when she suddenly looked up into his face. Finding herself observed, she made an effort to look unconcerned, but it did not succeed, for she burst into tears.

"I'm sorry to see you here, Sarah," said Mr. Weston, "you look too respectable to be in such a situation." Sarah smoothed down her apron, but did not reply. " What induced you to run away ? You need not be afraid to answer me truthfully. I will not do you any harm."

" My blessed grief!" said Bacchus. " No, master couldn't do no harm to a flea."

"Hash, Bacchus," said Mr. Weston.

There was something in Mr. Weston's appearance that could not be mistaken. The woman gave him a look of perfect confidence, and said—

" I thought I could better myself, sir."

" In what respect ? Had you an unkind master ?" said Mr. Weston.

"No," said the woman, "but my husband I was afear'd might be sold, and I thought I could make so much money at the North, that I could soon help him to buy himself. He's a barber, sir, lives on the Avenue, and his master, when he was young, had him taught the barber's trade. Well, his. master told him some time ago that he might live to himself, and pay him so much a month out o' what he made, but seemed as if he couldn't get along to do it. My husband, sir, drinks a good deal, and he couldn't do it on that account; so, a year or two ago his master sent for him, and told him that he was worthless, and unless he could buy himself in three years he would sell him. He said he might have himself for five hundred dollars, and he could have earned it, if he hadn't loved whiskey so, but 'pears as if he can't do without that. We aint got no children, thank God! so when the Abolitionists advised me to go off, and told me they would take care of me until I got out of my master's reach, and I could soon make a sight of money to buy my husband, I thought I would go ; and you see, sir, what's come of it."

Sarah tried to assume the same look of unconcern, and again she wept bitterly.

" I don't mean to reproach you, now that you are in trouble," said Mr. Weston, « but you colored people in this city have got into bad hands. God has made you slaves, and you should be willing to abide by his will, especially if he give you a good master."

" Yes, sir, it was mighty hard though, to think of my poor husband's being sold,—he and I don't belong to the same person."

" So, I suppose," said Mr. Weston; « but you have only made your condition worse."

" Yes, sir ; but I didn't think things would turn out so. The Abolitionists said they would see that I got off free."

" They ought to be cotched, and tied up, and have a good whaling besides," said Bacchus, indignantly.

"'Taint no use wishin'em harm," said Sarah; "the Lord's will be done," at the same time her pale lips qui vered with emotion.

Mr. Weston paused a few moments in deep thought, then went into the other room. When he returned, she was sitting as when he first entered, her face buried in her lap.

" Sarah," he said, and she looked up as before, without any doubt, in his open countenance, "are you a good worker ?"

"I am, at washin and ironin. I have been makin a good deal for my master that way." .

"Well," said Mr. Weston, "if I were to purchase you, so as you could be near your husband, would you conduct yourself properly ; and if I wish it, endeavor to repay me what I have given for you ?"

Such a thought had not entered the despairing woman's mind. She was impressed with the idea that she should never see her husband again; other things did not effect her. It was necessary, therefore, for Mr. Weston to repeat what he had said before she comprehended his meaning. When she heard and understood, every energy of her soul was aroused. Starting from her seat, she clasped her hands convulsively together; her face became death like with agitation.

« Would I, sir ? Oh! try me ! Work! what is work if I could be near my poor husband as long as I can. Buy me, sir, only for Jesus' sake, buy me. I will work day and

night to pay you, and the blessing of God Almighty will pay you too, better than any money I could earn."

Bacchus, the tears rolling down his cheeks, looked earnestly at his master's face.

"Buy her, master, buy her, for the love of God," he said.

" Sarah," said Mr. Western, "I do not like to be in a public place; do not, therefore, become excited, and say any thing that will draw observation to me. I have bought you, and I will not require you to repay me. Come to me to-night, at Willard's, and I will give you your free papers ; I will see also what I can do for your husband. In the mean time, Bacchus will help you take your things from this place. Stay here though a few moments, until he gets me a carriage to go home in, and he will return to you."

Sarah perfectly understood that Mr. Weston wanted no thanks at that time. With streaming eyes, now raised to heaven—now to her benefactor, she held her peace. Mr. Weston gladly left the dreadful place. Bacchus assisted him to a hack, and then came back to fulfil his directions as regards the woman.

Oh ! noble heart, not here thy reward! Thy weak arid trembling frame attests too well that the scene is too trying to afford thee pleasure. The All-seeing Eye is bent upon thee, and thine own ear will hear the commendation from the lips of Christ: " Inasmuch as ye have done it unto the least of these, my brethren, ye have done it unto me." Nor thou alone! Many a generous act is done by the slaveholder to the slave. God will remember them, though here they be forgotten or unknown.

We need not dwell on the unhoped-for meeting between Sarah and her husband, nor on Bacchus's description of it to his master. It suffices to close the relation of this incident by saying, that at night Sarah came to receive directions from Mr. Weston; but in their place he gave her the

necessary free papers. "You are your own mistress, now, Sarah," said he. "I hope you will prove yourself worthy to be so. You can assist your husband to pay for himself. If you are honest and industrious, you cannot fail to do well."

Sarah's heart overflowed with unlooked-for happiness. She thanked Mr. Weston over and over again, until, fearing to be troublesome, she withdrew. Bacchus went as far as the corner, and promised to look in upon herself and husband, repeatedly; which he did. He impressed his new acquaintances with a proper sense of his own importance. With the exception of one grand spree that he and Sarah's husband had together, the three enjoyed a very pleasant and harmonious intercourse during the remainder of the Westons' stay at Washington.

******

The gay winter had passed, and spring had replaced it; but night after night saw the votaries of fashion assembled, though many of them looked rather the worse for wear. Ellen and

Alice tired of scenes which varied so little, yet having no regular employment, they hardly knew how to cease the round of amusements that occupied them. Ellen said, "Never mind, Alice, we will have plenty of time for repentance, and we might as well quaff to the last drop the cup of pleasure, which may never be offered to our lips again." Very soon they were to return to Virginia, and now they proposed visiting places of interest in the neighborhood of the city.

One morning, after a gay party, and at a later hour than usual, the three ladies entered the breakfast-room. Mr. Weston was waiting for them. "Well, young ladies," he said, "I have read my paper, and now I am ready to hear you give an account of your last evening's triumphs. The winter's campaign is closing; every little skirmish is then of the greatest importance. How do you all feel?"

"I do not know how I feel, uncle," said Alice, languidly.

"Alice has expressed my feelings exactly, and Mrs. Weston's too, I fancy," said Ellen.

Mr. Weston smiled, but said he should not excuse them from their promise of giving him a faithful description of the scene.

"Well, my dear sir," said Ellen, "I have a decided talent for description; but remember, Mrs. Weston, my genius must not be cramped. Do not break the thread of my discourse by <Ellen, do not talk so!' A Washington party is what you have called it, Mr. Weston, a skirmish. You remember how the wind blew last night. When we reached Mr.

's front door, the people had collected in such crowds

in the hall, to get a little air, that it was fully ten minutes before we could get in. ' We had the benefit of a strong harsh breeze playing about our undefended necks and shoulders. As soon as we were fairly in, though, we were recompensed for our sufferings in this respect. We went from the arctic to the torrid zone; it was like an August day at two o'clock.

" We tried to make our way to the lady of the house, but understood, after a long search, that she had been pushed by the crowd to the third story; and being a very fat person, was seen, at the last accounts, seated in a rocking-chair, fanning herself violently, and calling in vain for ice cream. After a while we reached the dancing-room, where, in a very confined circle, a number were waltzing and Polka-ing. As this is a forbidden dance to Alice and me, we had a fine opportunity of taking notes. Mrs. S. was making a great exhibition of herself; she puffed and blew as if she had the asthma; her ringlets streamed, and her flounces flew. I was immensely anxious for the little lieutenant her partner. He was invisible several times; lost in the ringlets and the flounces. There were people of all sizes and ages dancing for a wager. I thought of what our good bishop once said : < It was very pretty to see the

young lambs gambolling about; but when the old sheep began to caper too, he'd rather not look on.' There was poor old Mr. K., with his red face and his white hair, and his heels flying in every direction. (I am ashamed of you for laughing at Mr. K., Mrs. Weston, when I am trying to impress upon Alice's mind the folly of such a scene.) I dare say Mr. K.'s wife was at that very moment, five hundred miles off, darning her children's stockings.

"All the people did not dance the Polka," continued Ellen; "and I was dazzled with the pretty faces, and the wise-looking heads. Mr. Webster was there, with his deep voice, and solemn brow, and cavernous eyes; and close up to him, where she could not move or breathe, there was a young face, beautiful and innocent as a cherub's, looking with unfeigned astonishment upon the scene. There was Gen. Scott, towering above everybody; and Mr. Douglass, edging his way, looking kindly and pleasantly at every one. There were artists and courtiers; soldiers and sailors; foolish men, beautiful women, and sensible women; though I do not know what they wanted there. There were specimens of every kind in this menagerie of men and women. Dear Mr.

Weston, I have not quite done. There was a lady writer, with a faded pink scarf, and some old artificial flowers in her hair. There was a she Abolitionist too ; yes, a genuine female Abolitionist. She writes for the Abolition papers. She considers Southerners heathens; looks pityingly at the waiters as they hand her ice cream. She wants Frederick Douglass to be the next President, and advocates amalgamation. I am quite out of breath; but I must tell you that I looked at her and thought Uncle Bacchus would just suit her, with his airs and graces; but I do not think she is stylish enough for him."

"But, my dear," said Mrs. Weston, "you forget Bacchus has a wife and twelve children."

" That is not of the least consequence, my dear madam," said Ellen; «I can imagine, when a woman ap-

proves of amalgamation, she is so lost to every sense of propriety that it makes no difference to her whether a man is married or not. Now, Alice, I resign my post; and if you have any thing to say I will give you the chair, while I run up to my room and write aunt a good long letter."

CHAPTER XXIV.

afternoon is so delightful," said Mr. Weston, " that we had better take our ride to the Congress burial ground. Your time is short, young ladies; you cannot afford to lose any of it, if all your plans are to be carried out."

The ladies gladly agreed to go, and were not long in their preparation. Mark was a perfect prince of a driver. When the ladies had occasion to go into the country, he entreated them to hire a carriage, but he was always ready to display his handsome equipage and horses in the city, especially on the Avenue.

He drove slowly this afternoon, and Mrs. Weston remembered, as she approached Harper's, that she had one or two purchases to make. Fearing it might be late on their return, she proposed getting out for a few moments.

A stream of gayly-dressed people crowded the pavements. The exquisite weather had drawn them out. Belles with their ringlets and sun-shades, and beaux with canes and curled moustaches. Irish women in tawdry finery, and ladies of color with every variety of ornament, and ridiculous imitation of fashion. Now and then a respectable-looking negro would pass, turning out of the way, instead of jostling along.

"Truly," said Mr. Weston, «Pennsylvania Avenue is

the great bazaar of America. Here are senators and members—three and four walking arm in arm. Here are gay young men, dressed in the latest style; here is the army and navy button ; old people and young children with their nurses ; foreigners and natives ; people of every shade and hue. There is our President, walking unattended, as a republican president should walk. And see ! there are a number of Indians, noble-looking men, and a white boy throwing a stone at them. I wish I had the young rascal. On our right, in their carriages, are the wives and children of the rich; while, scattered about, right and left, are the representatives of the poor. But what is this, coming along the side-walk?"

The girls put their heads out of the window, and saw a colored man, sauntering along in an impudent, dont-carish manner. His dress—indeed his whole appearance—was absurd. He wore a stylish, shiny black hat; the rim slightly turned up in front, following the direction of the wearer's nose, which had « set its affections on things above." His whiskers were immense; so were his moustaches, and that other hairy trimming which it is the* fashion to wear about the jaws and chin; and for which I know no better name than that which the children give—goatee; a tremendous shirt collar; brass studs in his bosom; a neck handkerchief of many colors, the ends of which stood out like the extended wings of a butterfly; a gorgeous watch chain; white kid gloves; pantaloons of a large-sized plaid, and fitting so very tightly that it was with the greatest difficulty he could put out his feet; patent leather gaiter-boots, and a cane that he flourished right and left with such determined strokes, that the children kept carefully out of his way. Several persons looked back to wonder and laugh at this strange figure, the drollery of which was greatly enhanced by his limber style of walking, and a certain expression of the whole outer man, which said, "Who says I am not as good

AUXT PHILLIS'S CABIX; OR,

as anybody on this avenue; Mr. Fillmore, or any one else?"

Now it happened, that walking from the other direction toward this representative of the much-injured colored race, was a stranger', who had come to Washington to look about him. He was from Philadelphia, but not thinking a great deal of what he saw in our capital on a former visit, he had quite made up his mind that there was nothing to make it worth his while to come again; but hearing of the convalescing turn the city had taken since the immortal supporters of the Compromise and the Fugitive Slave law had brought comparative harmony and peace, where there had been nought but disorder and confusion, he suddenly fancied to come and see for himself. He was not an Abolitionist, nor a Secessionist, nor one of those unfortunate, restless people, who are forever stirring up old difficulties. He had an idea that the Union ought to be preserved in the first place; and then, whatever else could be done to advance the interests of the human race in general, without injury to our national interests, should be attendee! to. He was always a good-tempered man, and was particularly pleasant this afternoon, having on an entire new suit of clothes, each article, even the shirt-collar, fitting in the most faultless manner.

As he walked along, he noticed the colored man advancing towards him, and observed, too, what I forgot to mention, that he held a cigar, and every now and then put it to his mouth, emitting afterwards a perfect cloud of smoke.

The thought occurred to him that the man did not intend to turn out of the way for anybody, and as they were in a line, he determined not to deviate one way or the other, but just observe what this favorite of fashion would do. They walked on, and in a minute came up to each other, the colored man not giving way in the least, but bumping, hat, goatee, cane, cigar, and all, against our

Philadelphia!!, who, with the greatest coolness and presence of mind, doubled up his fist and giving the colored Adonis two blows with it, (precisely on the middle brass stud which confined his frilled shirt-bosom,) laid him full length upon the pavement.

"Now," said the Philadelphian, "you've had a lesson; the next time you see a gentleman coming along, turn out of the way for him, and you'll save your new clothes." Without another glance at the discomfited beau, who was brushing his plaid pantaloons with his pocket-handkerchief, and muttering some equivocal language that would not do here, he went on his way to see the improvements about the City Hall.

Mark's low laugh was heard from the driver's seat, and Bacchus, who was waiting to open the carriage door for Mr. Weston, stood on the first step, and touching his hat, said, with a broad grin, " Dat's de best thing we've seen since we come to Washington. Dat beats Ole Virginny."

Mrs. Weston came from the store at the same moment, and Bacchus gallantly let down the steps, and, after securing the door, took his place beside Mark, with the agility of a boy of sixteen.

Mr. Weston, much amused, described the scene. Mrs. Weston declared "it served him right; for that the negroes were getting intolerable."

"I can hardly believe," she said, "the change that has been made in their appearance and conduct. They think, to obtain respect they must be impertinent. This is the effect of Abolition.

"Yes," said Mr. Weston, "this is Abolition. I have thought a great deal on the condition of the negroes in our country, of late. I would like to see every man and woman that God has made, free, could it be accomplished to their advantage. I see the evils of slavery, it is some times a curse on the master as well as the slave.

" When I purchased Sarah; when I saw those grieving, throbbing souls, my own was overwhelmed with sympathy for them. This is slavery, I said to myself. Poor creatures, though you have done wrong, how severe your punishment ; to be separated from all that your life has had to make it pleasant, or even tolerable. This is slavery indeed, and where is the man, come from God, who will show us a remedy ? I look at the free blacks of the North and South. I say again, this is Abolition ! How worthless, how degraded they are, after they imbibe these ridiculous notions. When I behold the Southern country, and am convinced that it is impossible to manumit the slaves, I conclude that here, at least, they are in their natural condition. Heretofore, I feel that I have only done my duty in retaining mine, while I give them every means of comfort, and innocent enjoyment, that is in my power. Now I have seen the result of the Abolition efforts, I am more convinced that my duty has been, and will be, as I have said. Could they be colonized from Virginia, I would willingly consent to it, as in our climate, white labor would answer; but farther South, only the negro can labor, and this is an unanswerable objection to our Southern States becoming free. Those servants that are free, the benevolent and generous Abolitionists ought to take North, build them colleges, and make good to them all the promises they held out as baits to allure them from their owners and their duties."

Mr. Weston found he had not two very attentive listeners in the young ladies, for they were returning the many salutations they received, and making remarks on their numerous acquaintances. The carriage began slowly to ascend Capitol Hill, and they all remarked the beautiful prospect, to which Washingtonians are so much accustomed that they are too apt not to notice it. Their ride was delightful. It was one of those lovely spring days when the air is still fresh and balmy, and the promise of a summer's sun lights up nature so joyfully.

There were many visitors at the burial-ground, and there had been several funerals that day. A woman stood at the door of the house, at the entrance of the cemetery, with a baby in her arms; and another child of two years old was playing around a large bier, that had been left there until it should be wanted again.

Mrs. Weston met with an acquaintance, soon after they entered the ground, and they stopped to converse, while Mr. Weston and the younger ladies walked on. Near a large vault they stopped a moment, surprised to see two or three little boys playing at marbles. They were ruddy, healthy-looking boys, marking out places in the gravel path for the game ; shooting, laughing, and winning, and so much occupied that if death himself had come along on his pale horse, they would have asked him to wait a while till they could let him pass, if indeed they had seen him at all. Mr. Weston tried to address them several times, but they could not attend to him until the game was completed, when one of them sprang upon the vault and began to count over his marbles, and the others sat down on a low monument to rest.

" Boys," said Mr. Weston, " I am very sorry to see you playing marbles in a burial-ground. Don't you see all these graves around you?"

" We don't go on the dead people," said an honest-faced little fellow. " You see the grass is wet there ; we play here in the walk, where its nice and dry."

"But you ought to play outside," said Mr. Weston. "This is too sacred a place to be made the scene of your amusements."

"We don't hurt any body," said the largest boy. "When people are dead they don't hear nothin; where's the harm?"

" Well," said Mr. Weston, "there's one thing certain, none of you have any friends buried here. If you had, you would not treat them so unkindly."

" My mother is buried over yonder," said the boy on the

vault; " and if I thought there was any thing unkind in it, I would never come here to play again."

"You are a good boy," said Mr. Weston. "I hope you will keep your word. If you were buried there, I am sure your mother would be very sad and quiet by your grave."

The boy drew the string to his bag, and walked off with out looking back.

"I wish," said Mr. Weston, "you would all follow his example. We should always be respectful in our con duct, when we are in a burial-ground."

As soon as they were gone, the boys laughed and marked out another game.

Mrs. Weston joined her party, and they went towards the new portion of the cemetery that is so beautifully situated, near the river.

"I think," said Mr. Weston, "this scene should remind us of our conversation this morning. If Washington be the meeting-place of all living, it is tjie grand cemetery of the dead. Look around us here! We see monuments to Senators and Members; graves of foreigners and stran gers ; names of the great, the rich, the powerful, men of genius and ambition. Strewed along are the poor, the lowly, the unlearned, the infant, and the little child;

"Head the inscriptions—death has come at last, watched and waited for; or he has come suddenly, unexpected, and undesired. There lies an author, a bride, a statesman, side by side. A little farther off is that simple, but beau-ful monument."

They approached, and Alice read the line that was in scribed around a cross sculptured in it, "Other refuge have I none!" Underneath was her name, "Angeline."

"How beautiful, how much more so in its simplicity than if it had been ornamented, and a labored epitaph written upon it," said Mr. Weston. "Here too are mem bers of families, assembled in one great family. As we walk along, we pass mothers, and husbands, and children;

but in life, they who lie here together, were possibly all strangers."

"What is that large vault open to-day for ?" said Ellen, to a man who seemed to have some charge in the place.

"That is the public receptacle," said the man. "We are obliged to air it very often, else we could never go in and out with the coffins we put there. There's a good many in there now."

"Who is there?" said Mr. Weston.

"Well," said the man, "Mrs. Madison is there, for one, and there are some other people, who are going to be moved soon. Mrs. Madison, she's going to be moved, too, some time or another, but I don't know when."

Ellen stooped down and looked in, but arose quickly and turned away. Two gentlemen were standing near observing her, and one of them smiled as she stepped back from the vault. Mr. Weston knew this person by sight; he was a clergyman of great talent, and almost equal eccen tricity, and often gave offence by harshness of manner, when he was only anxious to do good to the cause in which his heart was absorbed.

"Ah! young ladies," he said, looking kindly at them both, "this is a good place for you to come to. You are both beautiful, and it may be wealthy; and I doubt not, in the enjoyments of the passing season, you have forgotten all about death and the grave. But, look you! in there, lies the mortal remains of Mrs. Madison. What an influence she had in this gay society, which you have doubtless adorned. Her presence was the guarantee of propriety, as well as of social and fashionable enjoyment; the very contrast that she presented to her husband made her more charming. Always anxious to please, she was constantly making others happy. She gave assistance and encouragement to all, when it was in her power. She had more political influence than any woman in our country has had, before or since. But think of her now! You could not bear to approach the coffin that contains her remains. Where is her beauty—and her grace and talent ? Ah! young ladies," he continued, " did she rightly use those talents?"

1 i It is hardly a fair question to ask now," said Mr. Weston. "Let us tread lightly o'er the ashes of the dead."

"Let the living learn a lesson from the dead," said the clergyman, sternly. "You are leading, it may be, a heartless life of pleasure, but, young ladies, forget not this grave. She could not escape it, nor will you. Pause from your balls, and your theatres, and your gay doings, and ask, what is the end of it all. Trifle not with the inestimable gift of life. Be not dead while you live. Anticipate not the great destroyer. Hear the appeal of one who was once the idol of every heart; she speaks to you from the grave, <Even as I am, shalt thou be !"

He turned from them, and wandered over the ground. Mr. Weston led the way to the carriage, and Ellen and Alice thought, that if a lesson of life was to be learned in the gay ball of the night before, a still more necessary one was found in the cemetery which they were now leaving, as the shadows of the evening were on the simple monument and the sculptured slab, and their silent tenants slept on, undisturbed by the gambols of thoughtless children, or the conversation of the many who came to visit their abode.

*****

The next morning, Bacchus brought no letter for Mr. Weston, but one for each lady; for Ellen from her aunt, for Alice from Arthur, and Cousin Janet's handwriting was easily recognized on the outside of Mrs. Weston's. Hardly had the girls arisen from the table to take theirs' to their rooms for a quiet perusal, when an exclamation from Mrs. Weston, detained them.

'•'Is anything the matter at home, Anna?" said Mr. Weston, "Is Cousin Janet ?"

" Cousin Janet is well, my dear brother," said Mrs. Weston. " I was very thoughtless, but our dear neighbor, Mrs. Kent, is no more."

« Can it be possible ?" said Mr. Weston, much agitated. "Read the letter aloud."

Mrs. Weston, turned to the beginning, and read aloud,

« MY DEAR ANNA :

" The time is near which will bring you all in health and happiness, I trust, to your home; and could you see how lovely it looks, I think you would be tempted to fix upon an earlier day. You see how selfish I am, but I confess that I quite 1 count the days, as a child does to Christmas, and am ashamed of my impatience.

" Throughout the winter I had no care. My kind friends did all the housekeeping, and the servants in the house, and on the plantation, were so faithful, that I feel indebted to all who have made my time so easy; and your absence has not, I am sure, been attended wTith any ill effects, without you find me a little cross and complaining, and Mr. Barbour out of his senses with joy, on your return. Good Mr. Barbour! he has superintended and encouraged the servants, and visited us forlorn ladies frequently, so that he must come in for a portion of our thanks too.

"You will perhaps think I ought only to write you cheerful news, but it is best to let you know as well as I can, the condition that you will find us in, on your return. Phillis is the only one of us, whose concerns are of any immediate importance, but I am sorry to have to tell you that she is now seriously indisposed. Her cough has never really yielded—her other symptoms have varied; but for the last few weeks, her disease has not only progressed, but assumed a certain form. She is in consumption, and has no doubt inherited the disease from her mother.

" I have, throughout the winter, felt great anxiety about her, and have not permitted her to work, though some-

times I found it hard to prevent her. Her children have been constantly with her; indeed, I have passed a great deal of my own time in her cabin, which, under Martha's superintendence, is so neat and comfortable.

"You will all perhaps blame me that I have not been thus plain with you before, but Dr. Lawton said it was not necessary, as she has never been in any immediate danger, and Phillis would not consent to my doing so. She wanted you to enjoy yourselves, and Alice to have a good chance to regain her health. <No doubt. Miss Janet,' she said, <the Lord will spare me to see them yet, and I have every thing I want now—they couldn't stop my pains any more than you, and I feel that I am in the Lord's hands, and I am content to be.' She has not been confined to her bed, but is fast losing strength, though from my window now I see her tying up her roses, that are beginning to bud. Some other hand than hers will care for them when another Spring shall come.

" Her nights are very restless, and she is much exhausted from constant spitting of blood; the last week of pleasant weather has been of service to her, and the prospect of seeing you all at home gives her the most unfeigned pleasure.

"I have even more painful intelligence to give you. Our young neighbor, Mrs. Kent, has done with all her trials, and I trust they sanctified her, in preparation for the early and unexpected death which has been her lot. You are not yet aware of the extent of her trials. A fortnight ago her little boy was attacked with scarlet fever, in its most violent form. From the first moment of his illness his case was hopeless, and he only suffered twenty-four hours. I went over as soon as I heard of his death; the poor mother's condition was really pitiable. She was helpless in her sorrow, which was so unexpected as to deprive her at first of the power of reason. The Good Shepherd though, had not forgotten her—he told her that

he had taken her little lamb, and had gently folded it in his bosom, and that he would wander with it in the lovely pastures of Paradise, She was soon perfectly reconciled to the sad dispensation; sad indeed, for the child was her only earthly solace. Victim of an unhappy marriage, the dear engaging little boy was a great consolation to her, and his amusement and instruction occupied her mind, and passed away happily many a weary hour.

" She insisted upon attending the funeral, and I accompanied her. Mr. Kent was with her, too, much distressed, for this hard man loved his child, and keenly felt his loss.

" She got out of the carriage to hear the funeral service read, and was calm until they took up the coffin to lower it into the grave. Then it was impossible to control her. Placing her arms upon it, she looked around appealingly to the men; and so affected were they, that they turned from her to wipe away their own tears. Her strength gave way under the excitement, and she was carried, insensible, to the carriage, and taken home,

«I found her very feverish, and did not like to leave her, thinking it probable that she might also have the disease which had carried off her child. Before night she became really ill, and Dr. Lawton pronounced her complaint scarlet fever. The disease was fearfully rapid, and soon ended her life. She was, I think, well prepared to go. Her solemn and affectionate farewell to her husband can not fail to make an impression upon him.

"I shall have a great deal to tell you of her when you return. The past winter has been a sad one; a constant coolness existing between her and her husband. A short time ago he was brutally striking that faithful old man of her father's, Robert, and Mrs. Kent interfered, insisting upon Robert's returning tfec his cabin, and in his presence forbidding Mr. Kent again to raise his hand against one servant on the plantation; Mr. Carter's will, allowing

Mr. Kent no authority over his servants, and commending them to his daughter's kindness and care, showed great discrimination of character. This, though, has been a constant source of irritation to Mr. Kent, and he has never been kind to the people. Mrs. Kent, usually so timid, was roused into anger by his treatment of Robert, and interfered, as I have related to you. She told me of this, and said how unhappy it had made her, though she could not blame herself. Since then there has only been a formal politeness between them ; Mr. Kent not forgiving his wife for the part she took against him. Poor little woman! Robert had been her father's faithful nurse in his long illness, and I do not wonder at her feelings on seeing him struck.

" Yesterday the will was read, arid Dn Lawton, who was present, informed us of the result. Mrs. Kent has left most of her property to her husband, but her servants free ! The plantation is to be sold, and the proceeds ex pended in preparing those who are willing to go to Liberia, or where they choose; as they cannot, manumitted, re main in Virginia. The older servants, who prefer stay ing in Virginia as they are, she has left to you, with an allowance for their support, considering you as a kind of guardian; for in no other way could she have provided for their staying here, which they will like better.

" Who would have thought she could have made so wise a will?

" Dr. Lawton says that Mr. Kent showed extreme anger on hearing it read. He intends returning to the North, and his $30,000 will be a clear gain, for I am told he had not a cent when he married her.

"Write me when you have fixed the time for your return, and believe me, with love to all,
" Your affectionate relative,
JANET WILMER."

Bacchus entered in time to hear the latter part of this letter. He had his master's boots in his hands. When Mrs. Weston stopped reading, he said, " That's good; bound for Mister Kent. I'm glad he's gwine, like Judas, to his own place."

CHAPTER XXV.

THE carriage was slowly ascending the road to the old church, a familiar and dear object to each member of the Weston family. A village churchyard fills up so gradu ally, that one is not startled with a sudden change. Mr. Weston looked from the window at the ivy, and the gothic windows, and the family vault, where many of his name reposed.

The inmates of the carriage had been conversing cheer fully, but as they approached the point where they would see home, each one was occupied with his or her musings. Occasionally, a pleasant word was exchanged, on the ap pearance of the well-known neighborhood, the balmy air, and the many shades of green that the trees presented; some of them loaded with white and pink blossoms, pro mising still better things when the season should ad vance.

Alice leaned from the window, watching for the first glimpse of the well-remembered house. She greeted every tree -they passed with a lively look, and smiled gaily as the porter's lodge presented itself. The gates of it flew open as the carriage approached, and Exeter in its beauty met their view. " Oh, uncle," she said, turning from the window, «look! look ! Is there any place in the world like this?"

"No, indeed, Alice;" and he took a survey of the home which had been so blessed to him. " How beautiful every thing looks! and how we will enjoy it, after a crowded, noisy hotel. Anna, you are not sorry to see its familiar face again. Ellen, my darling, we have not forgotten you— Exeter is your home, too; you are as welcome as any of us. Why, you look sober; not regretting Washington already?"

"No sir," said Ellen, "I was thinking of other things."

"Well," said Mrs. Weston, "we must look very happy this evening. I wonder, Ellen, Mr. Barbour has not met us."

"I suppose," said Alice, laughing, "he is too much agitated at the thought of meeting Ellen again—he will be over this evening, I dare say."

"I am sorry I can't keep my word with Mr. Barbour," said Ellen, " but I have concluded to marry Abel Johnson, on Arthur's recommendation, and I ought not to give good Mr. Barbour any false expectations."

"You must know, dear uncle," said Alice, "that Ellen and Arthur have been carrying on a postscript correspon dence in my letters, and Arthur has turned matchmaker, and has been recommending Abel Johnson to Ellen. They have fallen in love with each other, without having met, and that was the reason Ellen was so hard-hearted last winter."

"Ah! that is the reason. But you must take care of these Yankee husbands, Miss Ellen, if Mr. Kent be a spe cimen," said Mrs. Weston.

"I am quite sure," said Alice, "Arthur would not have such a friend."

Mr. Weston smiled, and looked out again at home. They were rapidly approaching the gates, and a crowd of little darkies were holding them open on each side. "I wish Arthur were here," said he. "How long he has been away ! I associate him with every object about the place,"

Alice did not answer; Arthur was in her thoughts. This was his home, every object with which she was surrounded breathed of him. She had thought of it as her home, but she had no right here—she was really only a guest. The thought was new and painful to her. Could the whole of her past existence have been dreamed away ?—had she in deed no claim to the place she loved best on earth—was she dependant on the will of others for all the gay and joyous emotions that a few moments before filled her breast ? She thought again of Arthur, of his handsome appearance, his good and generous heart, his talents, and his unchanging love to her— of Walter, and of all with which he had had to contend in the springtime of his life. Of his faults, his sin, and his banishment; of his love to her, too, and the delusion under which she had labored, of her returning it. Arthur would, ere long, know it all, and though he might forgive, her proud spirit rebelled at the idea that he would also blame.

She looked at her uncle, whose happy face was fixed on the home of his youth and his old age—a sense of his pro tecting care and affection came over her. What might the short summer bring? His displeasure, too—then there would be no more for her, but to leave Exeter with all its happiness.

Poor child! for, at nearly nineteen, Alice was only a child. The possibility overpowered her, she leant against her uncle's bosom, and wept suddenly and violently.

" Alice, what is the matter?" said her mother. "Are you ill?"

"What is the matter?" said her uncle, putting his arm around her, and looking alarmed.

"Nothing at all," said Alice, trying to control herself. " I was only thinking of all your goodness to me, and how I love you."

"Is that all," said Mr. Weston, pressing her more closely to his bosom. "Why, the sight of home has turned your little head. Come, dry up your tears, for my old eyes can distinguish the hall door, and the servants about the house collecting to meet us."

" I can see dear Cousin Janet, standing within—how happy she will be," said Mrs. Weston.

" Well," said Ellen, "I hope Abel will make a fuss over me, for nobody else ever has."

"If you are to be married," said Alice, smiling through her tears, "you must have his name changed, or always call him Mr. Johnson."

"Never," said Ellen. " I have a perfect passion for the name of Abel. There was a picture in my room of Abel lying down, and Cain standing, holding the club over him. Whenever I got into a passion when I was a child, mammy used to take me to the picture and say, < Look there, honey, if you don't learn how to get the better of your temper, one of these days you will get in a passion like Cain and kill somebody. Just look at him, how ugly he is—because he's in such a rage. But I always looked at Abel, who was so much prettier. I have no doubt Abel Johnson looks just as he does in the picture."

They w^ere about to pass through the gates leading to the grounds; some of the servants approached the car riage, and respectfully bowing, said, < Welcome home, mas ter," but passed on without waiting to have the salutation returned. Mrs. Weston guessed the cause of there not being a general outbreak on the occasion of their return. Miss Janet had spoken to a number of the servants, telling them how unable Mr. Weston was to bear any excitement, and that he would take the earliest opportunity of seeing them all at their cabins. As he was much attached to them and might feel a good deal at the meeting after so long a separation, it would be better not to give him a noisy welcome.

She had, however, excepted the children in this prohibi tion, for Miss Janet had one excellent principle in the management of children, she never forbade them doing what she knew they could not help doing. Thus, as the carriage passed the lodge, a noisy group of small-sized darkies were making a public demonstration. " Massa's come home," says one. "I sees Miss Alice," says an other. "I sees Miss Anna, too," said a third, though, as yet, not a face was visible to one of them. They put their heads out of the carriage, notwithstanding, to speak to them, and Alice emptied a good-sized basket of sugar plums, which she had bought for the purpose, over their heads.

" Take care, Mark," said Mr. Weston, " don't cut about with that whip, while all these children are so near."

"If I didn't, sir," said Mark, some of 'em would a been scrunched under the carriage wheels 'fore now. These little niggers," he muttered between his teeth, "they're always in the way. I wish some of 'em would get run over." Mark's w^ife was not a very amiable character, and she had never had any children.

"Hurrah! daddy, is that you?" said an unmistakeable voice proceeding from the lungs of Bacchus the younger. " I been dansin juba dis hole blessed day—I so glad you come. Ask mammy if I aint?"

"How is your mother, Bacchus?" said Mr. Weston, looking out the window.

"Mammy, she's well," said the young gentleman; "how's you, master?"

"Very well, I thank you, sir," said Mr. Weston. "Go down there and help pick up the sugar-plums."

Bacchus the elder, now slid down from the seat by Mark, and took a short cut over to his cabin.

"Poor Aunt Phillis!" said Mrs. Weston, looking after him, "I hope she will get well."

"Ah!" said Mr. Weston, "I had forgotten Phillis on this happy day. There is something, you see, Anna, to make us sigh, even in our happiest moments.

"But you shall not sigh, dearest uncle," said Alice, kissing his hand, "for Aunt Phillis will get well now that we are all back. Oh, there is Cousin Janet, and little Lydia—I wish the carriage would stop."

"You are the most perfect child Iever saw, Alice," said Mrs. Weston. "I think you are out of your senses at the idea of getting home."

The carriage wheeled round, and William let down the steps, with a face bright as a sunflower. Miss Janet stood at the top of the portico steps, in her dove-colored gown, and her three-cornered handkerchief, with open arms. Alice bounded like a deer, and was clasped within them. Then Mrs. Weston, then Ellen; and afterwards, the aged relatives warmly embraced each other. Little Lydia was not forgotten, they all shook hands with her, but Alice, who stooped to kiss her smooth, black cheek. William was then regularly shaken hands with, and the family entered the large, airy hall, and were indeed at home.

Here were collected all the servants employed about the house, each in a Sunday dress, each greeted with a kind word. Alice shook hands with them two or three times over, then pointing to the family pictures, which were arranged along the hall, "Look at them, uncle," said she; "did you ever see them so smiling before?"

They went to the drawing-room, all but Alice, who flew off in another direction.

"She is gone to see Phillis," said Mr. Weston, gazing after her. "Well, I will rest a few moments, and then go too."

Never did mother hold to her heart a child dearer to her, than Phillis, when she pressed Alice to her bosom. Alice had almost lived with her, when she, and Walter, and Arthur were children. Mrs. Weston knew that she could not be in better hands than under the care of so faithful and respectable a servant. Phillis had a large, old clothes' basket, where she kept the toys, all the little plates and

cups with which they played dinner-party, the dolls with out noses, and the trumpets that would not blow. Her children were not allowed to touch them when the owners were not there, but they took a conspicuous part in the play, being the waiters and ladies' maids and coach-drivers of the little gentlemen and Alice. After Walter and Arthur went

o

away, Alice was still a great deal with Phillis, and she, regarding her as Arthur's future wife, loved her for him as well as for herself. Alice loved Phillis, too, and all her children, and they considered her as a little above mortality. Bacchus used to insist, when she was a child, that she never would live, she was too good. When, during her severe illness, Phillis would go to her cabin to look around, Bacchus would greet her with a very long face, and say, "I told you so. I know'd Miss Alice would be took from us all." Since her recovery, he had stopped prophesying about her.

"Aunt Phillis," said Alice, "you don't look very sick. I reckon you will work when you ought not. Now I intend to watch you, and make you mind, so that you will soon be well."

"I am a great deal better than I was, Miss Alice, but there's no knowing; howsomever, I thank the Lord that he has spared me to see you once more. I want to give Master time to talk to Miss Janet a little while, then I am going in to see him and Miss Anna."

"Oh! come now," said Alice, "or he will be over here."

Phillis got up, and walked slowly to the house, Alice at her side, and Bacchus stumping after her. As they went in, Alice tripped on first, and opened the drawing-room door, making way for Phillis, who looked with a happy expression of face towards her master.

"Is this you, Phillis?" said Mr. Weston, coming forward, and taking her hand most kindly. Mrs. Weston and Ellen got up to shake hands with her, too. "I am very glad to find you so much better than I expected," continued Mr. Weston; "you are thin, but your countenance is good.

I hope you will get perfectly well, now that we are going to have summer weather."

"Thank you", sir," said Phillis. "I am a great deal better. Thank God, you all look so well, Miss Anna and all. Miss Janet began to be mighty lonesome. I've been a great trouble to her."

"No, you have not," said Miss Janet; "you never were a trouble to any one."

"Master," said Bacchus, "I think the old ooman looks right well. She aint nigh so bad as we all thought. I reckon she couldn't stand my bein away so long; she hadn't nobody to trouble her."

"You will never give her any more trouble," said Alice. "Aunt Phillis, you don't know how steady Uncle Bacchus has been; he is getting quite a temperance man."

"Old Nick got the better of me twice, though," said Bacchus. "I did think, master, of tryin to make Phillis b'lieve I hadn't drank nothin dis winter; but she'd sure to find me out. There's somefin in her goes agin a lie."

"But that was doing very well," said Alice; "don't you think so, Aunt Phillis? Only twice all through the winter."

"Its an improvement, honey," said Phillis; "but what's the use of getting drunk at all? When we are thirsty, water is better than any thing else; and when we aint thirsty, what's the use of drinking?"

Phillis had been sitting in an arm-chair, that Mrs. Weston had placed for her. When she first came in, her face was a little flushed from pleasure, and the glow might have been mistaken as an indication of health. The emotion passed, Mrs. Weston perceived there was a great change in her. She was excessively emaciated; her cheek-bones prominent, her eyes large and bright. The whiteness of her teeth struck them all. These symptoms, and the difficulty with which she breathed, were tokens of her disease. She became much fatigued,

and Miss Janet advised her to go home and lie down. « They shan't tell you of their grand doings to-night, Phillis," she said; "for you have been excited, and must keep quiet. In the morning you will be able to listen to them. Don't tell any long stories, Bacchus," she continued. "Dr. Lawton wants her to keep from any excitement at night, for fear she should not sleep well after it. All you travelers had better go to bed early, and wake up bright in the morning."

Alice went home with Phillis, and came back to welcome Mr. Barbour, who had just arrived. The happy evening glided away; home was delightful to the returned family.

Bacchus gave glowing descriptions of scenes, in which he figured largely, to the servants; and Bacchus the younger devoutly believed there had not been so distinguished a visitor to the metropolis that winter, as his respected father.

Dr. Lawton came regularly to see Phillis, who frequently rallied. Her cheerfulness made her appear stronger than she was; but when Alice would tell her how well she looked, and that the sight of Arthur would complete her recovery, she invariably answered, "I want to see him mightily, child; but about my gettin well, there's no tell ing. God only knows."

CHAPTER XXVI.

"Do sit down, my dear cousin," said Miss Janet to Mr. Weston, who was walking up and down the drawing-room. " Here, in August, instead of being quiet and trying to keep cool, you are fussing about, and heating yourself so uselessly."

"I will try," said Mr. Weston, smiling, and seating himself on the sofa; but you must recollect that for three years I have not seen my only son, and that now he is coming home to stay. I cannot realize it; it is too much happiness. We are so blessed, Cousin Janet, we have so much of this world's good, I sometimes tremble lest God should intend me to have my portion here."

"It is very wrong to feel so," said Cousin Janet; « even in this world, He can give his beloved rest."

"But am I one of the beloved?" asked Mr. Weston, thoughtfully.

"I trust so," said Cousin Janet. "I do not doubt it. How lamentable would be your situation and mine, if, while so near the grave, we were deprived of that hope, which takes from it all its gloom."

"Are you talking of gloom?" said Mrs. Weston, "and Arthur within a few miles of us ? It is a poor compliment to him. I never saw so many happy faces. The servants have all availed themselves of their afternoon's holiday to dress; they look so respectable. Esther says they have gone to the outer gate to welcome Arthur first; Bacchus went an hour ago. Even poor Aunt Phillis has brightened up. She has on a head-handkerchief and apron white as snow, and looks quite comfortable, propped up by two or three pillows.

"Arthur will be sadly distressed to see Phillis, though he will not realize her condition at first. The nearer her disease approaches its consummation, the brighter she looks."

"It seems but yesterday," said Mr. Weston, "that Phillis sat at her cabin door, with Arthur (a baby) in her arms, and her own child, almost the same age, in the cra dle near them. She has been no eye-servant. Faithfully has she done her duty, and now she is going to receive her reward. I never can forget the look of sympathy which was in her face, when I used to go to her cabin to see my motherless child. She always gave Arthur the preference, putting her own infant aside to attend to his wants. Phillis is by nature a conscientious woman; but nothing but the grace of God could have given her the constant and firm principle that has actuated her life. But this example of Christian excellence will soon be taken from us; her days are numbered. Her days here are numbered; but how blessed the eternity! Sometimes, I have almost reproached myself that I have retained a woman like Phillis as a slave. She deserves every thing from me: I have always felt under obligations to her."

" You have discharged them," said Mrs. Weston. " Phil lis, though a slave, has had a very happy life; she fre quently says so. This is owing, in a great measure, to her own disposition and rectitude of character. Yet she has had every thing she needed, and a great deal more. You have nothing with which to reproach yourself."

«I trust not," said Mr. Weston. «I have endeavored, in my dealings with my servants, to remember the All-seeing eye was upon me, and that to Him who placed these human beings in a dependant position, would I have to render my account. Ah! here are the girls. Alice, we had almost forgotten Arthur; you and Ellen remind us of him."

"Really," said Ellen, "I am very unhappy; I have no lover to expect. You see that I am arrayed in a plain black silk, to show my chagrin because JVlr. Johnson could not come now. Alice has decked herself so that Arthur can read her every thought at the first glance. She has on her blue barege dress, which implies her unvarying constancy. Then "

"I did not think of that," said Alice, blushing deeply, and looking down at her dress ; " I only "

"Miss Alice," said Lydia, "I hears somethin." "No, no," said Miss Janet, looking from the window,

"there is nothing "

" Deed the is," said Lydia. "Its Mas' Arthur's horse, I know."

Mr. Weston went out on the porch, and the ladies stood at the windows. The voices of the servants could be dis tinctly heard. From the nature of the sound, there was no doubt they were giving a noisy welcome to their young master.

" He is coming," said Miss Janet, much agitated; " the servants would not make that noise were he not in sight." "I hear the horses, too," said Ellen; "we will soon see him where the road turns."

"There he comes," said Mrs. Weston. "It must be Arthur. William is with him; he took a horse for Arthur to the stage house."

The father stood looking forward, the wind gently lift ing the thin white hair from his temples ; his cheek flushed, his clear blue eye beaming with delight. The horseman approached. The old man could not distinguish his face, yet there was no mistaking his gay and gallant bearing. The spirited and handsome animal that bore him flew over the gravelled avenue. Only a few minutes elapsed from the time he was first seen to the moment when the father laid his head upon his son's shoulder; and while he was clasped to that youthful and manly heart experienced sen sations of joy such as are not often felt here.

Alice had known, too, that it was he. But when we long to be assured of happiness, we are often slow to be lieve. It was not until her eyes could distinguish every feature that her heart said, "It is Arthur." Then all was forgotten—all timidity, all reserve—all, save that he was the dearly loved brother of her childhood; the being with whom her destiny had long been associated. She passed from the drawing-room to the porch as he alighted from his horse, and when his father released him from a long embrace, Arthur's eyes fell upon the dear and un changed countenance, fixed upon him with a look of wel come that said more than a thousand words.

******

" Aunt," said Arthur, a week after his return, as he sat with Mrs. Weston and Alice in the arbor, " before you came, Alice had been trying to persuade me that she had been in love with Walter ; but I can't believe it."

" I never did believe it for a moment. She thought she was, and she was seized with such a panic of truth and honor that she made a great commotion; insisted on writing to you, and making a full confession; wanted to tell her uncle, and worry him to death; doing all sorts of desperate things. She actually worked herself into a fever. It was all a fancy."

"I have too good an opinion of myself to believe it," said Arthur.

"I am sorry," said Alice, "for it is true. It is a pity your vanity cannot be a little diminished."

" Why, the fact is Alice, I remember Uncle Bacchus's story about General Washington and his servant, when the general's horse fell dead, or rather the exclamation made by the servant after relating the incident: 'Master, lie thinks of everything.' I do too. When we were children, no matter how bad Walter was, you took his part. I re member once he gave William such a blow because he stumbled over a wagon that he had been making, and broke it. I asked him if he were not ashamed to do so, and you said, «Hush, Arthur, he feels bad; if you felt as sorry as he does, you would behave just in the same way.' So, the fact is, last summer you saw lie felt bad, and your tender heart inundated with sympathy."

" That was it," said Mrs. Weston ; «it was a complete inundation."

"You are not in love with him now, are you, Alice?" said Arthur, smiling.

" No, indeed," said Alice, " I am not in love with him, or you either—if being in love is what it is described in novels. I never have palpitation of the heart, never faint away, and am not at all fond of poetry. I should make a sad heroine, I am such a matter-of-fact person."

" So as you make a good w r ife," said Arthur, " no mat ter about being a heroine."

"A planter's wife has little occasion for romance," said Mrs. Weston ; "her duties are too many and too im portant. She must care for the health and comfort of hei family, and of her servants. After all, a hundred ser* vants are like so many children to look after."

"Ellen would make an elegant heroine," said Alice. " She was left an orphan when very young; had an ex acting uncle and aunt; was the belle of the metropolis ; had gay and gallant lovers; is an heiress—and has fallen , in love with a man she never saw. To crown all, he is not rich, so Ellen can give him her large fortune to show her devotion, and they can go all over the world together, and revel in romance and novelty."

"Well," said Arthur, "I will take you all over the world if you wish it. When will you set out, and how will you travel ? If that is all you complain of in your destiny, I can easily change it."

"I do not complain of my destiny," said Alice, gaily. " I was only contrasting it with Ellen's. I shall be satis fied never to leave Exeter, and my migrations need not be more extended than were Mrs. Primroses's, < from the green room to the brown.' Poor Walter! I wish he would fall in love with some beautiful Italian, and be as happy as we are."

" Do not fear for Walter," said Mrs. Weston. " He will take care of himself; his last letter to Cousin Janet was very cheerful. I shall have to diminish your vanity, Alice, by telling you Walter will never < die for love of Alice Weston.' He will be captivated some day with a more dashy lady, if not an Italian countess. I have no doubt he will eventually become a resident of Europe. A life of repentance will not be too much for a man whose hands are stained with the blood of his fellowman. The day is past in our country, and I rejoice to say it, when a duellist can be tolerated. I always shudder when in the presence of one, though I never saw but one."

Mr. Weston now entered, much depressed from a recent interview with Phillis. This faithful and honored servant was near her departure. Angels were waiting at the throne of the Eternal, for his command to bear her purified spirit home.

* * * *

The master and the slave were alone. No eye save their Maker's looked upon them; no ear save his, heard what passed between them.

Mr. Weston was seated in the easy chair, which had been removed from the other room, and in which his wife had died.

Phillis was extended on a bed of death. Her thin hands crossed on her bosom, her eyes fearfully bright, a hectic glow upon her cheek.

"Master," she said, "you have no occasion to feel uneasy about that. I have never had a want, I nor the children. Tnere was a time, sir, when I was restless about being a slave. When I went with you and Miss Anna away from home, and heard the people saying colored people ought to be free, it made me feel bad. I thought then that God did not mean one of his creatures to be a slave; when I came home and considered about it, I would often be put out, and discontented. It was wicked, I know, but I could not help it for a while.

"I saw my husband and children doing well and happy, but I used to say to myself, they are slaves, and so am I. So I went about my work with a heavy heart. When my children was born, I would think ' what comfort is it to give birth to a child when I know its a slave.' I struggled hard though, with these feelings, sir, and God gave me grace to get the better of them, for I could not read my Bible without seeing there was nothing agin slavery there; and that God had told the master his duty, and the slave his duty. You've done your duty by me and mine, sir; and I hope where I have come short you will forgive me, for I couldn't die in peace, without I thought you and I was all right together."

"Forgive you, Phillis," said Mr. Weston, much affected. "What have I to forgive ? Rather do I thank you for all you have done for me. You were a friend and nurse to my wife, and a mother to my only child. Was ever servant or friend so faithful as you have been !"

Phillis smiled and looked very happy. " Thank you, master," she said, "from my heart. How good the Lord is to me, to make my dying bed so easy. It puts me in mind of the hymn Esther sings. She's got a pleasant voice, hasn't she, sir ?

' And while I feel my heart-strings break,

How sweet the moments roll ! A mortal paleness on my cheek And glory in my soul.'

"Oh! master,its sweet for me to die, for Jesus is my friend; he makes all about me friends too, for it seems to me that you and Miss Janet, and all of you are my friends.

Poor Bacchus ! he takes on sadly about me; he always was a tender-hearted soul. Master, when I am gone, I know you will be good to him and comfort him, but, please sir, do something else. Talk to him, and pray for him, and read the blessed Book to him ! Oh ! if he would only give up liquor! I trust in the Lord he will live and die a sober man, else I know we'll never meet again. We won't be on the same side at the Judgment Seat. There's no drunkards in that happy place where I am going fast. No drunkards in the light of God's face—no drunkards at the blessed feet of Jesus."

"I think Bacchus has perfectly reformed," said Mr. Westori, « and you may feel assured that we will do every thing for his soul as well as his body, that we can. But, Phillis, have you no wishes to express, as regards your children?"

Phillis hesitated—»My children are well off," she said; " they have a good master; if they serve him and God faithfully they will be sure to do welL"

" If there is any thing on your mind," said Mr. Weston, " speak it without fear. The distinction between you and me as master and slave, I consider no longer existing. You are near being redeemed from my power, and the power of death alone divides you from your Saviour's pre sence. That Saviour whose example you have tried to follow, whose blood has washed your soul from all its sin. I am much older than you, and I live in momentary expec tation of my summons. We shall soon meet, I hope, in that happy place, where the distinctions of this world will be forgotten. I have thought of you a great deal, lately, and have been anxious to relieve your mind of every care. It is natural that a mother, about to leave such a family as you have, should have some wishes regarding them.

"I have thought several times," continued Mr. Weston, " of offering to set your children free at my death, and 1 will do so if you wish. You must be aware that they could not remain in Virginia after they were manumitted. In the Middle and Northern states free blacks are in a degraded condition. There is no sympathy for or with them. They have no more rights than they have as slaves with us, and they have no one to care for them when they are sick or in trouble. You have seen a good deal of this in your occasional visits to the North. In Washington, since the Abolitionists have intermeddled there, the free blacks have become intolerable; they live from day to day in discomfort and idleness. I mean as a general thing; there are, of course, occasional exceptions. Bacchus is too old to take care of himself; he would not be happy away from Exeter. Consider what I say to you, and I will be guided by your wishes as regards your children.

" They might go to Liberia; some of them would be willing, no doubt. I have talked to William, he says he would not go. Under these circumstances they would be separated, and it is doubtful whether I would be doing you or them a favour by freeing them. Be perfectly candid, and let me know your wishes."

"As long as you, or Master Arthur and Miss Alice live, they would be better off as they are," said Phillis.

" I believe they would," said Mr. Weston, "but life and death cannot be too much considered in connection with each other. I must soon go. I am only lingering at the close of a long journey. Arthur will then have control, and will, I am certain, make his servants as happy as he can. My family is very small; you are aware I have no near relations. I have made my will, and should Arthur and Alice die without children, I have left all my servants free. Your children I have thus provided for. At my death they are free, but I would not feel justified in turning them into the world without some provision. The older children can take care of themselves; they are useful and have good principles. I have willed each one of them to be free at the age of twenty years. Thus, you see, most of them will soon 1 e free, while none will have to wait very long. In the mean dme they will be well taught and cared for. My will is made, and all the forms of law attended to. Arthur and Alice are very much pleased with it. Your older children know it; they are very happy, but they declare they will never leave Exeter as long as there is a Weston upon it.* And now, Phillis, are you satisfied ? I shall experience great pleasure in having been able to relieve you of any anxiety while you have so much pain to bear."

"Oh! master," said Phillis, "what shall I say to you? I haven't no learning. I am only a poor, ignorant woman. I can't thank you, master, as I ought. My heart is nigh to bursting. What have I done that the Lord is so good to me. He has put it into your heart to make me so hap py. Thank you, master, and God for ever bless you."

The tears streamed down her cheeks, as Mr. Weston arose to go. Esther had come to see if her mother wanted any thing.

"Master," said Phillis, "wait one moment—there's no thing between me and Heaven now. Oh ! sir, I shall soon be redeemed from all sin and sorrow. I think I see the glory that shines about the heavenly gates. I have never felt myself ready to go until now, but there is nothing to keep me. The Lord make your dying bed as easy as you have mine."

Mr. Weston endeavored to compose himself, but was much agitated. "Phillis," he said, "you have deserved more than I could ever do for you. If any thing should occur to you that I have not thought of, let me know, it shall, if possible, be done. Would you like again to see Mr.

Caldwell, and receive the communion?"

"No, master, I thank you. You and Miss Janet, and Miss Anna, and poor Bacchus, took it with me last week,

* A number of slaves have been manumitted recently at the South— in one instance more than half preferred to remain in slavery in New Orleans, to going to the North.

and I shall soon be where there will be no more need to remind me of the Lamb that was slain; for I shall be with him; I shall see him as he is. And, master, we will all meet there. We will praise him together."

Esther was weeping; and Mr. Weston, quite overcome, left the room.

"Esther, child," said Phillis, "don't do so. There's nothing but glory and peace. There's no occasion for tears. God will take care of you all here, and will, I hope and pray, bring you to heaven at last. Poor master! To think he is so distressed parting with me. I thought I should have stood by his dying bed. The Lord knows best."

"Mother," said Esther, "will you take this medicine— it is time?"

"No, honey. No more medicine; it won't do me no good. I don't want medicine. Jesus is what I want. He

is all in all.

*****

Reader! have you ever stood by the dying bed of a slave? It may be not. There are those who are often there. The angels of God, and One who is above the angels. One who died for all. He is here now. Here, where stand weeping friends—here, where all is silence. You may almost hear the angel's wings as they wait to bear the redeemed spirit to its heavenly abode. Here, where the form is almost senseless, the soul fluttering between earth and heaven. Here, where the Spirit of God is overshadowing the scene.

"Master," said Phillis, "all is peace. Jesus is here. I am going home. You will soon be there, and Miss Janet can't be long. Miss Anna too. Bacchus, the good Lord will bring you there. I trust in Him to save you. My children, God bless them, little Lydia and all."

"Master Arthur," said she, "as Arthur bent over her, "give my love to Master Walter. You and Miss Alice will

soon be married. The Lord make you happy. God bless you, Miss Ellen, and make you his child. Keep close, children to Jesus. Seems as if we wasn't safe when we can't see him. I see him now; he is beckoning me to come. Blessed Jesus! take me—take me home."

Kind master, weep not. She will bear, even at the throne of God, witness to thy faithfulness. Through thee she learned the way to heaven, and it may be soon she will stand by thee again, though thou see her not. She may be one of those who will guide thee to the Celestial City; to the company of the redeemed, where will be joy forever. "Weep not, but see in what peace a Christian can die. Watch the last gleams of thought which stream from her dying eyes. Do you see any thing like apprehension? The world, it is true, begins to shut in. The shadows of evening collect around her senses. A dark mist thickens, and rests upon the objects which have hitherto engaged her observation. The countenances of her friends become more and more indistinct. The sweet expressions of love and friendship are no longer intelligible. Her ear wakes no more at the well-known voice of her children, and the soothing accents of tender affection die away unheard upon her decaying senses. To her the spectacle of human life is drawing to its close, and the curtain is descending which shuts out this earth, its actors, and its scenes. She is no longer interested in all that is done under the sun. Oh! that I could now open to you the recesses of her soul, that I could reveal to you the light which darts into the chambers of her understanding. She approaches that world which she has so long seen in faith. The imagination now collects its diminished strength, and the eye of faith opens wide.

"Friends! do not stand thus fixed in sorrow around this bed of death. Why are you so still and silent? Fear not to move; you cannot disturb the visions that enchant this holy spirit. She heeds you not; already she sees the spirits of the just advancing together to receive a kindred soul. She is going to add another to the myriads of the just, that are every moment crowding into the portals of heaven. She is entering on a noble life. Already she cries to you from the regions of bliss. "Will you not join her there? Will you not taste the sublime joys of faith? There are seats for you in the assembly of the just made perfect, in the innumerable company of angels, where is Jesus, the — Mediator of the New Covenant, and God, the Judge of all."

CONCLUDING REMAKES.

I MUST be allowed to quote the words of Mrs. Harriet B. Stowe:

"The writer has often been (or will be) inquired of by correspondents from different parts of the country, whether this narrative is a true one; and to these inquiries she will give one general answer. The separate incidents that compose the narrative are to a very great extent authentic, occurring, many of them, either under her own observation, or that of her personal friends. She or her friends have observed characters the counterpart of almost all that are here introduced; and many of the sayings are word for word as heard herself, or reported to her."

Of the planter Legree, (and, with the exception of Prof. Webster, such a wretch never darkened humanity,) she says:

" Of him her brother wrote, he actually made me feel of his fist, which was like a blacksmith's hammer or a nodule of iron, telling me that it was calloused with knocking down niggers."

Now as a parallel to this, I will state a fact communicated to me by a clergyman, (a man of great talent, and goodness of character, and undoubted veracity,) that a superintendent of Irishmen, who were engaged on a Northern railroad, told him he did not hesitate to knock any man down that gave him the least trouble; and although the clergyman did not « examine his fist and pronounce it like a blacksmith's hammer," yet, I have not the slightest doubt it was « calloused with knocking down Irishmen." At any rate, I take the license of the writers of the day, and say it was.

23

Mrs. Stowe goes on to say, " That the tragical fate of Tom also has too many times had its parallel, there are living witnesses all over our land to testify." Now it would take the smallest portion of common sense to know that that there is no witness, dead or living, who could testify to such a fact, save & false witness. This whole history is an absurdity. No master would be fool enough to sell the best hand on his estate ; one who directed,, and saved, and managed for him. No master would be brutish enough to sell the man who had nursed him and his children, who loved him like a son, even for urgent debt, had he another article of property in the wide world. But Mr. Shelby does so, according to Mrs. Stowe, though he has a great many other servants, besides houses and lands, £c. Pre posterous!

And such a saint as Uncle Tom was, too! One would have thought his master, with the opinion he had of his religious qualifications, would have kept him until he died, and then have sol,d him bone after bone to the Roman Catholics. Why, every tooth in his head would have brought its price. St. Paul was nothing but a common man compared with him, for St. Paul had been wicked once; and even after his miraculous conversion, he felt that sin was fetill impelling him to do what he would not. But not so with 'Uncle Tom! He was the very perfection of a saint. Well might St. Clare have proposed using him for a family chaplain, or suggested to himself the idea of ascending to heaven by Tom's skirts. Mrs. Stowe should have carried out one of her ideas in his history, and have made him Bishop of Carthage, j I have never heard or read of so perfect a character. All the saints and martyrs that ever came to unnatural deaths, could not show such an amount of excellence. I only wonder he managed to stay so long in this world of sin.

When, after fiery trials and persecutions, he is finally purchased by a Mr. Legree, Mrs. Stowe speaks of the horrors of the scene. She says though, "it can't be

helped." Did it ever occur to her, that Northerners might go South, and buy a great many of these slaves, and manumit them? They do go South and buy them, but they keep them, and work them as slaves too. A great deal of this misery might be helped.

Tom arrives at Legree's plantation. How does he fare? Sleeps on a little foul, dirty straw, jammed in with a lot of others; has every night toward midnight enough corn to stay the stomach of one small chicken; and is thrown into a most dreadful state of society—men degraded, and women degraded. We will pass over scenes that a woman's pen should never describe, and observe the saint-like perfection of Tom. He was, or considered himself, a missionary to the negroes, evidently liked his sufferings, and died, \ by choice, a martyr's death. He made the most astonishing number of conversions in a short time, and of characters worse than history records. So low, so degraded, so lost were the men and women whose wicked hearts he subdued, that their conversion amounted to nothing less than miracles. No matter how low, how ignorant, how depraved, the very sight of Tom turned them into advanced, intelligent Christians.

Tom's lines were indeed cast in a sad place. I have always believed that the Creator was everywhere.; but we are told of Legree's plantation "The Lord never visits these parts." This might account for the desperate wickedness of most of the characters, but how Tom could retain his holiness under the circumstances is a marvel to me. His religion, then, depended on himself. Assuredly he was more than a man! J

Legree had several ways of keeping his servants in order—"they were burned alive; scalded, cut into inch pieces; set up for the dogs to tear, or hung up and whipped to death." Now I am convinced that Mrs. Stowe must have a credulous mind; and was imposed upon. She never could have conceived such things with

all her talent; the very conception implies a refinement of cruelty. She gives, however, a mysterious description of a certain "place way out down by the quarters, where you can see a black blasted tree, and the ground all covered with black ashes." It is afterward intimated that this was the scene of a negro burned alive. Reader, you may depend, it was a mistake; that's just the way a tree appears when it has been struck by lightning. Next time you pass one, look at it. I have not the slightest doubt that this was the way the mistake was made. We have an occasional wag at the South, and some one has practised upon' a soft-hearted New Englander in search of horrors; this is the result. She mentions that the ashes were black. Do not infer from this that it must have been a black man or negro. But I will no longer arraign your good sense. It was not, take my word for it, as Mrs. Stowe describes it, some poor negro «tied to a tree, with a slow fire lit under him."

Tom tells Legree "he'd as soon die as not." Indeed, he proposes whipping, starving, burning; saying, "it will only send him sooner where he wants to go." Tom evidently considers himself as too good for this world; and after making these proposals to his master, he is asked, "How are you?" He answers: "The Lord God has sent his angel, and shut the lion's mouth." Anybody can see that he is laboring under a hallucination, and fancies himself Daniel. Gassy, however, consoled him after the style of Job's friends, by telling him that his master was going "to hang like a dog at his throat, sucking his blood, bleeding away his life drop by drop."

In what an attitude, O Planters of the South, has Mrs. Stowe taken your likenesses!

Tom dies at last. How could snich a man die? Oh! that he would live forever and convert all our Southern slaves. He did not need any supporting grace on his

deathbed. Hear him—« The Lord may help me, or not help, but I'll hold on to him."

I thought a Christian could not hold on to the Lord without help. "Ye can of yourself do nothing." But Tom is an exception—to the last he is perfect. All Christians have been caught tripping sometimes, but Tom never is. He is "bearing everybody's burdens." He might run away, but he will not. He says, " The Lord has given me a work among these yer poor souls, and I'll stay with 'em, and bear my cross with 'em to the end." Christian reader, we must reflect. We know where to go for one instance of human perfection, where the human and the Divine were united, but we know not of another.

Tom converts Cassy, a most infamous creature from her own accounts, and we are to sympathize with her vileness, for she has no other traits of character described. Tom converts her, but I am sorry to see she steals money and goods, and fibs tremendously afterwards. We hope the rest of his converts did him more credit.

The poor fellow dies at last—converting two awful wretches with his expiring breath. The process of conversion was very short. " Oh! Lord, give me these two more souls, I pray." That prayer was answered.

The saddest part of this book would be, (if they were just,) the inferences to be drawn from the history of this wretch, Legree. Mrs. Stowe says, " He was rocked on the bosom of a mother, cradled with prayer and pious hymns, his now seared brow bedewed with the waters of baptism. In early childhood, a fair-haired woman had led him, at the sound of Sabbath bells, to worship and to pray. Far in New England that mother had trained her only son with long unwearied love and patient prayers." Believe it not, Christian mother, North or South! Thou hast the promises of Scripture to the contrary. Rock thy babe upon thy bosom—sing to him sweet hymns—carry him to the baptismal font—be unwearied in love—-patient in

prayers; he will never be such a one. He may wandei but he will come back; do thy duty by him, and God will not forget his promises. « He is not man that he will lie; nor the son of man that he will repent."

Legree is a Northerner. Time would fail me to notice all the crimes with which Southern men and women are charged; but their greatness and number precludes the possibility of their being believed. According to Mrs. Stowe, mothers do not love their beautiful children at the South. The husbands have to go to New England and bring back old maids to take care of them, and to see to their houses, which are going to rack and ruin under their wives' surveillance. Oh! these Southern husbands, a heart of stone' must pity them.

Then again, Southern planters keep dogs and blood hounds to hunt up negroes, tear women's faces, and commit all sorts of doggish atrocities. Now I have a charitable way of accounting for this. I am convinced, too, this is a misapprehension; and I'll tell you why.

I have a mortal fear of dogs myself. I always had. No reasoning, no scolding, ever had the slightest effect upon me. I never passed one on my way to church with my prayer-book in my hand, without quaking. If they wag their tails, I look around for aid. If they bark, I immediately give myself up for lost, I have died a thousand deaths from the mere accident of meeting dogs in the street. I never did meet one without believing that it was his destiny to give my children a step-mother. In point of fact, I would like to live in a world without dogs; but as I cannot accomplish this, I console myself by living in a house without one. I always expect my visitors to leave their dogs at home; they may bring their children, but they must not bring their dogs. I wish dogs would not even look in my basement windows as they pass.

I am convinced therefore, that some Northerner has passed a plantation at the South, and seen dogs tied up. Naturally having a horror of (loirs, he has let his imao-ina-tion loose. After a great deal of mental exercise, the brain jumps at a conclusion, " What are these dogs kept here for?" The answer is palpable : " To hunt niggers when they run away." Reader, imitate my charity; it is a rare virtue where white faces are concerned.

All the rest of Mrs. Stowe's horrors can be accounted^ for satisfactorily. It is" much better to try and find an excuse for one's fellow-creatures than to be always calling them « story-tellers," and the like. I am determined to be charitable.

But still it is misrepresentation ; for if they took proper means, they would find out the delusions under which they labor.

Abolitionists do not help their cause by misrepresenta tion. It will'do well enough, in a book of romance, to describe infants torn from the arms of their shrieking

O

mothers, and sold for five and ten dollars. It tells well, for the mass of readers are fond of horrors; but it is not true. It is on a par with the fact stated, that masters advertise their slaves, and offer rewards for them, dead or alive. How did the snows of New England ever give birth to such brilliant imaginations !

Family relations are generally respected; and when ~~-they are not, it is one of the evils attendant on an institu tion which God has permitted in all ages, for his inscruta ble purposes, and which he may in his good time do away with.

The Jews ever turn their eyes and affections toward Jerusalem, as their home ; so should the free colored peo ple in America regard Liberia. Africa, once their mother country, should, in its turn, be the country of their adop tion.

As regards the standard of talent among negroes, I fancy it has been exaggerated ;-* though no one can, at present, form a just conclusion. Slavery has, for ages, pressed like a band of iron round the intellect of the

colored man. Time must do its work to show what he is, without a like hindrance.

The instance mentioned in « Uncle Tom's Cabin," of a young mulatto, George Harris, inventing a machine, is very solitary. The negroes, like a good many of their owners, are opposed to innovations. They like the good old way. The hot sun under which they were born, and the hotter one that lighted the paths of their ancestors, prejudices them against any ncw effort. I think, when they do get in Congress, they will vote for agricultural against manufacturing interests. I am sure they would rather pick cotton than be confined to the din and dust of a factory. An old negro prefers to put his meal bags in a covered wagon, and drive them to market at his leisure, with his pocket full of the tobacco he helped to raise, and the whole country for a spit-box, to being whirled away bodily in a railroad car, in terror of his life, deaf with the whistling and the puffing of the engine. When Liberia or Africa does become a great nation, (Heaven grant it may soon,) they will require many other buildings there, before a patent office is called for.

George Harris is a natural Abolitionist, with a dark complexion. He is a remarkable youth in other respects, though I should first consider the enormous fact of George's master appropriating to himself the benefit of his servant's cleverness. Even with a show of right this may be a mean trick, but it is the way of the world. A large portion of New England men are at this time claiming each other's patents. I know of an instance down East, for South erners can sometimes « tak notes, and prent 'em too." A gentleman took a friend to his room, and showed him an invention for which he was about to apply for a patent. The friend walked off with his hands in his pocket; his principles had met, and passed an appropriation bill; the invention had become his own—in plain English, he stole it. Washington is always full of people claiming each other's brains. The lawyers at the Patent Office have their hands full. They must keep wide awake, too. Each inventor, when he relates his grievances, brings a witness to maintain his claim. There is no doubt that, after a while, there will be those who can testify to the fact of having seen the idea as it passed through the inventor's mind. The way it is settled at present is this—whoever can pay the most for the best lawyer comes off triumphant ly ! Poor George is not the only smart fellow in the world outdone by somebody better off than himself.

George positively refuses to hear the Bible quoted. He believes in a higher law, no doubt, Frederic Douglas being editorial expounder; a sort of Moses of this century, a little less meek, though, than the one who instructed the Israelites. George won't hear the Bible; he prefers, he says, appealing to the Almighty himself. This makes me fear his Abolitionist friends are not doing right by him; putting him up to shooting, and turning Spanish gentle man, and all sorts of vagaries ; to say nothing of disobey ing the laws of the country. No one blames him, though, = for escaping from a hard master ; at least, I do not.

It would be a grand thing to stand on the shore of a new country, and see before you, free, every slave and prisoner on the soil of the earth; to hear their Te Deum as cend to the listening heavens. Methinks the sun would stand still, as it did of old, and earth would lift up her voice, and lead the song of her ransomed children; but, alas ! this cannot be yet—the time is not come. Oppres sion wears her crown in every clime, though it is some times hidden from the gaze of her subjects.

George declares he knows more than his master; "he can read and write better;" but his logic is bad. He thus discusses the indications of Providence. A friend reminds him of what the apostle says, « Let every man abide in the condition in which he is called," and he immediately uses this simile: "I wonder, Mr. Wilson, if the Indians should

come, and take you a prisoner, away from your wife and children, and want to keep you all your life hoeing corn for them, if you'd think it your duty to abide in that con dition in which you were called. I rather think, that you'd think the first stray horse you could find an indica tion of Providence—shouldn't you T T

This does not apply to slavery. A man born a slave, in a country where slavery is allowed by law, should feel the obligation of doing his duty while a slave; but Mr. Wilson, carried off by Indians, would feel as if he had been called to a state of life previous to the one in which he was so unfortunate to be doomed, while he was among savages.

George goes on to say—« Let any man take care that tries to stop me, for I am desperate, and I'll fight for my liberty. You say your fathers did it: if it was right for them, it is right for me."

Too fast, George! You are out in your history, too. Your master must be a remarkably ignorant man if you know more than he. Our glorious ancestors were never condemned to slavery, they nor their fathers, by God him self. Neither have they ever been considered in the light of runaways; they came off with full permission, and having honestly and honorably attained their liberties, they fought for them.

Besides being of a prettier complexion, and coming of a better stock than you, they were prepared to be free. There is a great deal in that.

Then, those very ancestors of ours—ah! there's the rub —(and the ancestors of the Abolitionists, too,) they got us and you into this difficulty—think of it! They had your ancestors up there in New England, until they found you were so lazy, ami died off so in their cold climate, that it, did not pay to keep you. So I repeat to you the stdvice of Mr. Wilson, "l>c careful, my boy; don't shoot

anybody, George, unless—well—you'd better not shoot, I reckon; at least, I wouldn't hit anybody, you know."

As regards the practice of marking negroes in the hand, I look upon it as one of the imaginary horrors of the times—a delusion like spiritual rappings, got up out of sheer timidity of disposition, though I have heard of burning old women for witches in New England, and placing a scarlet letter on the bosom of some unhappy one, who had already sorrow and sin enough to bear.

It won't do; the subject has, without doubt, been duly investigated already. I'd be willing (were I not opposed to betting) to bet my best collar and neck ribbon, that a committee of investigation has been appointed, consisting of twelve of Boston's primmest old maids, and they have been scouring the plantations of the South, bidding the negroes hold out their hands, (not as the poor souls will at first suppose, that they may be crossed with a piece of silver,) and that they are now returning, crest-fallen, to their native city, not having seen a branded hand in all their journeying. Could aught escape their vigilance? But they will say they saw a vast number, and that will answer the purpose.

(Ah! Washington Irving, well mayest thou sigh and look back at the ladies of the Golden Age. " These were the honest days, in which every woman stayed at home, read the Bible, and wore pockets." These days arc for ever gone. Prophetic was thy lament! Now we may wear pockets—but, alas ! we neither stay at home, nor read our Bible. We form societies to reform the world, and we write books on slavery!)

Talking of our ancestors, George, in the time of the Revolution, (by-the-by, yours were a set of dear, honest old creatures, for there were no Abolitionists then among us,) reminds me of an anecdote about George Washington and a favorite servant. Billy Lee was an honest, faithful

man, and a first-rate groom, and George Washington—you need not blush to be a namesake of his, though he was a slaveholder.

The two were in a battle, the battle of Monmouth, the soldiers fighting like sixty, and Billy Lee looking on at a convenient distance, taking charge of a led horse, in case Washington's should be shot from under him.

0, but it was a hot day! Washington used to recall the thirst and the suffering attendant upon the heat, (thinking of the soldiers' suffering, and not of his own.) As for Billy Lee, if he did not breathe freely, he perspired enough so to make up for it. I warrant you he was anxious for the battle to be over, and the sun to go down. But there he stood, true as steel—honest, old patriot as he was—quiet ing the horse, and watching his noble master's form, as proud and erect it was seen here and there, directing the troops with that union of energy and calmness for which he was distinguished. Washington's horse fell under him, dying from excessive heat; but hear Billy Lee describe it:

"Lord! sir, if you could a seen it; de heat, and dust, and smoke. De cannons flyin, and de shot a whizzin, and de dust a blowing, and de horses' heels a kickin up, when all at onct master's horse fell under him. -It warn't shot— bless your soul, no. It drapped right down dead wid de heat. Master he got up. I was scared when I see him and de horse go; but master got up. He warn't hurt; couldn't hurt him.

" Master he got up, looked round at me. <Billy,' says he, 'give me the other horse, and you take care of the new saddle on this other poor fellow.'

"Did you ever hear de like?" added Billy Lee, "thinking of de saddle when de balls was a flyin most in our eyes. But it's always de same wid master. He thinks of every thing."

I agree with the humane jurist quoted by Mrs. Harriet Beecher Stowe : " The worst use you can put a man to is to hang him." She thinks slavery is worse still; but when "I think of every thing," I am forced to differ from her.

The most of our Southern slaves are happy, and kindly cared for; and for those who are not, there is hope for the better. But when a man is hung up by the neck until he is dead, he is done for. As far as I can see, there is nothing that can be suggested to better his condition.

I have no wish to uphold slavery. I would that every human being that God has made were free, were it in accordance with His will;—free bodily, free spiritually— 4 'free indeed!"

Neither do I desire to deny the evils of slavery, any more than I would deny the evils of the factory system in England, or the factory and apprenticeship system in our own country. I only assert the necessity of the existence of slavery at present in our Southern States, and that, as a general thing, the slaves are comfortable and contented, and their owners humane and kind.

I have lived & great deal at the North—long enough to see acts of oppression and injustice there, which, were any one so inclined, might be wrought into a " living dramatic reality."

I knew a wealthy family. All the labor of the house was performed by a "poor relation," a young and delicate girl. I have known servants struck by their employers. At the South I have never seen a servant struck, though I know perfectly well such things are done here and every where. Can we judge of society by a few isolated incidents? If so, the learned professors of New England borrow money, and when they do not choose to pay, they murder their creditors, and cut them in pieces! or men kill their sleeping wives and children !

Infidelity has been called a magnificent lie ! Mrs. Stowe's

24

"living dramatic reality" is nothing more than an interesting falsehood; nor ought to be offered, as an equivalent for truth, the genius that pervades her pages; • rather it is to be lamented that the rich gifts of God should be so misapplied.

Were the exertions of the Abolitionists successful, what would be the result ? The soul sickens at the thought. Scenes of blood and horror—the desolation of our fair Southern States— the final destruction of the negroes in them. This would be the result of immediate emancipation here. What has- it been elsewhere ? Look at St. Domingo. A recent visitor there says, " Though opposed to slavery, I must acknowledge that in this instance the experiment has failed." He compares the negroes to "a wretched gibbering set, from their appearance and condition more nearly allied to beasts than to men." Look at the free colored people of the North and in Canada.

I have lived among them at the North, and can judge for myself. Their « friends" do not always obtain their affection or gratitude. A colored woman said J^o me, " I would rather work for any people than the Abolitionists. They expect us to do so much, and they say we ought to work cheaper for them because they are < our friends.' ' -Look at them in Canada. An English gentleman who has for many years resided there, and who has recently visited Washington, told me that they were the most miserable, helpless human beings he had ever seen. In <fact he said, " They were nuisances, and the people of Canada would be truly thankful to see them out of their country." He had never heard of "a good missionary" mentioned by Mrs. Stowe, "whom Christian charity has placed, there as a shepherd to the outcast and wandering." He had Been no

good results of emancipation. On one occasion he hired a colored man to drive him across the country.

did you get here?" he said to the man. "Are you not a runaway?"

" Yes, sir," the man replied. « I came from Yirginny."

" Well, of course you are a great deal happier now than when you were a slave ?"

"No, sir; if I could get back to Virginny, I would be glad to go." He looked, too, as if he had never been worse off than at that time.

The fact is, liberty like money is a grand- thing; but in order to be happy, we must know how to use it.

It cannot always be said of the fugitive slave,—

11 The mortal puts on immortality, When mercy's-hand has turned the golden key, And mercy's voice hath said, Rejoice, thy soul is free."

The attentive reader will perceive that I am indebted to Mrs. Stowe for the application of this and other quota tions.

The author of Uncle Tom's Cabin speaks of good men at the North, who " receive and educate the oppressed" (negroes). I know"'lots" of good men there, but none good enough to befriend colored people. They seem to me to have an unconquerable antipathy to them. But Mrs. Stowe says, she educates them in her own family with her own children. I am glad to hear she feels and acts kindly toward tfyem, and I wish others in her region of country would imitate her in this respect; but I would rather my children and.negroes were educated at different schools, being utterly opposed to amalgamation, root and branch.

She asks the question, " What can any individual do ?" Strange that any one should be at a loss in this working world of ours.

Christian men and women should find enough to occupy

them in their families, and in an undoubted. sphere of duty.

Let the people of the North take care of their own poor.

Let the people of the South take care of theirs.

Let each remember the great and awful day when they must render a final account to their Creator, their Re deemer, and their Judge.

THE END.

Made in the USA
Middletown, DE
13 October 2020